JACQUELINE JAMES is a retired GP now living in Menton on the French Riviera. Born in Solihull she went to Sheffield University Medical School, qualifying in 1980 and, after a stint in hospitals, became a GP and family planning doctor in 1986, first in inner city Sheffield and then in rural Cambridgeshire. She retired in 2016 after thirty-six years in medicine and in 2021 her first novel, *Rude Awakening* was published. *Let's Escape* followed a year later and this book completes the Barwell Trilogy. Visit www.jacquelinejames.co.uk to sign up for news and events.

Also by Jacqueline James

Rude Awakening
Let's Escape

Journey's End

Jacqueline James

Book 3
in The Barwell Trilogy

BARWELL
PRESS

Published in 2023 by Barwell Press

ISBN 978-1-7393593-0-0 (paperback)

Also available as an ebook

Page design and typesetting by SilverWood Books
www.silverwoodbooks.co.uk

JOURNEY'S END

To Margaret, a good friend

ONE

A Walk by the Sea

The clouds rushed across the April sky above the car park at the top of the cliffs. Suzanne parked the Range Rover in the space next to Liz's old SEAT. Liz grabbed her coat and bag from the child seat strapped into the passenger seat and leaped out to greet Suzanne, Carol and Janet as they emerged from the car into breezy Debden-on-Sea. They laughed as their words were drowned out by a motor-mower, driven by a council worker, mouth set in concentration, making turns as if he were on a race track, leaving perfect straight lines in the damp grass.

They were prepared for a walk on the beach. Liz and John had recently discovered a lovely restaurant and she wanted to share it with her friends. *They serve the biggest, the best, the freshest seafood platters*, her email had read, and a lopsided photo of an article from a Sunday newspaper supplement supported her opinion.

She'd included the husbands in the invitation, even though her own, John, was away at a conference, and there was an unspoken relief among the women when none of the other husbands could or wanted to come. Carol had asked Jonathan in the certain knowledge that he had arranged to help her brother Dan collect new furniture for his flat. Suzanne had mentioned the outing to David, who, with no prompting, had assumed that it was just for *the girls*. Janet knew that Richard wouldn't want to join them if none of the other men were going. The girls had the day to themselves.

It was now three months since Liz and John had moved to be nearer to their daughter, Lisa, and to their grandchildren. Liz had missed seeing five-year-old Siobhan every day and the arrival of her baby brother, Sonny, confirmed Liz's belief that she and John had done the right thing in following them to the seaside. Lisa's partner, Jason, lived in a tiny house on a new estate on the edge of town, where Lisa had somehow found space for herself, Siobhan and baby Sonny. Massive billboards advertised seaside living, but with no sea view and a walk to the beach that was just a little too far, 'seaside living' wasn't how Liz would have described the part of town where her daughter lived.

She was still getting used to the town, to its car parks and one-way system, and to the visitors who came whatever the weather. She had found a good supermarket and a nice coffee shop and had figured out the best route to Siobhan's school.

She loved her own new house, with its expansive rooms and sea views from the bedrooms. Despite needing some work, it already felt like home. The garden, sloping slightly towards the salt marshes, was home to spiky plants and tall grasses that rustled in the wind and clung to the sandy borders that surrounded the lawn. Liz couldn't wait to see what summer would bring.

But she missed her friends and missed seeing people she knew every time she left the house. She even missed her old next-door neighbours with their suburban small-mindedness. Although she and John had never been close to them, they had been a familiar annoyance, with their petty squabbles over dustbins, overhanging honeysuckle, and borrowed tools not returned, that she and John laughed about in the privacy of their own home. Their children had played together for a time and one of the neighbours watered the plants whenever she and John were away, and kept a spare key in case Liz ever locked herself out. They weren't friends exactly, but they were reassuringly familiar.

Even though some of the houses changed hands, there had been a sameness about the road that she had lived on for thirty years. Life on the road never seemed to change but, looking back, she knew that the Liz and John who had moved from Barwell bore no resemblance to the young couple who had moved into that house all those years before. They initially caused ripples by not being married and by having a house interior that did not conform to the magnolia norm. Over time, though, and with the arrival of their children, their differences had been accepted and they had become part of the neighbourhood.

Her new neighbours, Rupert and Rowena—or "R-squared" as Rupert announced with a guffaw when they called round to introduce themselves—were pleasant enough but, as Liz found out when Siobhan was helping her in the garden one afternoon, quick to show their disapproval. She was cutting back a rhododendron that threatened to block the gate leading to the back garden. Siobhan, bored with dragging the branches into a pile, was playing at being a witch on a broomstick and had strayed onto R-squared's drive, when the couple arrived home and turned into their drive. Nothing was said but Rowena's pointed stare from the passenger seat of the car spoke volumes. Liz, feeling wrong-footed, gathered Siobhan to her and mouthed a silent apology.

"She wasn't doing anything wrong," she told John later. "She was just playing. I swept up the leaves that ended up on their drive. Should I invite them round for a drink or something? I don't want to fall out with them."

"You could invite them round to share that half bottle of Prosecco they gave us as a house warming present," John replied. Liz giggled.

"Perhaps I'll wait. They said they'd have us round for a drink once we'd settled in. Let's just wait and see."

They had been in the house three months now and were still waiting.

Liz talked to some of the other neighbours, passed the time of day with parents and grandparents outside the school gates and had long chats with the coffee shop owner when she wasn't busy. It was true that she was getting to know people, but she still missed her friends. Although they kept in regular contact, this was the first time she had seen them since the move.

"Are we all ready?" she asked, as Suzanne put the parking ticket in the windscreen and locked the car.

"Yes," said Janet. "It's such a shame Hilary can't be here." She rolled up her cagoule and stowed it in her rucksack.

"I wonder how they're getting on," mused Carol. "Is it just me, or do some of the smiles in the photos look a bit forced?"

"I think the photos are lovely, especially as some of them must be selfies," said Suzanne.

"I've never managed to take a selfie," said Janet. "I always look hideous or ridiculous."

"Why don't we take one now and send it to Hilary?" suggested Liz, as she pulled her phone from her pocket. "Come on, sea in the background, smile…" She stretched her arm out above their heads and quickly took the picture before the wind coming in off the sea blew their hair across their smiling faces.

"See? Lovely!" she said, showing them the phone. A few taps on the screen and she had sent the photo to Hilary. "A true representation of how happy we are."

The others laughed, and followed her rapid steps as she headed down the steep path towards the base of the cliffs.

She turned immediately right and started clambering nimbly over the rocks.

"Slow down a bit," called Janet, struggling to keep her footing on the slippery seaweed-strewn rocks.

"Our legs aren't as long as yours," Carol said, laughing.

While Liz strode ahead, Suzanne held out a hand to steady Janet as she stepped uncertainly from one rock to the next. They both waited for Carol, and then ventured to catch up with Liz.

"Sorry. I'm used to chasing down here with Siobhan," she said, as the others joined her on the beach. "She absolutely loves it here, loves school, loves the seaside, the new baby. It couldn't be better." She pointed to a rock pool. "There's a fairy castle and all sorts in there, crabs guard it and that bit of seaweed hides the door to the castle. She has such an imagination."

"I love that stage when reality and imagination merge," said Carol. "When Father Christmas is real, and there might be dragons under the bed. Sadly, Lucy is just growing out of it, becoming all sensible and cynical."

"I'm sure I believed in Father Christmas till I was ten," said Janet.

"Pearl disabused me of the idea when I was very little," said Liz.

"And I don't think Lisa and Edward were very interested either, as long as they got their presents. So, it's lovely to play along with Siobhan."

"How is Pearl these days?" asked Carol.

"Oh, you know. Pearl's Pearl. Never changes."

"I wish I could say the same for my mum," said Janet. "Dad says she sometimes has hallucinations. It must be horrible for him." She regretted the words as she said them. She had promised herself that she would enjoy the day and leave thoughts of her parents at home.

At that moment, a ball narrowly missed Suzanne's shoulder and landed at their feet. An over-excited terrier chased around the women's legs and grabbed the ball in his mouth.

"Sorry," a plump, elderly man shouted, as he came panting towards them. "Drop it, Tiger! Drop it…" he said over and over. The dog resisted all the man's attempts to secure either the ball or his collar; he thought it was a great game. He enjoyed it even more when the women joined in the chase.

Finally, amid much hilarity, Janet secured the sand-encrusted ball and handed it to the owner to stow in his pocket. Tiger's collar came within grabbing distance at last, as he leaped up and down at the man's side. He was recaptured and put back on his lead.

"I don't know how to thank you," he said. "I'm so sorry. He's the wife's dog, spoilt rotten. I'd better get him back to our caravan. Doris will be worried sick."

"No problem at all," said Janet, grateful for the diversion.

He started to walk slowly up the beach, Tiger leaping about on his lead, yapping and trying to get at the ball in the man's coat pocket.

"Hector would have loved this walk," mused Carol.

"Yes, and he'd have been a lot better behaved than that one!" said Janet. "I bet he's having a great time in some Bavarian forest."

"Will they have got there yet?" asked Suzanne. "I hope they don't come face to face with a wild boar. All those new smells for Hector…"

"And all those new experiences for the two humans!" Carol laughed.

At that moment, Liz's phone pinged.

"Oh look." The others crowded around to see a picture of a smiling Hilary perched on the parapet of a bridge, a medieval town on the hill behind her.

"Well, that answers that. That looks like France to me," said Suzanne.

"Doesn't she look happy and relaxed?" said Liz. "I don't think we need worry about how they are getting on, do you?"

They continued along the beach at a leisurely pace and rounded the headland as the sea started to come up the beach. Liz mentally congratulated herself for having the forethought to check the tide times and patted her pocket to make sure that she still had the time-table for the bus that would take them back to the car park.

"It must be great to get to the beach every day?" said Janet.

"It would be. I wish I did," said Liz. "But just knowing how close it is and that I could go every day is somehow enough. And I still find the view from the bedroom windows exciting. Daft, aren't I?"

"I'm quite envious," admitted Carol.

"Me too," said Janet. "But I'll make do with visiting for now. I can't imagine living anywhere but where we do. And Jonathan would never move…"

"I think John likes living here," said Liz. "Although he hasn't said much."

"David thought he might see him around Barwell," said Suzanne. "He still covers that area, doesn't he?"

"He does, but he covers such a big area, even when we lived there, he only visited the Barwell surgeries occasionally," explained Liz. "I think David may be seeing more of him though. There's some problem with the golf club here—I wasn't listening properly. Anyway, there's no way he's going to give up his golf, so I expect he'll find a way of carrying on at the old club."

"And then there's the rugby," put in Carol. "I'm surprised he hasn't been back to some of the matches."

"Oh, I'm sure he will," said Liz. "I could come back too. I really miss you lot, but I'm trying to find my feet here. I can't believe it's taken three months to organise this get-together. And then Hilary's not here, nor Chahna—too busy, as ever! Thinking of missing people, have you heard from Esmée recently, Suzanne?"

"I hear from her pretty regularly," said Suzanne. "I can't believe how she has pulled herself round since that first time we met her." Suzanne shuddered as she remembered her failed attempts to resuscitate Esmée's husband on a beach in the Seychelles eighteen months ago. "She's getting married, to Erik. I think I told you that she brought him to meet us last year. They've known each other for ages. Lovely man. I'm so happy for her. Her boys get on really well with him. She was worried…didn't want them to think that she was trying to replace their dad. They're not children, but what they think still matters."

"Of course it does. That's wonderful news," said Liz. She started to quiz Suzanne about the forthcoming wedding.

Carol and Janet dropped behind them.

"You're very quiet, Janet."

"Just enjoying the moment, listening to the waves, remembering times on the beach when Mum and I used to go off looking for shells. Julia could never be bothered. She was perfectly happy to sit on a deck chair with a stick of rock and a magazine."

"Have you seen much of her lately?"

"Not really. But she did visit us for a few days, to meet Jasmine," said Janet. "She was lovely with Jasmine. Although she got quite stroppy when I called her Great Aunt Julia. She does ask about Mum a bit more, and Dad said that she phones most weeks. In fact, there are going to be some changes that will make everything a bit easier, so things aren't too bad at the moment. Touch wood." She bent down and touched a piece of driftwood.

"Come on, you two slow-coaches," shouted Liz, interrupting any further conversation. "I'm going to take my socks off and paddle in the sea." She matched the action to the words and soon they were all walking barefoot along the water's edge.

"Not exactly the balmy sea of the Seychelles or even the Mediterranean," said Suzanne, as her toes turned blue. "I think we have to say this is exhilarating!"

"At least it's exfoliating your feet," said Liz. They all laughed and started to run, the cold water splashing around their ankles.

"Did anyone bring a towel, or something to get the sand off our feet?" asked the ever-sensible Janet as they slowed and began to walk up the beach.

"Of course," said Carol. "Standard equipment when you take grandchildren out."

They were quiet for a while. When they reached the path that led to the restaurant, they leaned against the railings to brush the sand off their feet.

"What a sight we must be," said Janet, trying to balance on one leg to get at the sole of her foot.

When they were all dry and decently shod again, Carol rolled the towel up and put it back in her bag.

"What a performance!" said Liz. "Let's get some lunch. I'm starving."

They opted for a table on the veranda, overlooking the sea. As they pinned down napkins and menus that threatened to blow away, another photograph pinged through to all their phones—Hilary and Tobiasz again, this time with two beers and a sandwich on the table in front of them.

"Perfect timing," said Carol.

Later, when Carol and Janet had gone in search of the toilets, Liz admitted to Suzanne that her granddaughter's new life was not quite as rosy as she had painted it.

"Siobhan, understandably, feels pushed out. She's just started school, which she absolutely loves, but it has been hard. Five years of being number one for her mummy's attention and now, not only has Jason come along, but this new and very demanding baby.

"Lisa is beginning to realise how spoiled she was with Siobhan, who seemed to just sail through every stage. Sonny—daft name—is lactose-intolerant or something. Which basically meant that for the first few weeks he cried constantly and was uncomfortable, until they finally got to the bottom of it. I know Lisa and Jason tried not to push Siobhan away, tried to stop her feeling left out, but they were both exhausted and worried.

"I've done what I can. Most of the time, that means having Siobhan at mine and I'm not sure that's the best solution. It might just be delaying problems until later. She's still lovely, don't get me wrong, and she's not hitting him or biting him, or any of the other horrible things children can do to each other. But she's definitely quieter than she was and has lost some of her sparkle.

"Now that they've got a diagnosis and a milk that doesn't upset Sonny, we've had him overnight a couple of times. That was terrifying the first time for both Lisa and me, but at least it gave Siobhan a bit of time with her mummy and her new daddy."

Suzanne poured more coffee from the cafetière and added milk to her own. She put the jug down in front of Liz.

"If Sonny…" Suzanne grimaced at the name, "…had been the perfect baby, Siobhan would still have felt left out. At least you were on hand to be a constant in her life and I bet that she has your undivided attention when she's with you."

"Of course she does," said Liz. "I know it's just time, but it just hasn't been quite as great as we thought it would be, and whatever I was saying earlier, I know John is missing his friends. Working the hours he does and being away so much, it's difficult to get to know people and he's not a great one for going into a pub on his own. It will all be fine, I know it will, and I do love living here. It's just taking a bit of time to adjust."

At that moment, Janet and Carol returned to the table and the four friends got down to the business of dividing and paying the bill.

Liz insisted they sit across the back seat of the small bus back to the car park. As it hurtled along the narrow coast road, she made dramatic gestures to point out landmarks and laughed uproariously as they were thrown together when the bus swung around corners. She knew that she was overcompensating, but she felt that she had let both Lisa and John down by admitting that things weren't perfect.

They staggered, laughing, off the bus, relieved to be on solid ground again. The bonhomie continued until Suzanne drove off, with Carol and Janet waving madly out of the windows.

"See you soon," shouted Liz. As they turned out of the car park, she got into her car and sat for a moment.

She started the engine and drove slowly towards the road.

What a lovely day, she thought. She smiled as she went back over it and was still smiling when she drove past the little harbour, her smile broadening even more when one of Siobhan's little friends, crossing the pelican crossing with her grandma, recognised Liz and waved excitedly. She negotiated a shortcut that she had recently discovered and, in no time, was pulling onto the drive.

She felt very alone as she closed the front door and took off her shoes and coat. The sand that scattered from her shoes onto the carpet somehow deepened the feeling. She missed her friends. Phone, text and email contact, however regular, was no replacement for the spontaneity of meeting in the street, or for text messages that read, *did you see…?* or *meet in 10?* or simply, *coffee?* Everything had to be planned and she felt out of the loop, at a remove from the news and gossip of Barwell.

Don't spoil the day, she told herself, as she climbed the stairs to her bedroom to get changed.

She was interrupted by a ping from her phone. It was a message thanking her for the photos and saying it looked as though they'd had a great day. Even without the name, Liz would have known the text was from Hilary, with its impeccable grammar and spelling. Hilary added, poignantly, *We are having a wonderful trip, but I wish I could have been with you all.*

TWO

Road Trip Through Europe

Hilary and Tobiasz were in France. After much discussion and detailed planning, they had set out in late March, on a month-long road trip across Europe to Tobiasz's homeland, Poland. The map of their route looked like a massive grand prix circuit, taking in places that Hilary remembered from childhood holidays. She was also keen to go to Bavaria, to see if she was right in her belief that this was where her mother had set some of the story told in the manuscript that Hilary had found in the back of her mother's wardrobe shortly after she died. Now they were nearing the German border and things were not going as well as Hilary had hoped.

Before leaving England, they had almost had an argument. It had arisen over how to cross the channel and, strictly speaking, it was more of a prolonged discussion punctuated by long silences than an argument. Hilary hated the sea and Tobiasz didn't like the idea of being confined underneath it.

At first, Hilary had given in. But when she looked into what would happen to Hector on the ferry, the discussion had begun again.

In the end, it was Hector who decided for them. The thought of leaving him alone in the car for the whole of the ferry crossing, and the possibility of him being seasick, upset them both too much. Tobiasz gracefully agreed to the tunnel.

Hilary was convinced that they wouldn't get away at all when, on route to the channel tunnel, the traffic ground to a halt on the M25. A travel bulletin on the radio alerted them to a problem ahead but, after a brief discussion, Tobiasz gently overruled Hilary's suggestion that they get off the motorway. Now, a line of stationary cars extended far into the distance in front of them.

"We should have come off at the last junction. We'll never make it now…"

"It does not matter. There will be another train," Tobiasz reassured her.

"But I don't want to spend the whole of your birthday on the M25."

"I have spent it in worse places. I don't have to work. I am with someone I love. We have food and drink on the back seat."

Hilary switched off the engine and turned the radio down.

"Well, I suppose we don't have a choice," she said. She leaned back against the seat and closed her eyes.

After half an hour, they watched the air ambulance coming in to land up ahead. Tobiasz poured two cups of coffee from the flask, glad that he had at least won that point and not relied on being able to stop for refreshments.

Hilary thanked him grudgingly for the coffee and, taking care not to spill it, twisted around in her seat to pick up the crossword book from the floor. Hector nudged her hand with his nose.

"Good boy," she said automatically.

Tobiasz quickly finished his coffee, put the cup back on the flask and got out of the car. He went around to the driver's side and unclipped Hector's lead from the harness. Hector jumped out eagerly and Hilary watched them walk towards a group of people standing by the central reservation, trying to see what was going on. Some went back to their cars when the air ambulance took off but the traffic remained stationary. Tobiasz continued chatting, while Hector sniffed around and accepted pats and compliments from the other people as his due. Before long, the cold forced them back into the car.

Hilary switched the engine on to warm the car and offered Tobiasz a boiled sweet from her precious stash.

She was puzzling over the final clue in her crossword when the sound of car engines made her look up. The red brake lights of the cars ahead came on and soon they were on the move again.

The remainder of the journey to France passed without incident and they arrived at a small hotel just outside Calais in time to enjoy a relaxing dinner to celebrate Tobiasz's birthday and the start of the trip.

Staying off the autoroute as much as possible allowed them to lunch in little roadside cafés and stay in quaint and very French *chambre d'hôtes*. On the second night, their hosts were a retired English policeman and his French wife. They treated Hilary and Tobiasz like family, spoiled Hector with meaty snacks and sent them on their way with a jar of home-made apricot jam and promises to keep in touch. The drive through the countryside to the vineyards of the Champagne district was idyllic and Hilary felt herself relax. They meandered along tiny roads under a pale blue sky, until they reached Épernay in the early afternoon. It was one of the places Hilary had insisted they include in their trip. Tobiasz had suggested Reims but, with its massive cathedral, ghost of Joan of Arc and pretentious champagne caves, Reims reminded Hilary too much of a school outing and a WI coach trip she had taken with her mother.

They chose a small hotel near the centre of Épernay and, although their room was charming and they had been greeted with glasses of champagne (and had sampled several more as they explored the town), the bed was far too hard for Hilary and the bolster like a lump of concrete.

"We should have brought our own pillows," she said, after a sleepless night. She hoped she would feel better after a long, hot shower.

The warmish water, more a trickle than a torrent, did nothing to ease the ache in her neck or clear the gritty feeling from her eyes. When she finally managed to rinse the shampoo from her hair, she came out of the shower to find Tobiasz looking very pleased with himself.

"I have walked Hector, he is in the car, and I have bought you these," he said, as he held a paper bag out towards her. Inside she could see a selection of mini croissants and pains au chocolat.

"Breakfast is included here," she said.

Tobiasz had forgotten. He carefully rolled down the top of the bag and placed it next to his suitcase.

Checking out after breakfast—which could have included more champagne if Hilary hadn't been driving—was a hurried affair because Hilary was worried about Hector being alone in the car. Besides, they had a lot of miles to cover. At each distance marker, Hilary silently converted the kilometres to miles using the formula that had been drummed into her at school. She felt more comfortable with miles than with the rapidly passing kilometres. It rained on and off all day, not heavily but enough to need the windscreen wipers, which screeched annoyingly when there was not enough water on the screen. Hilary sighed and slowed, as the third section of roadworks they'd met that day impeded their progress.

"Oh no," she almost shouted.

"What?" Tobiasz asked anxiously. He looked out of the window to see what disaster awaited them but saw only a short line of slow-moving cars and lorries.

"I think I've left my face cream and deodorant in the bathroom. Did you see them when you went back to the room?"

"I'm sorry, I didn't look. I didn't go in the bathroom. I just picked up the bags."

"You always check the room. What else might we have left? We're too far along to turn around now!" Hilary's tiredness heightened her irritation.

"I am sorry. It may be that you packed them. It is not the end of the world. We can buy what you need when we stop for lunch."

The search to find somewhere suitable for lunch, hampered by Hilary's simmering resentment, took a long time. Tobiasz apologised again and, aware that Hilary was tired, offered to drive. Hilary refused to accept either the apology or his offer to drive and allowed her irritation to develop into anger. The anger was directed at herself but Tobiasz felt it, nevertheless. By the time they stopped at an unprepossessing café in a small down-at-heel town, they had been sitting in uncomfortable silence for several miles.

"I'm sorry," she said, taking a small sip from a glass of red wine that Tobiasz had ordered for her, after he had finally persuaded her to let him drive after lunch. "I overreacted. I hope that I have a better night's sleep tonight."

"It is all right. I understand. But you must let me help you."

When they had finished what turned out to be a delicious lunch,

Tobiasz took advantage of a lull in the rain and left Hilary dozing in the car while he took Hector for a short walk. Hilary woke to the sound of the engine starting, but was asleep again before they reached the autoroute.

She felt stiff and almost drugged when they reached their destination. She couldn't match Tobiasz's enthusiasm for the town, which looked dull and uninspiring under grey skies.

The hotel was off the main square and the car, complete with all their belongings and Hector, had to be parked a short distance away.

"We'll come and get you soon," Hilary said to Hector. "We need to book into the hotel first." Hector took the proffered treat but dropped it on the seat as he stood and watched Tobiasz and Hilary take their overnight bags from the boot. He barked once, making Hilary turn, but then lay down on the back seat.

The hotel reception was manned by a large middle-aged woman who waved aside their attempts at French and pushed a registration form towards them. She gave directions to the room in heavily accented, exaggeratedly slow, English. The room, at the top of two flights of stairs, was a disappointment. It was small, painted in a harsh terracotta and furnished with angular modern furniture. After her previous sleepless night, Hilary sat down on the bed hopefully, but hit her calf on the metal bed-frame as she sank into the lumpy softness of the thin mattress.

"I'll take Hector for a walk," she said, pushing herself up off the bed.

"Shall I come?"

"No. I won't be long."

She checked her coat pocket for the car keys, left the room and started down the stairs, frustrated by the light switch that clicked off just before she reached the first landing.

It started to rain again as she reached the town square, and even Hector seemed subdued. She soon gave up the pretence of a walk and found a seat under the awning of a café.

I mustn't cry, she told herself as the rain got heavier. *I just mustn't cry.*

She was angry at herself, ashamed of feeling homesick, and of her inability to cope on this, only the third day of their trip. She couldn't have stayed in the room a moment longer; Tobiasz's persistent niceness was making her feel even more annoyed and his calm understanding only added to her feeling of hopelessness. He didn't seem to see that there was anything to complain about, and he slept wherever he was put. She wondered if they had been too ambitious, if they should have simply gone away for a weekend together. The trip stretched endlessly before her.

What is the matter with me? she thought.

The waiter placed a cup of coffee in front of her. Looking at the tiny cup of inky black liquid, she realised that her French had failed her again. *I must stop feeling sorry for myself!*

After securing Hector to the pedestal of the wrought iron table, she picked up the cup and went inside. In a mixture of French, English and pointing, she secured the cup of coffee that she wanted.

"You didn't get very far," said Tobiasz, as she came out again, carrying the coffee.

The waiter appeared at the table as Tobiasz pulled the chair opposite further under the awning.

Tobiasz pointed at Hilary's cup and said, "Un autre comme ça, s'il vous plait."

The correct coffee appeared in seconds, sending Hilary's mood plummeting further.

"Come on, you are tired, don't be upset." Tobiasz took her hand.

"I feel all at sixes and sevens," she said.

Tobiasz looked puzzled.

"Out of sorts, not myself, fed up!"

"Why are you not yourself?" he asked.

"Oh, I don't know. I just feel all upside down for no reason, nothing is right. Oh, I don't know."

They drank the coffees in silence, neither knowing what to say.

As if coming to a decision, Hilary put her cup down.

"Come on," she said. "The rain is slowing. Let's go for a walk. I'm sure that will make me feel better."

Tobiasz looked relieved as he went to pay for the coffee. Hilary untied Hector and they set off towards the river. Hector scampered about in his boisterous way. His joie de vivre brought a smile to Hilary's face and his antics offered a safe topic of conversation.

Later, exhausted, replete and secure in Tobiasz's arms, Hilary slept soundly, in spite of the lumpiness of the bed.

After a good night's sleep, she felt her good humour returning and, with it, the realisation that, to avoid future upsets, she needed some time apart from Tobiasz.

She felt a bit silly that neither of them had anticipated how different the trip would be to their life together at home in her extensive bungalow, with their separate rooms, their own space and their own time at work. Now, they spent each day cooped up in a car for hours, shared a room, and were isolated from others in unfamiliar places where they didn't speak the language. She didn't want her irritation to grow into something bigger. She simply wanted to feel comfortable again.

She broached the subject as she drove.

"I had thought the same thing," said Tobiasz. "I thought this last night, when you were upset with me."

"I wasn't upset with you, really. I just needed space."

"We must give each other space and I will try not to worry when you are not near me."

As the days passed, they began to find a balance. When the constant proximity became too much, Hilary took solitary walks or even a drive and started to feel more relaxed. Tobiasz accepted Hilary's need for space but, when he was apart from her, he needed to be surrounded by people. While Hilary walked in solitude or drove to some scenic spot, he went in search of a busy bar or coffee shop.

Now that they had established the ground rules, the silences were decidedly comfortable for the remainder of the drive across France and into Germany.

THREE

In the Pub

"I can't imagine taking a month off and driving all over the continent," said Jonathan. "They could easily have flown to Poland."

"Not with the dog," said Richard. "Ah! There's a table."

"I'll bring the drinks. You go and sit down," said Jonathan. He handed a £20 note to the young girl behind the bar. "Are you new?" he asked.

She turned to the till without answering. Jonathan gave her the benefit of the doubt and suspected that she hadn't heard him. Carol often accused him of mumbling.

He thanked her as she put the change into his hand and topped up one of the pints without being asked.

He made his way towards Richard across the Friday evening pub, already busy with afterwork drinkers.

"I wonder who's doing all the driving," said Richard, as Jonathan eased himself onto the settle at the back of the table.

"What? Oh, Tobiasz, I expect."

"I must admit there's something appealing about going away for a month," said Richard, taking a swig of his pint. "I feel as though I need a break. I'm exhausted."

"How come?"

"I'm not used to having a baby in the house. Don't get me wrong. I love having Claire living with us. Jasmine is an absolute delight. But, big as the house is, baby things seem to take up every corner of it. Claire was already a toddler when I met Janet, so I missed the screaming and the broken nights. According to both Janet and Claire, Jasmine is a very good baby—hardly cries at all, apparently—but any crying in the middle of the night is too much for me. I don't know how these older dads manage. I know, in no time at all, she'll be running about all over the place and I'll want to go back to this more controlled stage but, at the moment, I'm just exhausted. I don't even have to get up, but I'm no good if my sleep is disturbed. Now that Claire is feeling a bit stronger, got over all that upset over Jasmine's father, she's started looking at a few flats, but Janet's in her element. She's in no rush for her to leave."

"Grandchildren certainly get more interesting as they get older," said Jonathan.

"I don't know how you cope with your grandchildren, all of them around all the time," Richard mused.

"You get used to it, and they're not there all the time," replied Jonathan. "I know what you mean about all the baby paraphernalia though. I'm sure our children managed to survive babyhood without a quarter of the equipment that they seem to need now. I suppose I'm used to it. All of ours are of an age now where they just get on with things. Trouble is, then they start to get independent and, sadly, that means we won't be needed for much longer. It's all change." Jonathan took a long drink of his pint and leaned back gloomily in his chair.

"I could never understand you saying that you had to escape to the pub, but I do now!" said Richard with a rueful smile. "But, having said that, Janet is so much better. She's far less stressed now that she has something positive to concentrate on. Her mum is not any better. If anything, she's worse. Just as well she'll be moving soon. I don't know how her dad has carried on all this time."

"Nor me," agreed Jonathan. "I'm afraid I left all that to Carol. She knows I'm hopeless with illness. Anyway, have you heard from John recently? I honestly thought we'd see more of him than we have."

"I've hardly seen him since they moved," said Richard, glad of the change of subject. Janet had asked him not to say anything about her mother until it was all settled. "I've seen his car a couple of times; he still covers this area for work. I'm surprised he hasn't dropped in for a drink."

"Who hasn't dropped in for a drink?" asked John as he sat down between them. "Can I join you? I thought my ears were burning. David's at the bar. I'm staying at theirs tonight. So, if you're going to the rugby, you'll see me tomorrow as well."

"Why on earth didn't you tell us you were coming?" asked Richard.

"It was all a bit spur of the moment. David texted to say he had a spare ticket for the rugby. I wasn't needed for babysitting duties…"

"Richard was just moaning about a house full of baby," put in Jonathan.

"…and I could guarantee that I'd find you in here, at this time, on a Friday night."

"So, are you going to tell us how life is at the seaside?" asked David as he joined them with a pint in each hand. Sheila followed him with a bowl of pistachios for the table.

"Hello, stranger," she said to John, as she leaned between him and Richard. "What's brought you back to town?"

"This lot," he replied, his arms wide. "Oh, and, of course, the rugby."

"Well, I hope Liz is making the most of her freedom," she said, as she collected the empty glasses and headed back to the bar.

"Liz has settled in really well," said John, taking a handful of pistachios and splitting the shells. He absentmindedly scattered the pieces on the table. "You know Liz. She gets talking to everybody and, of course, having to do the school run a couple of days a week helps."

"Yes, you have to be a very odd sort of person not to get to know anyone outside the school gates," said Jonathan, scooping up John's scattered shells and placing them in the spare bowl that Sheila had left on the table, before securing his own supply of nuts.

"She's tried all the coffee shops and found her favourite already; knows the whole life-history of the owner. It's a bit more difficult for me. The immediate neighbours are a bit odd—Rupert and Rowena."

"Says it all doesn't it, with names like that?" said David.

"There's a nice couple opposite though," John continued. "I had quite a chat with him the other day. He's into vintage cars. Very knowledgeable." David looked interested but didn't interrupt. "I've been to the local pub but I'm not very good at going in on my own and it's not like this. More of a country pub, where everybody has their own seat. I'll have to see if there's another one." He took a long drink from his pint. "Tell you what though. There are some really good places to eat. I suppose if the seafood is not good at the seaside, it's not going to be good anywhere, is it?"

The others murmured their agreement.

"Golf?" asked Richard.

"The local club has a waiting list as long as your arm," John replied. "I've put myself on it but I've decided—and Liz said it's okay—to keep my membership up here, until I can get in there. So sorry, but you'll be seeing more of me. We're settling in, hoping for lots of visitors over the summer, but not too many..."

"That's great. Shall we get some dates in the diary?" asked Richard. "Don't look so worried... I meant for a few rounds of golf."

Looking relieved, John pulled his phone out of his pocket.

"Anyway, I didn't come all this way to talk about me. What's been going on?"

FOUR

Home Again

The day before Hilary and Tobiasz returned from their trip, Janet and Carol met for coffee in the town centre. Chahna had offered Carol a job in her new shop and Carol was keen to tell Janet all about it and about the possibility of giving up her work at the charity shop. She seemed very excited about the possibilities opening up for her. But Janet was distracted.

"What's the matter?" Carol asked. "Is something wrong?"

"I wanted to tell you the other week," she said. "When we all met up. But I couldn't face Liz pooh-poohing all my concerns or even Suzanne being all reasonable about it."

"Tell me what?"

Janet leaned across the table and, without stopping for breath, as her coffee went cold, told Carol about her father's plans to move with her mother into the new care home just outside Barwell.

Carol smiled.

"How do you feel about it?" she asked.

"Relieved, frightened, apprehensive," Janet replied. "I cannot believe Dad's strength. He presented it to me as a fait accompli. I felt a bit hurt, at first, that he'd done it behind my back, and not needed me. But then, all I felt was grateful."

George had called Janet one Wednesday in late January to check when she would next visit. Janet assumed that the call was simply because of his concern about the weather. Indeed, the drive had taken longer than usual and spray from the recently melted snow had made driving difficult.

She was alarmed to find her father waiting in the hall when she arrived. He seemed impatient as she took off her coat, hung it up on the hall stand and slipped her feet out of her shoes. He directed her into the dining room.

"Is Mum okay?" she asked, looking towards the closed living room door.

"Fine, just having a snooze. I just want a quick word with you. I'll make some coffee." With that, he went out, pulling the door to behind him. Janet heard him clattering about in the kitchen. She sat down at the table and began to wonder what had happened.

After a few minutes, he pushed the door open and came in with a tray that held two cups of coffee and a plate of biscuits. Janet jumped up and took the tray from him.

"Mum would be proud of you," she said.

"Can't let standards drop," he muttered, as he sat down at the head of the table.

Janet used her teaspoon to remove the rapidly forming skin from the milky coffee and sipped the comforting, familiar drink.

George took one of the bourbon biscuits and pushed the plate towards Janet.

"I had thought of booking your mother into a nursing home for respite care," he said. "But I realised that we need something more permanent."

Before Janet could finish her mouthful of biscuit, he continued, "I'm getting to the point where I know we can't carry on like this much longer."

And then he dropped the bombshell about the bigger plan. He had already had the house valued and planned to put it on the market in March. The estate agent had been very confident that it would sell quickly.

"Young whippersnapper had the cheek to say it would sell quickly in spite of being in need of updating," said George.

"People like to put their own stamp on a house," said Janet, looking around the dining room that, despite being regularly redecorated, hadn't changed much since she left home thirty-nine years ago.

"He also said I could get more if I got outline planning permission for an extension or even another house in the garden. I don't want more money. I'll get enough. Property values have gone up since your old school got that outstanding Ofsted report. I've been keeping an eye on the market."

Janet smiled. She felt a little sorry for the estate agent.

"You have done so much for us," her dad continued. "I wanted to carry out the whole plan without worrying you but, of course, I can't because, in part, it involves you."

"Me?" said Janet. "The two of you aren't moving in with Richard and me, are you?"

Ignoring her question, her father placed his cup carefully in the saucer and sat up a little straighter in his chair.

"I've found a nursing home, not far from Barwell, just over three miles from you and Richard," he said. "It opens in June. I've seen all the brochures. I haven't managed to have a look around yet, but there would be a place for both of us. It's nursing and residential. Your mother would have her own room on the dementia floor. We would be able to surround her with her familiar things. I will be there but not in the same room. They have lots of activities and there's a garden. It's expensive, but the money from the house would cover it for some time."

"James Place," said Janet. "I've seen it. Brand new. It's on the road to Warwick. It looks like a smart hotel. How did you find it?"

"Ian, next door, helped me on the internet. I bought him lunch. He's helped me with Beryl on a few occasions when she's fallen," he admitted, sounding ashamed. "I can't keep relying on neighbours."

Janet wanted to hug her dad but his upright posture and the history between them precluded this. He had needed to do this himself. She couldn't believe how far down the line he had got. The relief was immense; she wanted to cry but that was something else you didn't do around Dad.

"That sounds like a perfect plan," she said. "I can't believe how much you've done."

"Oh, it's only the bare bones. I think it's going to fall to you to make all the arrangements. Although, of course, I can sort out the sale of the house. But I will perhaps need some help clearing out all the stuff that we've accumulated. I've already been in touch with a house clearance company."

Janet was saddened by the lack of sentimentality in his voice.

"I'm going to have another cup of coffee. Do you want one?" She picked up the plate and cups and put them back on the tray.

"No, thank you, but you have one," he replied. "There's plenty of milk." He took the last biscuit as she walked past.

Janet's mind was in a whirl as she watched the pan of milk come to the boil. Lists, and lists of lists, formed in her head.

"Through here," shouted her dad as she came out of the kitchen.

He had gone into the living room. As Janet walked in, he placed a biscuit in Beryl's hand. She looked at it suspiciously, before putting the whole thing in her mouth and crunching greedily.

Janet later realised that she had underestimated the amount of organisation required to move her parents, but she was grateful to her dad for making the decision to move before things became unmanageable.

"It brings back all the feelings that I had when Mum had to go into a home," Carol said when Janet stopped to drink her now cold coffee, "and then Jonathan's dad, so soon afterwards. It was awful. I don't think the guilt ever goes completely. Even when Mum stopped asking me to take her home and even after Jonathan's dad had absolutely no idea where he was!"

"I think that was why I felt so grateful to Dad for making the decision. For being brave enough to accept that he couldn't do it any longer," said Janet.

"As a woman, I felt that I should have been able to cope," continued Carol. "That I shouldn't have to ask anybody else for help. In a way, I think that's what made me leave it for so long and that just made it more difficult. I'd looked after Mum for so long, that she simply refused to accept that I couldn't do it forever. She hated going into Oaklands."

"But she settled, didn't she?" said Janet, looking a bit worried. "She was happy before she got so poorly, wasn't she?"

"Oh yes," said Carol. She turned in her chair, to attract the attention of the waitress, wondering whether to tell Janet about the latest episode in her mother's care.

Carol had recently had a difficult discussion with her mother's doctor. She had witnessed a distressing battle as a care assistant tried to persuade her mum to take her medication. Carol couldn't bear it and had to leave the room. When the care assistant came out of the room, Carol asked her if it had happened before.

The young Filipina girl looked close to tears.

"She must have tablets," she said and scuttled off down the corridor.

Carol went to see the duty manager. She was dismayed to see that it was Margot, a large, efficient woman who was very skilful at looking busy.

Carol refused the offer of a chair and described what she had seen.

"Dr Potter insists that she has 'er tablets, they're keeping 'er alive," said Margot, moving a pile of papers from one side of the desk to the other. "My girls are pretty successful at getting the awkward ones to cooperate. Might be because they don't 'ave much English."

Carol wished that she hadn't started the conversation and had waited until Jennifer was on duty. But she knew that she had to stand her ground.

"I would like a list of Mum's medication, please."

"What for?"

"So that I can speak to Dr Potter."

Margot tutted and swung her chair around to reach into the filing cabinet behind her without getting up and, with a great show of effort, extracted a file. She sighed as she thumbed through the pages until she came to the two pages that listed Carol's mother's medication. She pushed her chair to the photocopier and grudgingly gave the copy to Carol.

Carol took it, offering effusive thanks for Margot's trouble, and left the room.

She planned to ask Suzanne for some advice first and then make an appointment with the doctor.

Dr Potter was relatively new to the practice, full of his own importance and extensive knowledge. He almost accused Carol of wanting to finish her mother off but, armed with some advice from Suzanne and with the feeling that her mother rarely took the tablets anyway, Carol stood her ground. Dr Potter, implying that he was afraid of being sued for negligence, suggested he call in one of the more senior doctors in the practice. Carol almost hugged Jag when he came into the room. He calmly listened while Dr Potter explained what Carol was trying to do and then patiently went through the medications one by one, praising the young doctor for his knowledge of the drugs and explaining the ethics and logic of continuing treatment against a patient's wishes. Carol was profuse in her thanks when she was reassured that, apart from an indigestion remedy and painkillers, all of her mother's medication would be stopped over a period of a few weeks.

Carol felt vindicated when she met Dr Potter in the corridor at the nursing home some days later. He stopped and apologised.

"It was a valuable lesson," he said. "It is always easier to start medication than to stop it."

"I know it was only a matter of time," said Carol, as she finished recounting the incident and the waitress brought their second coffee. "But I've removed one battle from Mum's life and, hopefully, ensured that what remains of her life will be more bearable––for everyone."

"That must have been awful for you," Janet said. "That's why I wanted to talk to you. I knew you'd understand, you've been through so much. It isn't nearly as bad for me. Dad is still in charge."

"I think that must be really important to him, to feel in control," said Carol.

"Absolutely, and the plan wouldn't have worked if he hadn't been able to go into the same home. Secretly, I think he's really looking forward to it, although I know that he will miss his friends—who are becoming fewer and fewer in number anyway. He seems to go to a funeral every week. He's become chief mourner, but he takes it all in his stride—but yes, I think he's looking forward to it. Going back to his days in the army when he first joined up. Living in a single room, dinners in the mess hall, everything provided, responsibilities lifted, simply orders to follow."

"When are they planning to move?" asked Carol.

"This summer, as soon as the home opens," said Janet. "They'll be in the first wave of residents. I've no doubt they'll be spoiled rotten at first, as the home is still trying to fill the other rooms and then things may change, but we'll cross that bridge when we come to it."

"That doesn't sound like you," Carol said, laughing.

"No, probably not, but I'm hoping it is the new me. I'll have all my family close by. I'll be able to keep an eye on them. Claire has been looking at flats, you know, but nothing too far away. She'll be going back to work in October and I think she'd like to be settled in by then."

"It's nice that she and Dan are still in touch, isn't it?" said Carol. "I can't get over them hitting it off like that. My brother isn't the easiest."

"I think it's lovely that what started because they were both at such a low ebb has developed into a real friendship," said Janet. "Anyway, you've let me witter on all this time, what did you say about Chahna renting a shop? I thought it was all online."

"It was."

Carol told Janet about the shop Chahna had found, her excitement and enthusiasm apparent.

"Sounds amazing. Fingers crossed it all goes ahead," said Janet.

She started to say something else and then looked at her watch.

"Oh goodness, look at the time. I've got to go." She stood up and started to gather her coat and bags. "Hilary comes back tomorrow, doesn't she?"

Carol got up too and shrugged her coat on. "Yes. I can't wait to hear how they got on."

"Nor me. She sent loads of texts and I even got a postcard…"

"Me too," said Carol.

"…but none of them said very much."

"Another excuse for a get-together."

"Definitely."

FIVE

Voices From the Past

Hilary had been dreading opening the front door of the bungalow after a month away but Suzanne, true to her word, had popped over frequently to water the plants, open doors and windows to keep the air fresh, and put lights on and close curtains to fool would-be burglars into believing that the bungalow was occupied.

"Bless her," said Hilary, as she put the light on and noticed the post neatly stacked on the hall table.

"There is even milk in the fridge," Tobiasz called from the kitchen.

"She is so kind."

Hilary went to let Hector out of the car and start bringing in the luggage.

A few moments later, Tobiasz followed her out.

"I have put the kettle on," he said. "We can finish this tomorrow." He took the suitcases from her and turned to go in.

Hilary gathered up Hector's things and locked the car. Hector checked the drive and its borders for strange smells and then followed her into the house.

Suddenly tired, Hilary flopped onto her chair and Hector, hearing the rattle of food in his bowl, dashed through to the kitchen.

"Welcome home," said Tobiasz a few minutes later, placing a cup of coffee next to Hilary.

"It is nice to be home," she said. "But, do you know, I'd have been happy just to carry on travelling around. I have loved it."

"I am sorry we did not go to all the places we planned. I still feel I let you down. What will your friends say?"

"It doesn't matter. You didn't let me down. I keep telling you. We are free to do as we please." Hilary took her feet off the footstool, picked up her coffee and went to sit next to Tobiasz on the settee. She placed her coffee next to his and leaned towards him, almost forcing him to put his arm around her. She snuggled into his side.

"What will impress them all is that we went away for a month and we are still friends."

Tobiasz smiled and squeezed her shoulder.

"It is because we are both kind people. We want happiness for each other."

The following morning Tobiasz glanced at his letters. He put the telephone bill to one side and dropped the junk mail into the recycling. He kissed Hilary on the cheek, as she joined him in the kitchen.

"I will take Hector out," he said. "Do you mind? You must not do all the unpacking and washing while I am out. We will do it together when I get back."

Hilary smiled as he left with Hector. She made a cup of coffee, picked up her pile of post and sat down at the breakfast bar. A bank statement and a couple of household bills held no surprises, but she was puzzled by a brown envelope addressed in handwriting that she didn't recognise and that suggested an older writer. It was addressed to Ms Walton. She slit open the envelope and took out folded blue notepaper and a matching sealed envelope. The letter started abruptly without any greeting.

You won't know me but when I was clearing my father's things after his death, I found photos of someone who I think could be your mother.

The words brought back all the feelings of turmoil that the original discovery of her mother's manuscript had produced. She felt dizzy and disorientated but pulled herself together, relieved that she was on her own and didn't have to explain. She paused, had a sip of her coffee and continued to read. The tone softened.

I understand she died last year. I am sorry for your loss. My daughter, Marianne, is doing a PhD. I can't think why at her age. It's called Erotic dancing in 1950s London – A female perspective. *I would have thought that everything that could be written about that had already been written, but obviously I'm wrong because the university accepted her research proposal. She knew that her granddad had worked at the Windmill Theatre, doing the lighting. Ogling probably, my dad was a bit of a dirty old man, by present standards. Anyway, my daughter showed me a picture of him with some of the dancers at the theatre that she found when she was doing her research and then, when I was clearing his things (ironically, he died at about the same time as your mother, cancer), I found this picture of him with one of them sitting next to the old Ford Anglia I remember from my childhood. The date was stamped on the back of the photo and he had written 'Phyllis, South Downs' under it. Surprisingly, there weren't that many dancers called Phyllis in the Windmill at that time. He was only there four years, which made the search easier. He will have blotted his copybook one way or another, he was always a bit of a chancer. Please don't think that I didn't love my father but he left me, my sister and my mum when I was 11. Mum and Georgina never forgave him, but I did. I always kept in touch with him. Secretly at first and then, when mum died, and in spite of Georgie's disapproval, I let him into my life again. It was difficult always having to juggle family parties so that it was either Dad or Georgie, never both. Her son staunchly took her side but I know he would have loved to have met his granddad. The way he leaves a trail of broken hearts behind him I think they would have had a lot in common.*

Anyway, Marianne and I researched this Phyllis together. It took a bit of time, not as straightforward as I imagined. But it finally led us to you.

I had no idea I was going to write all this and it probably won't be read. But I do find these little things help you get through the grieving process. Get in touch with me, if you think that you can.

The sealed envelope contained two photographs.

The first was a colour shot, obviously professional, of her mother dressed for the stage. It was a smaller copy of the picture that Hilary had found with her mother's manuscript.

The other was black and white, small and square with a narrow white border. The photograph showed a man and woman sitting on a plaid picnic rug, leaning against a white car, the remains of a picnic in front of them. The man was obviously older, more self-assured. Good-looking in a brash sort of way, Hilary thought uncharitably. The woman, who could definitely be her mother, was wearing a sundress. The material was pale with what looked like tiny sprigs of flowers. Hilary imagined pale blue with yellow flowers—her mother's favourite colours. The sweetheart neckline and cinched waist emphasised her trim figure. She looked carefree, happy and so very young. They were leaning towards each other, their shoulders not quite touching. They were looking towards the camera but Hilary felt that the smiles were for each other rather than for the photographer. The man's posture somehow implied ownership, but the more Hilary looked, the more she wondered if she just was being fanciful.

She needed to think carefully before replying to the letter. She needed time and space, so she refolded the letter and placed it with the photos back in the envelope. She found that she was curious to know more, in spite of having said to everyone, including herself, that she wanted to leave the past in the past, and, if her mother had wanted her to know, she would have told her.

With her mind in a whirl, she thought about getting the rest of the things out of the car, unpacking the bags and putting on the washing while Tobiasz and Hector were out of the way. She could hear her mother telling her to keep busy, but she needed to talk to someone to take her mind off what she had just learned. All the unpacking and washing in the world won't stop me thinking, she thought. And Tobiasz said that we should do it together.

She decided to pop across the road with Suzanne's gift and to see if her friend had time for a chat. She felt calmer having made a plan and took one of the suitcases into her bedroom, laid it on the bed, and unzipped it.

She rummaged through the carefully folded clothes and found the gift. She had alighted on it in a small antique shop in Germany and immediately loved it. A vase, not six inches high, shaped like a classical Greek vase and decorated with a magenta and cream, almost yellow, drip glaze. Tobiasz thought that it wasn't enough for looking after the bungalow but Hilary was adamant that Suzanne would love it; she could even picture a place for it among the other treasures in the house. Lifting the small tissue-wrapped parcel from her suitcase, she wondered if Tobiasz had been right. Feeling very unsure, she put two bottles of wine into a gift bag with the vase and went across the road. In her rush, she was already up Suzanne's drive before she realised her friend's car wasn't there. She dashed back across the road, dodging the traffic, and swapped the gift for a small decorative box of Bavarian sugar cookies. She crossed the road again, sure that Betty, Suzanne's mother-in-law, would be at home in her flat above the garage.

Betty smiled as she watched Hilary's antics from her armchair by the living room window. When she saw that Hilary was on her way across the road for a second time, she pushed herself up from her chair and put the kettle on in readiness.

"I'm so glad Suzanne has just popped out," she said as she opened the door. "I want to hear all about your trip first hand."

Hilary followed her into the kitchen and placed the biscuits on the counter top.

"Lovely, thank you," said Betty. She tore the cellophane off and put the open box on the tray with two mugs of coffee. "You carry it through, please."

"Well?" she said, as they sat down opposite each other.

"It was amazing, a wonderful trip. In a way, I didn't want it to end. But…"

Hilary tailed off awkwardly. She picked up her coffee and put it down again, took a biscuit, broke it in half and put both pieces next to her coffee.

"What?"

"We didn't get to Poland," said Hilary, in a rush. "We spent a couple of weeks in Germany instead."

"Oh," said Betty.

"We had a wonderful time. Brilliant," gushed Hilary. "There was me thinking that I'd learn all about what made Tobiasz tick, seeing him in his home country, meeting his relatives, but I have to admit I think we learned more about each other being cooped up in the car for so long!"

Betty laughed. "Yes, that was a very brave thing to do."

"I'm very naive," said Hilary. "I thought that because we had lived in the same place for several months that it would all be easy but, of course, it's very different when you can't find some space for yourself. There's no way you can just get out and go for a walk when you're on the autoroute. We didn't actually argue," she continued, "but there were some difficult moments… We got through them, and I think just being able to stay in one place for a week, in that lovely apartment, made everything right again. That was certainly fate."

Hilary went on to describe how she and Tobiasz had met Katja.

Tobiasz had grown unaccountably quiet as they neared the Polish border. Hilary, used to his chattering and observations, stopped at a roadside café and, without a word, took Hector from the back of the car and went and sat at one of the tables set precariously on the pavement. Tobiasz reluctantly got out of the car. Hilary ordered coffee. Tobiasz still said nothing.

"What's the matter?" she asked, feeling irritated. "Have I done something wrong?"

Tobiasz didn't answer immediately. He politely thanked the waitress for his coffee and sat staring down into the froth.

"Well?" asked Hilary, sounding like her mother. Her teaspoon clattered onto the saucer, splashing coffee onto her white blouse. She rubbed at it.

"I feel very foolish, very childish. But I cannot do it. I cannot go back there. I cannot go to Poland. It is not logical. I didn't experience anything bad. In spite of the times, I had a good life. A good childhood. So, why do I feel so reluctant now?"

"Is it me? Are you ashamed of me?"

"Of course I am not ashamed of you. I cannot explain here, but I will."

Hector chose that moment to jump up and pull on his lead that was attached to the leg of the table, sending the coffees flying.

Hilary was looking down at her now ruined blouse and trying to rein Hector in when a young woman crossed the road towards them. She was carrying the cause of Hector's escape attempt. Black eyes, surrounded by what looked like a ball of white fluff, peeped out from her shoulder bag.

"I am sorry, very sorry," she said. "Can I buy you a coffee, another coffee?"

"It's not your fault," said Hilary. "I'm the one with the dog who nearly pulled the table over."

"But perhaps we will all have a coffee," she said, seeing the young woman's distraught face. "I'll just go and see if I can do something about my blouse."

As she stood in the cramped toilet at the back of the café, holding the front of her blouse out under the hand drier, her mind went into overdrive. She forgot about the young woman and her dog and wondered if it had all been a lie, if the stories Tobiasz had told her had really been true.

She had read a translation of the book that he said had been written by his mother. It had been a harrowing read, disturbing in a different way from her own mother's book. She recalled the nights they had talked and talked, when he told her about his father's suicide, his wife's accident, the guilt that he felt for both. He couldn't have made it up. She couldn't be that wrong.

Tobiasz often told her what a great help it had been to talk to her; that he felt a weight lifted from his mind, a weight that had been there ever since his childhood. He told her about cousins that they might be able to get in touch with in Poland. At the time, she had been a bit curious as to why he hadn't got in touch with them before they left England. Why arrangements hadn't already been made to meet up. Every other aspect of the trip had been meticulously planned. It now crossed her mind that the cousins might not exist.

I have to go out and face him, find out what's going on, she thought. I wish we'd just booked a weekend coach trip with other people around.

When she got outside, she found Tobiasz and the woman deep in conversation. Hector was sitting with his head on Tobiasz's lap, warily eyeing the woman's handbag.

"Hilary, this is Katja," said Tobiasz.

"Hello, Hilary." Katja held out her hand. "Your blouse looks much better. I am so sorry," she said, with barely a trace of an accent.

Hilary shook her hand. "Nice to meet you." She sat down and Hector settled in the shade under the table.

"Anyway," continued Tobiasz. "I was telling Katja that we have changed our plans and decided to explore this area more." He ignored Hilary's quizzical glance. "And Katja says she knows of an apartment that we may be able to rent. She's not sure if it's free but she will find out. It's in the next town. What do you think?"

"Really?" asked Hilary.

"Yes," said Katja. "I'm not doing this because I feel guilty about disrupting your coffee. I'm doing this because I know last week my friend Peta didn't manage to rent it and she relies on the money. To me, it seems like fate but, then, of course, she might have rented it since I last saw her. I will find out when we finish coffee."

"It sounds too good to be true," said Hilary. "Let's hope that it is still free."

They exchanged phone numbers and Katja continued on her way.

"I can't believe how lucky we were to find this place," Tobiasz said two days later. He was sitting on the small balcony overlooking the town square, a clear blue sky outlining the mountains that towered above the buildings. "All the travelling has been good and we have seen wonderful places, but I think it is good to stop. To get out of the car and put down roots, however temporary. I do not regret cutting our trip short."

"After all that planning, it did make me a bit cross at first," said Hilary. "But you're right. Here is perfect and being in the car, together all the time, was getting a bit much, wasn't it?"

Hector put his head on Hilary's lap and she twisted his ears in her fingers, her own living security blanket.

"Hector didn't complain, did he? But he's certainly making the most of the long walks. I know, at first, he must have hated those walks around car parks and service stations."

"I do not think that he minded," said Tobiasz, "but I worried about what he would find among all the rubbish."

"Hector just accepts what he's offered, but he wasn't as joyous as he is now."

"So Hector saved us in a way," Hilary explained to Betty. "We got to stay in this lovely apartment for ten days and explored all round Regenstauf. It was lovely to unpack after nearly two weeks of overnight stays."

The sound of a car pulling into the drive brought Hilary to the window. She waved down at Suzanne, who soon joined them for a cup of tea and to hear all the news.

"I have a present for you," said Hilary. She leaped up and dashed out of the door, before either of them could say anything. Suzanne smiled at Betty as she collected the cups and went to put the kettle on again. Hilary was soon back.

"Thank you so much for looking after the bungalow," she said, pushing the bag towards Suzanne.

Suzanne was as enamoured with the vase as Hilary had hoped and she was sure that David would be pleased with the wine.

"So, what's this I hear about you not going to Poland?"

Hilary recounted the story again.

By the time she got home, Tobiasz was back. He had finished emptying the car and had unpacked his cases.

"I thought you had left me," he said, only half joking.

"I popped across to thank Suzanne and was there longer than planned," Hilary replied. "She loved the vase. I took some wine for David."

"That is good. Was there any news?"

"I didn't ask," Hilary said. "She and Betty were too interested in what we had been up to."

After lunch, Hilary unpacked her cases and sent Tobiasz to the shops to restock the fridge. She had to shoo Hector away as he tried to lie on the piles of sorted laundry.

"How come everything needs washing again?" she asked him.

She tidied away her jewellery and returned the toiletries to the bathroom, before stowing the suitcases on the high shelves in the garage.

"We'll have to have a go at the garden this weekend," she said to Hector, as she pegged the first load of washing on the line.

"I saw Dan in Sainsbury's," said Tobiasz, putting two bulging bags down in front of the fridge and pushing Hector's nose out of them. "We are meeting for a drink tonight. Is that okay?"

"Of course," said Hilary.

That'll give me a chance to phone Liz, she thought.

With Tobiasz and Hector out of the way, she settled in her chair with her feet up and a cup of coffee beside her. She dialled Liz's number and her friend answered straight away.

"How come you didn't send any pictures from Poland?" Liz asked, after a brief greeting. "Was it too difficult for you both?"

Hilary took a sip of her coffee. "We didn't go."

"What?" screeched Liz.

Hilary held the receiver away from her ear.

"We stopped in Germany," she replied.

"But I thought that was the whole point," said Liz. "I thought that's where you were going to meet his family, to see where he'd come from. What on earth did you do? What about all the hotel bookings in Poland? And the people you were supposed to meet up with?"

"It was the whole point of the trip," agreed Hilary. "Halfway across Germany, Tobiasz told me that he had cancelled all the bookings and secured refunds for the hotels in Poland. He'd done it before we left France. He hadn't said anything to me before that."

"I would have been absolutely furious," said Liz. "Didn't he even discuss it with you?"

"No," said Hilary. "I was a bit cross at first. I felt that he'd deceived me. I thought it was because he was ashamed of me, didn't want to introduce me to his family and friends."

"You are daft," said Liz. "How could he possibly be ashamed of you?"

"Well, I'm not very glamorous or interesting…"

Liz groaned.

"Anyway, it wasn't that at all," continued Hilary. "It was nothing to do with me. He couldn't face going back to Poland. I didn't realise that he hadn't been back since his wife's funeral all those years ago. And although he didn't say this directly, every association that he has with that country is related to loss. The one thing that all that time in the car did was give him lots of time to think and, as he said, the Poland that he knew doesn't exist any longer. I can understand that all his associations with the country are negative. He said that if his mother had been alive, he would have loved to introduce us, that I'm just like her, that we would have got on well, with lots of things in common."

"I hope that he doesn't think that you are going to become his mother," said Liz.

"Of course not. I think that he was just trying to reassure me that his decision to change his plans was nothing to do with me. I have thought about it a lot and I think, at first, I did give him a bit of a hard time…"

"Good for you!" said Liz.

"…all that planning. I still think that it's possible that he never intended to go to Poland, he just went along with my wishes. But he said that wasn't the case. From the safety of the bungalow in Barwell, he thought that he would be able to go through with it. He was ashamed of the deceit, and afraid to discuss it with me. He said he didn't tell me until it was too late because he didn't want to be persuaded to stick to the original plan. But when he realised how upset I was, he offered to rebook everything, take me anyway. But the trip wasn't for me, the trip was for us!"

"What on earth did you do?" asked Liz.

Hilary settled herself more comfortably into her chair to tell her tale.

"What did Janet say when you told her? Or Carol?" Liz asked when she'd finished.

"I haven't had a chance to speak to them yet. I told Betty and she didn't say anything really. She and Suzanne were just interested in what we'd seen and where we'd been."

"But surely they must have thought it strange," said Liz. "I shall have to talk to your Tobiasz."

SIX

Pondering a Big Question

Tobiasz didn't regret not going to Poland. But he felt guilty for cancelling without telling Hilary, for letting her think that they were going, for changing all their carefully laid plans. He wasn't proud of how he had done it and it could all have gone disastrously wrong had Katja's silly little dog not upset Hector.

He wanted to talk to Dan about what had happened on the trip, about why he had felt unable to continue with the journey into Poland; but, in truth, he found it difficult to explain it to himself. More importantly, he had an idea he wanted to run past Dan.

They met as usual in the local pub. Tobiasz secured a table while Dan went to get the drinks. Seeing the crush at the bar, Tobiasz settled back in his chair for a bit of a wait. The noisy chatter, shouts and laughter mixed with the ringing sounds of glasses, along with the smell of beer and perfumed bodies, took him back to the night when he had taken that fateful call from his father-in-law.

He had been working in a London bar frequented by city businessmen with loud voices and louder ties. He was serving a couple of giggling girls—dressed for the office but in every other way letting their hair down—when the phone behind the bar started to ring. He and the other bar staff ignored it for as long as possible, but its insistence made him grab it as he put the girls' money into the till. He was surprised when the heavily accented voice on the other end asked for him by name. He thought he recognised his father-in-law's voice but he couldn't hear what he was saying. He covered his other ear and tried to duck round the side of the bar but the telephone cord wasn't long enough.

He laid the handset on the bar and grabbed Josh, who was the nearest of the four bar staff serving the packed pub.

"The call is for me. I will take it upstairs," he said. "Can you put the receiver down when I answer?" Josh agreed with a grunt.

Tobiasz dashed upstairs and picked up the receiver of the phone on the landing.

"Got it," he yelled. He heard the click as Josh replaced the receiver downstairs.

"Is it important?" he asked in Polish. "I am working." He regretted the words as soon as his father-in-law told him the news.

"Krystyna is dead. She died instantly. Car accident."

Shocked and dazed, Tobiasz couldn't form the sentence to ask what had happened. His wife was dead.

"I will phone back later when I can get someone to cover my shift," he said.

"Tomorrow," his father-in-law said, as he put the phone down.

In the end, there was no one to take over from Tobiasz. The landlord, sitting at the other side of the bar, laughed with his cronies and acted as if he didn't believe Tobiasz. The others helped him as he stumbled through the shift but he took his money the next day and never returned.

Tobiasz had interpreted his father-in-law's shocked tone as callousness and his grief as blame. At the funeral, the coldness that his in-laws exhibited towards him added to his feelings of guilt. But now, thinking about it, and reliving their wedding with its few guests, he realised the coldness had been there that day too. Perhaps he had ignored the fact that Krystyna's family felt the same way about his wife as his own mother did.

His mother hadn't wanted him to marry Krystyna. She believed they were marrying for the wrong reasons and couldn't understand why he had chosen to marry someone that she knew he didn't really love. She couldn't understand why they couldn't just be business partners. But, for a while, Tobiasz thought that he loved Krystyna, with her liveliness and her head full of ideas. Her life was mapped out before her and the family business was ready for her to take over. Now that he knew what real love felt like, he realised that he had been in love with an idea.

With the distance that the years had given him, he could now see that the marriage had been doomed. His mother, who had never really liked Krystyna, died three weeks after the wedding. He wondered now if he had perhaps blamed Krystyna for his mother's death. The blame ate away at the already fragile relationship and probably prompted his move to London. He told Krystyna, and tried to convince himself, that it was in order to gain experience for the family hotel in Poland but, if he was being honest, it had been a new start. He could see now that there had been a lack of openness and honesty in their relationship. Perhaps his mother had been right; he and Krystyna should never have married. The feeling that he had perhaps used her added to his guilt. He now realised that he had wasted many years feeling guilty, feeling responsible for all that had happened over which he'd had very little control. This epiphany as they neared the Polish border had freed him and allowed him to shed some of his guilt, rid himself of the need to go back and make amends and to accept what had happened. The only person he had to make amends with was himself. For years he had felt responsible for his wife's accident. The weather had certainly played a part and perhaps she had been tired. But he had tortured himself for so long thinking that it was the last argument they'd had that had caused the fatal accident. It hadn't been a major argument, just a disagreement over when he would return to Poland. For years, he imagined that he had sent her, cross and upset, to her death. In reality, on the night of the accident, she had gone out to see a friend. It was raining hard and the roads were greasy after a dry spell. Her car had skidded into the path of a milk tanker. She was killed instantly and the tanker driver sustained hardly a scratch. In shock and grief, Tobiasz's mind condensed the time, altering his memory and compounding his guilt and self-blame. There had been an argument, there was no doubt of that, but the accident hadn't happened until three days later.

The tragedy had left him afraid of marriage and now, he realised, afraid of returning to Poland. At the time, he had felt angry and aggrieved that the family had blamed him but he came to realise the anger had come from the fact that he blamed himself. His mother's death a few weeks after the wedding had felt like a punishment. The grief that followed Krystyna's death brought all the distress and pain that had accompanied his mother's death to the fore.

After Krystyna's death, the anger turned inwards and he sank into a deep depression. In his lowest moments, he considered following his father to suicide. He moved out of London, drifting from job to job and only taking work that included accommodation. When he finally settled in the Lake District, he found peace and solace in the beauty of his surroundings and in people who valued his diligence and respected his privacy.

Life is cruel, he thought. *Guilt can be a very difficult emotion to break free from, the mind plays tricks and memories get distorted, keeping the feelings of blame and guilt alive. My life could have been so different, if I had come to this conclusion sooner. But then I may not have met Hilary…*

As Hilary came into his mind, it occurred to him that he was repeating previous mistakes, not being totally honest with himself or with those close to him.

He had wanted to show his country to Hilary, to be able to lay some ghosts to rest and put the past behind him once and for all. What he hadn't expected was the force of his feelings as the possibility of returning to Poland began to become a reality. He couldn't admit to Hilary how he felt. The shame, which he saw as a weakness, led him to cancel everything without telling her. Mixed with the shame and embarrassment, this feeling of failure, was the very real feeling that he couldn't bear to lose Hilary. He had thought he would never want to marry again but now it was more than a possibility in his mind.

"I thought I was never going to get served," said Dan, as he sat down opposite Tobiasz. "I lost some of your pint on the way back, sorry." He brushed his wet hand on the back of his jeans.

"So, come on. How come you only did half the trip? All that planning…"

"I change my mind," he said. He pushed the disturbing memories from his mind. "I wanted to show Hilary the beauty of my country. She really only had heard about the despair but I found that all my memories were associated with death, all those millions, my mother and grandmother and then Krystyna. I couldn't face it myself and I didn't want to put Hilary through it. She accept and understand without any explanation. I think it make me love her more."

Dan stared down at his pint.

"I regret that I did it without telling Hilary. I cancelled all the bookings that we have made in Poland, transferred the money back into her account. She was hurt and cross at first. She did not understand why I had not talked to her about it. I'm not sure she does now but we had a comfortable time in Bavaria. It was good to have a few days in one place."

Tobiasz told Dan about how they had met Katja, and how lucky they were to find the apartment. He went on for so long about how helpful and kind she was that Dan interrupted him.

"Are you smitten?"

Tobiasz looked puzzled at the word but when he realised what Dan was asking, said, "No. I am not! I want to marry Hilary."

Dan looked up from his pint in amazement.

"Why on earth do you want to do that? You seem to have the perfect arrangement. Does she want to marry you?"

"I have not asked her."

"Why would she want to marry you?"

"For love, for security. When everything went so wrong with my first marriage, I never wanted to marry again, but having met Hilary, I do."

"Don't get me wrong. I think you're a great match, but Hilary's already secure, rich, with property and income. People might think that you are doing it for the money."

Tobiasz looked hurt.

"I think she is lonely. I think she has difficulty trusting people. I think it would show how much I love her."

"She knows that, mate."

"I spent so many years being afraid of being married. I want to do it before it is too late."

"Well, if you're that set on it, it's not me you should be talking to."

"But you are not sure…"

"Well, perhaps I'm not the best person to be asking about marriage."

SEVEN

At the Motorway Services

Tobiasz had been late home from the pub the night before. Hilary was already in bed when she heard the front door open. He'd crept past her room, presumably not wanting to disturb her. He was still in his room when she clipped on Hector's lead the next morning and headed for the Garden of Remembrance. She needed to think.

She couldn't imagine her mother being comfortable, never mind in love, with the man that Gillian had described. He sounded exactly like the type of man that Hilary had been warned against as a teenager – a chancer, a risk taker, a charmer. The exact opposite of her father.

What if this man is my father? The thought stopped her in her tracks. Hector looked back at her to see why she had stopped. She pulled on his lead, turned around and went straight home.

She went to the bookcase and took down the photo albums. She wanted to look at photos of her and her father together. She studied them closely. There couldn't be any doubt; she was his daughter. Now that she was older, the likeness was quite striking—the shape of their noses, the slight downturn at the corner of the eyes; eyes that were perhaps too close together, which, with her dad's square chin, meant that she had never had that elfin look she so craved as a teenager. There was nothing of this other man in her appearance.

She took the letter to her laptop and carefully copied the email address that had been added in a different hand.

She typed 'Letter' into the subject box and then started, *Dear Gillian*. She sat back, not knowing what to write.

She closed the computer and put the letter in her pocket when she heard Tobiasz coming out of his room. She couldn't tell him about the letter. She justified the deception by reminding herself that Tobiasz had not told her of his change of plans for Poland until they had almost reached the border. She would tell him. But not yet.

"Just doing my emails," she said.

"Anything interesting?"

"No," she replied. "Just the usual."

"I was going to take Hector. Will you come too?"

"I think I'll stay here, if that's okay."

"Of course," said Tobiasz, looking a little disappointed. "I will be back in about an hour." *It's just as well Hector can't talk*, she thought as Tobiasz put his lead on and they headed out.

Hilary went straight back to her laptop.

Thank you for your letter. I was very interested to read what you had found out and the woman in the picture certainly seems to be my mother. I would like to meet up and hear more, if that is possible. What is your address?
Kind regards
Hilary

She added her phone number and pressed send.

"You're very quiet," said Tobiasz that evening.

"Just thinking," said Hilary. "The sales start next week. There's a lot to do at work tomorrow. In fact, I think I'll have an early night." Ignoring Tobiasz's concerned look, she picked up her laptop and went to her bedroom. She didn't like secrets but this was something that she had to process for herself, before sharing it with anyone else.

*

As predicted, she was very busy the following day getting ready for the sales and didn't get a chance to check her emails until she got home. She had received a reply.

Gillian sent her the name of the town where she lived and suggested they meet at a motorway service station an hour's drive from Barwell and midway between where the two women lived. Hilary thought the meeting place a little strange but agreed and suggested a couple of dates.

Over a couple more emails, they agreed on a meeting for the following week. The time had come to tell Tobiasz. She would need the car and, unless she took Hector with her, Tobiasz would have to feed Hector too.

She chose a moment when they were relaxing on deck chairs after a couple of hours of weeding and tidying in the garden.

"I've got something to show you," she said. "I'll just go and get it."

Thinking it was a new dress or something for the house, Tobiasz was surprised when she returned with an envelope. She handed it to him.

"It was waiting for me when we got back from our trip, but I needed to think about it before I shared it with anyone else," she said. "You're the first person I have mentioned it to."

Tobiasz opened the envelope and first looked at the two photographs before reading the letter.

"That is amazing," he said after a few moments. "Amazing that they found you, that this woman write to you. It is a shame that they are both dead. They cannot meet up again."

"I didn't even think of that as a possibility," said Hilary, trying to imagine what her mother's reaction would have been. "I have arranged to meet her. Gillian. Next Wednesday. That's why I'm telling you now, to check that you will be around for Hector, because I don't know exactly how long I'll be."

"Of course I can be here for Hector. But wouldn't it be better if I went with you?"

"No," said Hilary, emphatically. "I need to do this on my own, at least this first meeting."

Hilary showed him the email next and became upset when Tobiasz questioned why Gillian hadn't revealed her address and had asked to meet at a service station of all places. He suggested that it might all be a scam, that Gillian might not be who she purported to be, that it might be some sort of trap. The comfortable afternoon was spoiled, dinner was eaten in silence, and they each went to their separate rooms to sleep.

Hilary was determined to go. She hoped that Tobiasz was only acting this way because he cared about her and was genuinely worried. She could see the logic of meeting in a public place, midway between where they both lived, with easy parking, but she had to agree with Tobiasz that the choice of venue was a bit odd. They finally came to a compromise, and Hilary agreed to stay in touch by phone throughout the day.

It was raining when Hilary arrived at the motorway service station the following Wednesday. They had agreed to meet outside but, because of the rain, Hilary waited nervously between the two sets of doors. Gillian arrived carrying the red umbrella that she had told Hilary to identify her by, and which protected her carefully arranged hair from the downpour. They greeted each other awkwardly just as a coach disgorged its passengers into the building. Gillian made a beeline for the café as most of the coach party headed for the toilets. Hilary hurried to keep up with her.

"You find a table. I'll get the drinks. What do you want?" Gillian said, as she reached the queue. "Can you take this?" She pushed a canvass shopping bag into Hilary's hand.

"A cappuccino please. Do you want some money?"

Gillian waved the proffered note away and Hilary headed off to find a table by the window and placed the bag on the chair opposite.

"I don't know how they dare to charge these prices," said Gillian as she returned with the coffee. She waited for Hilary to move the bag to the adjacent chair before sitting down and placing two large, brimming cups of coffee on the table between them.

"No, I don't want your money," she continued, as Hilary again tried to pay her share.

Gillian was tall and self-assured; even sitting down she was an imposing presence. She reminded Hilary of the girls at school who had made her feel so inadequate. After a particularly difficult term, she remembered her father trying to convince her that they were acting that way to hide their own insecurities. She had not been convinced then, and was positive that Gillian had dealt with any insecurities long ago. She had the same haughtiness as those cruel schoolgirls and her attractive face seemed to have a permanent frown—a deep furrow bisected the skin between her thin eyebrows, and her dark red lips dipped down at the corners.

Hilary quietly listened to a diatribe about the state of the roads, traffic, litter and lack of respect. She agreed with it all, although with less vehemence, even though she wasn't required to agree. In fact, she wasn't required to have any opinion or make any contribution at all. She drank her coffee as Gillian went on to provide a potted life history. She described her father as a dashing hero—good-looking, charming, generous, fun and completely unreliable. She seemed to have little time for her mother, who, in her eyes, was a miserable drudge, given to bouts of depression, drowning her sorrows in cheap cider. Gillian glossed over what sounded like a pretty grim childhood, seeming proud that she had left school with few qualifications, had married soon after leaving and had never had to work. She reached into her bag and took out a photograph.

She showed Hilary a formal wedding picture of an attractive young couple. The groom, who Hilary recognised from the picnic photo, in an RAF uniform and hair marginally longer than regulation, stared defiantly at the camera. The bride wore a stiff-looking two-piece—Hilary wondered what colour it might have been. She held a small bouquet, the heads of the flowers pointing down to the ground; her smile appeared nervous.

"They got married in the war—1944," explained Gillian. "I don't think they'd known each other for very long. Dad, Lance, had a forty-eight-hour leave. I came along nine months later almost to the day and he didn't see me until I was able to sit up unaided.

"He told me it was love at first sight. He was besotted with me. Mum told me that he would parade around the streets with me in the pram. Ostensibly he was looking for work. I like to think he was genuinely proud of me, but Mum thought it was so that he could get other women to feel sorry for him. Mum and Dad must have got on well for a bit, on one level or another, because Georgina came along. There are quite a few photos from that time of the three of us. Dad must've bought a camera. He always liked to try out his new acquisitions."

Gillian pulled an album from the bag. It contained black and white photographs stuck to rough, grey card. She found a page with pictures of a family holiday on the beach. Gillian was a robust, solid-looking little girl in a knitted swimsuit. In one picture she brandished a spade, in another she had an arm wrapped protectively around her baby sister's shoulders.

Their mother appeared in all of the photos. She was not dressed for the beach, but seemed to be looking on from the outside. She didn't seem relaxed but, in fairness, Hilary had photos of her own parents from the same era, looking very formal, sitting on deckchairs fully clothed. In most of them, her father had his jacket on.

Hilary went to buy more coffee while Gillian put the albums back in her bag.

When Hilary returned, Gillian said, without preamble, "Marianne found someone who knew your mum. She advertised on Facebook or something. This woman's daughter replied, emailed Marianne, about her mother being a dancer—Doreen Harris." Gillian looked at Hilary expectantly. The name meant nothing to Hilary. "Marianne emailed the photos that I sent you, to the daughter. Apparently, Doreen recognised Phyllis and Dad straight away. She sent Marianne this letter, but it's taken so long to find you that Doreen has died now." Hilary muttered something about being away, but Gillian wasn't listening. She handed Hilary the letter. The spidery writing on the lined paper reminded Hilary so much of Phyllis's writing towards the end that it brought a tear to her eye. "She said that Phyllis was a great dancer. No one could understand why she left," continued Gillian before Hilary had a chance to read the letter. "Better than the rest of the chorus, but she never wanted to dance the solo; describes her as a bit of a loner. She says in the letter that she remembered Dad leaving not long after your mum did but then she said people came and went all the time."

Hilary read the letter and handed it back. Gillian finished her coffee.

"I have to go. I don't want to be driving back into town during rush hour," she said. She stood up abruptly, put on her coat, picked up her bag and umbrella and said a brief goodbye, leaving Hilary mid-sentence as she tried to say thank you for coming and how nice it had been to find out more about her mother.

Hilary stirred the dregs of her coffee as she sat thinking. She wished she had asked Gillian if she could have a copy of the letter. It hadn't said much more than what Gillian had told her, but one sentence had hit her—dancers always had to leave if they got in trouble. Did she mean pregnant? She hadn't had a chance to ask Gillian. In fact, she hadn't really had a chance to say, or ask, anything.

Do I have a sister or a brother somewhere? she wondered. *How can*

I find out? Is there a way to check records so I can find out if Mum had another baby? There was no one she could ask.

She wished that she could have liked Gillian, that she'd warmed to her in some way. But she seemed very hard, scathing, even about her own daughter, and especially about her mother. Hilary supposed that it was a defence mechanism, like her own shyness and reticence. She realised that if she was going to find anything else out about her mother's past, she would have to put her own feelings aside.

She gathered her things together and headed to the car. She started to compose an email in her head, wondering whether she should arrange another meeting, wondering if she could perhaps include the daughter. For all her harsh words, Gillian had obviously loved her dad; she was the one who had kept in touch throughout everything. There must be a chink in her armour somewhere, Hilary thought. After all, she told herself, it was Gillian who had contacted her and not the other way around. She would surely be open to more questions, would at least help her to find out if there had been another child.

Tobiasz opened the front door as Hilary pulled into the drive. Hector rushed out to greet her with his usual enthusiasm.

"I just need to send a thank you email," she said. "Then I'll tell you all about it." She hurried to her room and switched on the laptop and, before her resolve could weaken, wrote an email.

Dear Gillian,

I was delighted to meet you today. I hope that the drive home wasn't too trying.

Thank you so much for sharing your family history. I loved hearing it. And thank you for bringing all those photos. What a treat!

You and your daughter have been to so much trouble to find me, I am so grateful that you did. I know so little about my mother's life before I was born.

The trouble is, now I want to know more.

I wonder if you and Marianne would like to come for lunch one day. I have checked and there is a direct train, quite frequently, and I could collect you from the station.

I work on Tuesdays and Thursdays, so any other day suits me.

As soon as she had pressed send, she started to tell Tobiasz about Gillian—what she looked like, everything she had said, and the questions that remained in Hilary's own mind. "She hardly let me get a word in. I was interested in everything she said but she controlled the whole meeting. She's very strong. That's why I decided on the way home that I'd invite her here. I might be a bit better on my own territory and, of course, you can be here too. It is possible she will see through my ruse…" Hilary smiled. "She might refuse to come, but I have to try."

Tobiasz didn't hide his relief that Hilary had suggested a second meeting at the bungalow. He offered to collect them from the station and cook lunch.

"They haven't accepted yet. Let's wait and see."

A reply arrived two days later. Gillian accepted the invitation to the bungalow but refused lunch, claiming time pressures. She said that Marianne would drive and they would arrive at 2pm, a week on Monday. She confirmed that neither of them had any food allergies. Hilary wondered if she should check if either was allergic to dogs but she thought she would just risk it.

Hilary replied, telling Gillian how delighted she was that they had accepted her invitation.

EIGHT

Changes

While Hilary was in the motorway service station meeting Gillian, Janet was sitting on a bench in her local park, her hand resting on the handle of Jasmine's pram, which she gently pushed backwards and forwards. Her granddaughter had been fractious and difficult to settle, so Janet had decided to walk to the park on this damp May day. The walk and the rocking had lulled Jasmine to sleep, but Janet continued to rock the pram, not wanting to risk her waking up. That morning, before leaving for work, Claire announced that she had signed a lease on a flat and would be moving out in a couple of weeks. Janet tried to match her excitement, to feel pleased for her, but instead she felt cast aside. Claire didn't notice her silence because Richard was enthusiastic enough for the both of them. Janet wasn't surprised. She had helped Claire look for a flat, and she was pleased that her daughter felt well and confident enough to move out again; but she would miss her and Jasmine. Everything was changing again. Her parents' moving day was fast approaching. The sale of their house in Leckhampton had knocked her sideways. She was grieving for the house she had grown up in, the only home she had known until she went to university. That house always felt safe and secure, even over the last few difficult years. She had to keep telling herself that it was only a house, and remind herself how difficult and tiring the journey had become, how, without all the travelling to see her parents, she would now have more time for everyone, including herself. But she felt a real sense of loss, that she was being cut loose, cast adrift. She couldn't talk to Richard about how she felt. Even to herself her thoughts sounded disloyal, as if she didn't value the love and security that her husband gave her.

Jasmine murmured, but her blurred outline under the plastic rain cover remained still, her eyes closed.

However Janet felt about it, the plan for her parents move from Leckhampton was coming to fruition. She had stayed all day with her mother while Richard had brought George down to look at the care home. She felt anxious as she waved them off, her father smartly dressed in a shirt and tie, his blazer laid on the back seat next to the notebook that contained all his questions.

Richard and George both liked the woman who had shown them round. She didn't gush too much, she was very knowledgeable and, as Richard reported to Janet later, she stood up well to George's questions. The inspection met with George's approval and the details were finalised. The moving date was set for early July.

George had been visibly exhausted on his return home. He looked close to tears when he said, "I had no idea what you have had to do for all these months. All that driving. You should have said something."

"I got used to it. I did what had to be done," Janet replied, putting their relationship back on its more familiar footing. She gave him a brief report about how Beryl had fared in his absence.

After they had eaten the meal that Janet had prepared—one of the chores that had occupied her while her mother slept—she helped her mother to bed. She came downstairs to find George and Richard asleep in front of the television.

The following morning, her dad was back to full strength and full of pr*aise for James* Place. He told Janet all the details as they sat eating breakfast in the kitchen. Richard was still asleep and the carers were upstairs helping Beryl to wash and get dressed.

"Now that we know that the move is definitely going to happen, can I suggest something?" Janet asked her dad when she managed to get a word in. "It's about the house contents."

George grunted his assent but didn't look up from his Bran Flakes.

During her last few visits, she and her father had been going through his and Beryl's lifetime of possessions. George wanted to remove the things that he wanted and Beryl needed, and then arrange a house clearance company to come and do the rest. He was completely unsentimental about objects, unless they related to his long-ago army days. To Janet, it felt as though he was erasing decades of memories.

"Would you agree to me putting the furniture and the things from the house that you and Mum won't need into storage?" she asked. "I can't do this all in a rush."

"Do you really want to do that?" George replied. "It'll be very expensive. There's nothing of any value."

"It's not about money. I'll pay for the storage. At least that will ensure that I don't take too long over it," she said with a smile. "I'm not looking for secrets. I don't imagine you wrote a manuscript like Hilary's mum." George laughed. "But the whole of my childhood is in this house."

They were interrupted as a carer helped Beryl to sit down at the table.

"We'll be off now. See ya, Beryl luv." She patted Beryl's shoulder.

"Thank you," said George. "See you later."

The woman closed the front door gently as she left.

Beryl chose that moment to put her hand on Janet's arm. Janet covered her mother's hand with her own. If only it were her and her mum clearing the house, deciding what to keep, with reminiscences prompted by trivial objects and shared experiences.

"Well, I can't really see the point," said George. "But if that's how you want to do it, that is what we will do." The matter was decided.

Since that conversation, she and George had categorised and labelled almost everything in the house. There had been many journeys to the tip and the local charity shops.

Nearly there, she thought.

Consciously putting thoughts of the move to the back of her mind, she looked towards the leisure centre at the other end of the park and wondered who might be going swimming the following Monday. She pondered on the changes since Liz and John had moved away. Of course, that wasn't the only difference; all their lives had moved on, but that one thing had changed the dynamic between the friends. Things like trips to the swimming pool, coffees and lunches in town had somehow lost their sparkle, without Liz's caustic comments, cynicism and sense of fun.

Perhaps it's just where we all are in life at the moment, thought Janet. *Even Hilary has been a bit distracted recently. I hope that she is all right. Perhaps it's because of the trip. It all sounded a bit of a muddle.* She decided to phone Hilary later.

Jasmine's hungry cry roused Janet from her reverie. She moved the rain cover. Jasmine quietened momentarily and looked up at her. Janet retrieved the dummy and popped it into Jasmine's mouth before she could emit another cry and tucked her little hands under the blanket.

"I shall turn Claire's room into a room for you, so you can come and stay whenever you want, when you are a bit older," she said. "I could ask Carol, our new design guru. How about that?"

The idea took shape as she turned the pram and headed for home, hoping that Jasmine's dummy would pacify her until they got there.

Across town, Carol unlocked an unprepossessing shop door. A new sign above her head proclaimed *Chaja Bazaar* in ornate lettering. Chahna had suggested the name to Jag as a joke.

"It's probably a swear word in some language or other," he had replied, but when she checked, she discovered it was a rather ugly South American bird, it meant 'find' in Korean or, if you added an accent to the second a, it was a delicious-looking meringue dessert in Uruguay. They had gone through lots of other options using their daughters' names, their parents' names, places they had visited, but they kept coming back to Chaja Bazaar. It seemed to roll off the tongue. A business was born.

Carol walked in to the shop and smiled.

It's funny how smells define a place, she thought, as she took in the sweet smell of orange blossom and rose petals mingled with the tang of incense.

When she worked at the charity shop, no matter how much air freshener they used, the air was always stale, laden with the odour of old clothes and unwashed bodies. She had swapped the worthiness of the charity shop for the extravagant glamour of Chaja Bazaar, exchanging sad, worn clothes and battered ornaments for bolts of brightly coloured cloth, huge wallpaper books, intricate hand-knotted Indian rugs, exotic-looking lamps and tactile, tempting trinkets. Chahna had told Carol how she wanted things to run and had then left her to it. Carol loved the fact that, for much of the time, she worked alone, with no one to organise her and no compromises to make.

Chahna went back and forth to London—and had plans to go to India—collecting samples and ideas. A year ago, she had given up her job as a marketing manager for a cosmetics firm to join Jag on a year-long sabbatical in India. On their return, Jag couldn't wait to get back to the routine of general practice, to incorporate some of his newly gained knowledge and perhaps awakened spirituality into the care of the residents of Barwell. While Jag had visited Indian hospitals, toured remote medical centres and learned the value of diet and relaxation, Chahna had marvelled at the beauty and colour that surrounded them and had decided that, somehow, she wanted to take that feeling back to England. Her mother-in-law had proved surprisingly helpful and, with the aid of the innumerable relatives they visited, together they discovered the craftsmen, manufacturers, and business people that enabled her to set up a business in Barwell, selling the Indian goods that she loved.

Carol was surprised when Chahna contacted her shortly after the New Year's Eve party and asked her if she really was interested in helping with the new business. She didn't think Chahna would take her offer seriously. Chahna always seemed a little distant from the others. She and Jag had quiet, intelligent daughters, her slender beauty set her apart, and her ultra-busy life prevented her from joining in most of the coffee mornings and frivolous goings-on that the other women indulged in. Carol was a little in awe of her. At first, Carol had helped with packaging the online orders. The early clients were friends and family, but word soon spread. The website they had set up did not do the goods justice—the wood needed to be handled, the fabrics touched, the perfumes inhaled— so they were both delighted when a little shop just off Barwell High Street came up for rent. Carol had come into her own.

It had been Mr Weldon's electrical shop, where he continued to repair small household items long after replacing rather than repairing had become the norm. Jonathan was sad to see the shop go; there would be no one now to keep his and Carol's ancient vacuum cleaner going. People still occasionally came in expecting to see Mr Weldon in his brown overalls waiting to sell fuses, light bulbs or other electrical paraphernalia. The men tended to turn around and walk straight out again, but Carol was pleased with the number of women she had encouraged to stay and browse, many of whom departed with a purchase or an idea for new decor. Only the day before, a woman had come in with a lamp for Mr Weldon and had gone out with a pair of ornately decorated bronze lamps and two fringed lampshades. "Thank goodness Mr Weldon has retired," she said, as Carol carefully wrapped her purchases. "I've wanted to replace the bedside lamps for years but Julian wouldn't hear of it."

"You were a bit of a gamble," Chahna admitted one morning when she called into the shop. "But I have always thought, from the way you dress, that you are very good with colours. I imagine your home must be very stylish."

Carol hadn't disabused her. She had never thought about interior design. Their home was magnolia throughout; the furniture was functional, comfortable, and collected over time. But she discovered that she did have a good eye for colour and enjoyed advising the customers.

She treated Chahna with the deference due to an employer but, with time, gained confidence and put forward her own ideas. It was she who had suggested stocking wallpaper and Chahna, through her many contacts, had found an independent wallpaper company. There was certainly a market for wallpaper, and Chahna now hoped to persuade the company to create an exclusive range to complement the products sold in the shop.

At first, Carol had felt guilty about no longer working in the charity shop but, she reminded herself, she had devoted many years of her life to it. She felt that she had done her bit. They wanted her to carry on volunteering one day a week, which, in theory, she could have done. She worked for Chahna four days a week, but she liked to be available if needed when Chahna went on one of her trips and, when she wasn't needed at the shop, she wanted to devote more time to her own family. Her mother was still clinging to life against all the odds and her children continued to expect free childcare for their offspring, although Carol acknowledged that, these days, that duty mostly fell to Jonathan.

Carol placed her handbag in the big teak cupboard that took up most of the back of the shop. It was filled with stock, paperwork and other bits and pieces but, ever hopeful, Chahna had placed a label with a staggering price on it and told Carol that if it sold, she would be able to get another one. Carol couldn't imagine anyone in Barwell buying it.

Having returned to her car to retrieve two pairs of carefully wrapped curtains that she had finished the night before, she turned the OPEN sign on the door. The seamstress, a friend of Chahna's eldest daughter, had let them down at the last minute, choosing to go to a music festival rather than complete the job she had been hired to do. Carol didn't want Chahna to be yet another person she had difficulty saying no to, only to find herself making curtains and cushion covers for the shop's demanding customers. So, between customers, she made enquiries and found someone willing to take on the work. She hoped that Chahna would approve of her taking the initiative.

Towards the end of the day, she phoned Chahna to discuss the seamstress situation and to tell her about a customer who had bought almost the entire stock of sandalwood candles.

It had seemed an incongruous purchase for the immaculately made-up girl zipped into a voluminous puffer jacket, who reminded Carol of her granddaughter's Barbie. Carol asked the girl if she was buying the candles as gifts or if they were all for her own home.

"I work at Milton Spa. Beauty therapist," she replied, unzipping her puffer to reveal the dark lilac side-buttoned tunic and gold-lettered name badge. "A friend gave me one for my birthday. Got it online. I loved the smell and it's lasted ages, weeks. The ones we have in work aren't as nice. We're forever having to replace them and they smell chemically." She wrinkled her nose. "Mum said the chemicals might bring on my asthma, said I should tell the manager. So, I did. I showed her your website. We saw you had a shop. I live just up the road. The manager said I should get a candle for each of the treatment rooms, one for her office and three spare. Said to take the money out of petty cash—had to sign for it. Mum was going to come with me but Jayden fell over at school and she had to go and get him. I want to take them to work tomorrow." She stopped talking abruptly and carefully zipped the change into her pocket with the receipt.

"I'm very pleased you found us." Carol smiled as she pushed the two laden carrier bags towards the girl. "Tell your manager that if she speaks to the owner, Chahna—I've put one of her cards in the bag—I'm sure she'll be able to work out a deal, if it's going to be a regular order."

*

Chahna rubber-stamped her choice of seamstress and was delighted about the possibility of a regular order from the spa. "I'm a member," she said. "I'm going to phone in a day or two, see if we can draw up a contract. Brilliant, well done."

Carol put down the phone, glowing with pride.

NINE

Ironing

Liz was in the conservatory ironing John's shirts. The passion with which she hated this task almost exceeded the love she felt for John himself. John regularly offered to iron the shirts but, over the years, it had become a point of principle with Liz and, however much she disliked the task, she would not relinquish it. She liked how virtuous she felt when the job was done and she could shut the wardrobe door on the pile of immaculately pressed, precisely folded white shirts, having given them the care she never accorded to her own clothes. The task completed, she decided that she deserved a treat and, with just enough time before she had to collect Siobhan from school, she headed out to her favourite coffee shop.

"No little ray of sunshine today?" asked the plump woman behind the counter. Without asking what she wanted, she started to make Liz's coffee.

"Not today. She's still in school. This is a treat for me," replied Liz over the hiss of the coffee machine. "I'll have a toasted teacake too, Glenda, please."

"I can't believe it's only half two," said Glenda. "It's going so slow today. Could do with a few more customers."

Liz looked around the empty tables. "What's happened to everyone?"

"Can't decide if it's the weather or that new place over there." She flung her arm out in the direction of the rival coffee shop across the road, slopping the milk out of the jug as she did so. "But s'okay. I know me regulars'll come back. They always do." She mopped up the spilled milk with one hand and placed the half full jug under the steamer. "They have to try new places but they know that my cakes and coffee are the best. Always come back." Liz smiled at her confidence, which was probably well-founded, given that the notice over the door announced that Glenda's Glorious Goodies had been in Debden-on-Sea since 1977, with owner, staff, decor and clientele largely unchanged.

She paid Glenda the money and put a tip in the bowl by the till. Glenda didn't charge enough but, in the few months she'd been coming in, Liz had yet to convince her to raise her prices.

She carried her coffee to a table in the window and allowed herself to relax against the back of the chair. She heard her phone pinging to indicate a text and fished it out of her handbag. It was Janet. A sad face and washing-basket emoji told Liz that she too was about to face a pile of ironing. Liz replied with a picture of a cup of coffee and a cake.

Tia, a younger version of Glenda, placed a toasted teacake dripping with butter in front of Liz.

"Thank you," she said and glanced up to see a queue at the counter. "I didn't notice all those people coming in."

"They all followed you. At least it'll cheer Mum up," said Tia. "She gets real grumpy if we're not busy."

Liz smiled at her back as she bustled off to the counter.

Have you spoken to Hilary lately? A text appeared on her screen.

Few days. Why?

Not sure.

Intrigued, Liz finished her teacake, wiped her fingers on a serviette, and phoned Janet. She hated seeing people on their phone in cafés and restaurants but this felt like an emergency.

"What's all this about Hilary?" she asked without preamble.

"Probably nothing," said Janet, "but she seems a bit distracted since they got back from their trip, gone back into her shell a bit. I'm not sure. But yesterday I phoned her. I was a bit out of sorts because Claire is moving out soon."

"Oh great," Liz started to say.

"Yes, it is." Janet sounded unconvinced. "But yesterday when I phoned Hilary, she wasn't there and Tobiasz was a bit mysterious. It's the only word I can use. He wouldn't tell me where she was. I know there is no reason for him to tell me but it was as if there was some big secret. The oddest thing is, she hasn't phoned me back. It's just not like Hilary. It all seems a bit odd."

"I wouldn't worry too much. Tobiasz probably just forgot to tell her that you phoned. I'll have to see what I can get out of her. I hope there aren't any problems."

"I do too."

"Anyway, I'm pleased to hear that Claire has found somewhere but I know just how you feel. Why don't you and Richard come across on Saturday or Sunday for the day or even stay overnight?"

"Oh, Liz, that would be lovely. We can't stay because we have Jasmine on Sunday but that would be lovely. We'll treat you to lunch."

"Excellent. I'll see if I can get hold of Hilary in the meantime."

"I will too. See you Saturday."

Liz didn't have much time to ponder over Hilary before it was time to collect Siobhan from school.

TEN

Meeting on Home Ground

The following Wednesday promised to be warm and sunny. In honour of Gillian and Marianne's visit, Tobiasz had given the outside table and chairs a good clean. As the time of their arrival approached, Hilary rearranged the coffee cups on the tray, checked that the kettle was full and resisted the temptation to pour the coffee back into the canister to recheck the number of scoops. She touched the porcelain handle of her mother's cake slice as if it were a talisman.

A car pulled into the drive at 1.57pm. Hilary, who had been watching through the living room window, went towards the front door but Tobiasz was already there. Hector had been temporarily imprisoned in Hilary's bedroom, out of harm's way.

Gillian looked at Tobiasz with wide-eyed approval when he opened the door. Hilary introduced them and Gillian graciously held out her hand. Tobiasz took her hand and inclined his head towards her.

"I am very pleased to meet you," he said.

Gillian looked askance at Tobiasz, pulling her hand away and brushing it down her skirt. "You are not English," she said.

"No. Polish," he replied.

She turned from him and sketchily introduced her daughter, Marianne, to Hilary, before sweeping down the hall towards the living room. Hilary bustled after her.

Marianne smiled apologetically at Tobiasz as they followed the two women down the hall.

"I had thought that we could sit outside, as the weather is so lovely," said Hilary.

"I prefer not to," said Gillian. "Flies!" She shuddered as if already surrounded by swarms of biting insects.

Hilary thought of the citronella candles that she had placed on the patio but said nothing and went to prepare the coffee. Tobiasz followed, leaving the two guests to inspect the furnishings.

They prepared the coffee in silence. Tobiasz switched on the kettle, Hilary filled the milk jug, placed it on the tray, added two more shortbread biscuits to the plate and placed the cake slice alongside the cake. Taking a deep breath, she went back to the living room. Gillian had settled into Hilary's chair and Marianne was perched on the edge of the central cushion of the settee. It was difficult to know whether they had spoken to each other during the time they had been left alone in the room.

"How was the journey?" Hilary asked, for something to say. Gillian started to list her disgust at other drivers and hardly paused when Tobiasz came in with the refreshments.

A plaintive bark sent Hilary to her room to release Hector. He bounded in, ignored Gillian, who looked horrified, and headed straight for Tobiasz, who was pouring the coffee (and standing next to the biscuits).

"Lie down, Hector," he said and was greeted with obedience and a baleful glance. It was as if Hector knew that he would be sent out again if he misbehaved.

Gillian barely glanced at Tobiasz as he placed a cup of coffee on the table at her elbow. She waved away the plate of biscuits he offered and sat, with an empty plate in her lap, looking greedily at the Victoria sponge that Hilary had just offered to Marianne.

Hilary managed to keep smiling as Gillian, ignoring the slice of cake that Hilary had on the cake slice, reached out over the plate to secure the biggest piece.

Coffee distributed, Tobiasz and Hilary sat on the settee on either side of Marianne, who relaxed a little and shuffled back on the cushions.

There was silence as they all began to eat and drink. Gillian almost looked as though she was enjoying the cake, despite Hector jealously watching every mouthful.

Marianne was about to put her cup on the floor when she looked towards Hector, and instead placed it on the table that Hilary had put between them. She turned towards Hilary.

"I was so excited when it all tied up," she said, her face lighting up as she spoke. "I was really pleased when you suggested that we meet up. Knowing about your mum and Granddad will bring my whole dissertation to life. I think the personal involvement will really help me in my viva.

"I hope you'll read it when it's done," she continued. "Mum doesn't want to. She said she's heard me talking about it enough. It's not about your mum but it's about her era—and Granddad's," she added, glancing at Gillian. "And the environment they worked in, but from a very modern perspective, a feminist perspective." Her mother pulled a face.

"I would love to read it," said Hilary. She patted Marianne's arm and took a sip of her coffee. "In fact, I can't wait to read it. But what I really want to know is if you found out anything personal about Mum—whether she and Lance had a baby?"

The silence seemed endless. Hilary jumped as Gillian's coffee cup hit the saucer. Marianne shot her a meaningful glance. Gillian glared back but then seemed to reach a decision. She bent down and pulled a small blue envelope from her bag. From the crossing out on the front of the envelope it appeared to have been forwarded from its original destination. The top of the envelope had been sliced across precisely, as if with a knife, and PHYLLIS was written in black felt tip across the back flap. She slid the stiff blue paper out and unfolded the letter. "I wasn't going to show you this. It was with Mum's things," she said.

She held the letter out without getting up. Marianne jumped up from the settee, took it and handed it to Hilary.

Dear Lance,

I'm sure that you will have heard on the grapevine that I have married Gordon. What you will not know is that I had a miscarriage. Gordon was willing to bring up a child that was not his. He didn't even ask who the father was.

But in the end, it was not necessary. You know that I loved you but it is clear that you did not love me. That makes me very sad. I hope that you are back with your wife and children. I am only writing this letter to let you know that you are absolved of any responsibility. I wish this chapter of my life to be closed. Please do not try to contact me. With love always,

    Phyllis

"Well, that certainly answers my question," said Hilary, not sure whether she should feel sad or relieved. She handed the letter to Tobiasz to read.

"I found it when I had to sort Mum's things," said Gillian. "It must have been forwarded to our house when he moved on from the theatre. I showed it to him after she died. He told me that he'd never seen it. He said he'd been living in digs at the time, lost his job, thrown out by Mum. I suppose Mum kept it as proof, as if she needed it, something else she could use against him. It certainly would've fuelled her hatred and contempt for him. Dad never said anything but he was upset when I showed it to him. I could tell. He got all huffy, said it was nothing. He said he couldn't remember Phyllis at all, but then I found the photos after he died. Sadly, he got everything wrong. People loved him, he could charm the birds from the trees, but as soon as he charmed them, he'd shoot them down or cage them. His neighbours fell over themselves to help him at first when he was older but they soon saw through him and drifted away. He wasn't all bad. It was different then and it wasn't really just the men at fault."

Marianne pulled a face.

"Yes," her mother continued. "The women were treated as objects, both by their employers and by the audience. Objects to be admired and desired, but still objects, but they somehow colluded in this and it certainly wasn't all bad for either side." It sounded as though this was a discussion Marianne and her mother had had many times.

"Mum would never admit this," said Marianne, "but from what I've gathered from her and from the way Granddad talked about the dancers, I think he thought they were fair game. Put there for his enjoyment. Let's face it," she added when her mother looked as though she was going to interrupt. "He treated all women badly, the dancers, his wife, his daughters. They were all treated with the same disdain. It's all very well saying times were different, but he had choices. He didn't have to be like that. Circumstances meant that I didn't meet him very often but when I did, he was always very entertaining. He told me lots of stories about his time in the theatre. He lost jobs frequently but was never out of work for long. His skills were always in demand."

Hilary held out the cafetière, offering Marianne more coffee. She shook her head.

"Mum has always taken his side. When I've told her about some of the things that I've learned about the theatre and what went on in those days, she insists that Granddad wasn't like that, that it was other people. But what happened with your mum proves that it wasn't always just other people and she knows that there were others… He must have thought a lot of your mum to keep the photos, though. That letter to him about the pregnancy that he never saw until after Grandma's death. We have no idea what they went through. He might even have suggested an abortion."

"They were illegal then, weren't they? He wouldn't have suggested that." Hilary looked shocked.

"They still went on, for the right price. We have no idea really…"

In the silence that followed, Tobiasz asked Marianne if her father was proud of her doing a PhD.

"He died six years ago," Gillian said before Marianne could answer.

"Oh, I am sorry," said Tobiasz.

"It's okay," said Marianne. "He was ill for quite a while."

Gillian's tone suggested an annoying inconvenience rather than a great sadness.

The conversation wasn't flowing easily but now it became decidedly stilted and Hilary couldn't decide whether it was because of the question that Tobiasz had asked or the fact that he had asked it.

Gillian agreed reluctantly for Hilary to take a copy of the letter and the envelope it came in. As it had been written by her mother, Hilary didn't like to point out that, technically, perhaps the letter was more her property.

She printed a copy and then scanned it onto her computer, before putting the paper back into the envelope. She stroked it, touching yet another example of her mother's handwriting but, as she tapped the straight edge of the top of the envelope, she could only feel pleased that the letter confirmed that there would be no more surprises; no relations to connect her to this unpleasant woman. Here was a woman who seemed to carry all her mother's bitterness and all her father's 'don't care' attitude. Even the relationship with her daughter appeared difficult. Marianne seemed loyal to her mother but her body language and facial expressions demonstrated her discomfort.

The doorbell rang, interrupting her thoughts. She was delighted to see Sarah and Luke on the doorstep. Not questioning why they had come, she invited them in and propelled them into the living room.

"This is Sarah and her son Luke," said Hilary with a flourish, breaking an uncomfortable silence. "Hector was Sarah's dog before Luke came along. Weren't you, Hector?" She patted Hector on the head as she walked past him to give the letter back to Gillian, who quickly slipped it into her bag.

"I'll go and make some more drinks," Hilary said, going out of the door.

Tobiasz collected the cups and followed Hilary to the kitchen.

"I hope you don't mind," he said. "I told Sarah that Gillian was bringing her daughter round today. I thought it would help if she was here. I did not tell you. I thought you would put her off."

"I'm delighted she's here. Relieved," she said. She put her arm around him. "I don't know how you know what I need before even I do. You are a marvel."

"Glad to be of service, ma'am."

She punched him playfully on the arm as she leaned around him to get more cups out of the cupboard.

In the living room, Sarah had undone Luke's harness and lifted him out of his buggy. He toddled across to Hilary's chair and looked questioningly at Gillian. She pulled back and moved her skirt away from his possibly grubby hands. Then her features softened and she self-consciously pulled the cushion from behind her back and made Luke chuckle when she hid her face behind it and reappeared with "Boo".

Marianne could not have been more amazed if her mum had done a handstand.

"I can't believe she just did that," she said under her breath as Sarah sat down on the settee next to her.

"Luke has that effect on everyone," said Sarah, as the game of peekaboo continued. "Anyway, I have to admit I knew you and your mum were coming today, so this visit isn't as spontaneous as it appears. I want to hear about your research. It sounds fascinating."

"I've become completely immersed in it," replied Marianne. "I can't believe some of the things I've heard and read. I've met one or two of the dancers during my research and found it difficult to imagine those frail eighty-year-olds as dancers!"

"I didn't really know Hilary's mother, Phyllis, but I saw her when Hilary brought her into the Bistro. Not someone you could imagine dancing in a flimsy outfit."

"When I found the photo of Mum in her costume, you can imagine how hard it was to reconcile that gorgeous woman with the person that I knew," said Hilary as she walked in from the kitchen with the drinks. "Has your mum told you, Marianne, about the manuscript I found? I'm now pretty sure that it must be about her and your granddad." Hilary blushed and immediately wished that she hadn't mentioned it.

"It is very beautiful," said Tobiasz. "The words and the descriptions. But it is also very personal. We don't know if she meant it to be read. It was her own personal journey."

Gillian, who hadn't spoken for a while, looked at Tobiasz as if his opinion was worthless.

She turned towards Marianne. "I didn't tell her about it," she said. "I certainly don't want to read it and neither should she."

Marianne looked as though she was about to disagree, but stayed silent.

Hilary looked uncomfortable.

"I am sure that many of the places she describes are abroad. One chapter was definitely set in Bavaria—I remember going as a child. Mum and Dad had obviously been before but…" Hilary didn't know how to ask Gillian whether her father had visited Bavaria but Gillian answered the question without being asked.

"Dad would not go near Germany, not after the war. He hated the Germans, everything to do with the country. Hated it."

"I'll second that," said Marianne. "I remember when I was very little him going on about it, but if anyone should hate the Germans, Tobiasz has more reason than the rest of us."

Tobiasz looked as though he was about to speak, when he spotted Luke heading towards Hector. "Where are you going, young man?"

he asked, moving to head him off. Luke stopped, turned his head and chuckled. The tension was broken, the moment passed, and there was no further mention of the manuscript or Germany.

Luke gravitated towards Gillian, like a cat who always chooses to sit on the lap of the most ardent cat hater in the room. There was no more peekaboo, but she tolerated the toys he presented to her and even escorted him back to her chair when he was on the verge of annoying Hector with too much attention. While Marianne, Tobiasz and Sarah continued to chat, Hilary attempted to engage Gillian in conversation. She asked if she liked gardening (pointless hard work), reading (a waste of time), visiting galleries (full of noisy school children), walking (with my knees?) and travel (can't stand the sun). In the face of all that negativity, Hilary gave up and sat, with a fixed smile on her face, listening to the others.

Like the meeting at the service station, the afternoon ended abruptly. Ignoring the fact that Marianne was in the middle of a conversation, Gillian stood up suddenly and announced that they must leave. Luke, who had been leaning on her knee, landed on his bottom and sat there, too surprised to cry. Tobiasz leaped up to go to him but Hector beat him to it and placed his soft toy at Luke's feet. Everyone was on their feet then and Sarah, sensing that Luke, marooned in a sea of legs, was about to cry, scooped him off the floor.

Hilary tried to say the right things and regain some control of the situation but Gillian moved determinedly towards the door. Marianne gathered her things together, offering her thanks on behalf of both of them, while Gillian got into the car and sat impatiently in the passenger seat.

"She's always been like this," said Marianne to Hilary by way of an apology for her mother's rudeness. "It's as if there's a switch inside her and she has to get out. She'll never change, but it can be embarrassing."

Hilary patted her arm. "Don't worry..."

They stood on the drive as Marianne got into the car. Hilary went around to the passenger seat to thank Gillian again for coming, and Marianne leaned across and thanked Hilary for the coffee and cakes. Gillian muttered something, but Hilary didn't catch it. She felt relief as they reversed out of the drive. After closing the front door, she returned to the living room to find Luke in his buggy and Sarah retrieving his toys from Hector's basket.

"Oh, do you have to go too?" she asked. "I'm so glad you came. You and Marianne seemed to have a lot to say to each other."

"I liked her. I'm not surprised she doesn't live with her mother. What an odd woman. Quite rude, but then she was lovely with Luke. It was as if she didn't really want to have anything to do with you but she had been impelled by some outside force. Very odd."

"I think she is very lonely. She said her dad drove everyone away. She does the same," said Tobiasz.

"The trouble is, even if we understood why she is like she is, it doesn't make her any more likeable," said Hilary.

"True," said Sarah as she opened the front door and pushed Luke out. "Anyway, thank you for inviting me." She pecked Tobiasz on the cheek.

"Back to normal next week. See you at the swimming pool on Monday," she said to Hilary, giving her a quick hug.

"She's a bit of a drip, isn't she?" said Gillian, not looking back as Marianne pulled out of the driveway.

"I thought she was nice," said Marianne. She lifted her arm out of the driver's window and gave an enthusiastic wave to the group on the doorstep.

"Are they married, her and that foreigner?"

"No, but he lives there," replied Marianne. "They met on holiday. He was working in the hotel where she stayed. He came as a lodger last year but they are a couple now."

"Did she tell you all that?"

"No, Sarah did. I really liked her. And isn't Luke gorgeous? What a lovely little boy."

Gillian grudgingly agreed but quickly added, "I didn't like that great big dog, though. I didn't like the way he kept looking at me. He's obviously spoilt, his things all over the place. I thought at one point he was going to bite the baby but that foreigner got hold of him."

"Tobiasz," said Marianne. "His name's Tobiasz and Hector wasn't going to bite Luke. He was just being friendly."

Gillian looked unconvinced.

*

Hilary brought the last cups to the kitchen for Tobiasz to load into the dishwasher.

"Until I met Gillian, I had thought how lovely it would be to introduce her to my friends," said Hilary. "What a disaster that would be. She's very prickly, isn't she?"

Tobiasz nodded his agreement. "Her daughter seems nice. I think the husband had a lucky escape." They laughed.

"Luke had the measure of her, didn't he?" said Hilary.

"Yes, he played and then, when she didn't want him anymore, he went and found someone else."

"He is such a calm, amiable little boy. I do love him," said Hilary. "I'm so glad that you suggested that Sarah come around this afternoon. It eased the tension even if it only was for a short time."

"I wonder if Sarah ever regrets giving Hector away. He was very good with Luke. He didn't even object too much when Luke pulled his ears."

"I hope not," said Hilary. "She's never said anything and I think that this way suits everybody. Happy baby, happy parents, happy dog."

"And happy us," added Tobiasz, as Hector trotted through to the kitchen.

"Yes, you were a good boy," said Hilary. "It could have all gone quite differently if you had misbehaved." Hector stared hopefully at the treat jar. His patience was rewarded.

ELEVEN

Post-Mortem

When Janet and Liz met the previous weekend, Hilary had featured heavily in their conversation. They had both been in touch with her but had been left with the impression that she was hiding something.

When Janet finally met up with Hilary, she was shocked when Hilary blurted out, "We've found the man in Mum's manuscript."

"Where? During your trip? Why didn't you say?" She felt that she had been excluded, upset that Hilary hadn't trusted any of her friends with the news.

Hilary explained about the letter.

"I didn't want to tell anyone," Hilary explained. "Not until I knew for sure. Until I knew how I felt. I had to tell Tobiasz when I arranged to meet Gillian, because of Hector, the car…"

Janet didn't understand, but she listened patiently as Hilary described her less than successful meetings with Gillian.

"I don't like her," Hilary admitted.

Somewhat mollified, Janet's reaction to the first letter was the same as Tobiasz's.

"What a shame that you didn't find all this out until after they had both died.”

“Lance could have looked for her if he’d wanted to, when Gillian showed him the letter her mum had kept.”

“Mmmmm,” said Janet.

“And I know there are lots of things I didn’t know about my mum, but I do know that when she made a decision, she stuck to it. That letter to Lance was very definite, so perhaps if he had succeeded in finding her it would have just been too upsetting. Anyway, we’ll never know. I must admit it has explained a few things to me and perhaps the manuscript was like a journal that she wrote, trying to get him out of her system. I’m so glad that I didn’t publish it. Imagine if I had and then Gillian turned up. I told her about the manuscript but she didn’t seem at all interested in reading it or even knowing any more about it. It was really awkward when I mentioned it. I’m not sure, but I think Marianne would have liked to read it but she took her mother’s lead. Said that there were some things about her granddad that she didn’t need to know.”

“I couldn’t agree more,” said Janet.

“I wonder if I ought to destroy it, now that I know the history of it. It won’t be of interest to anyone else. In a way, I feel better about it all. If it was a journal, she was doing what she always told me to do when something had upset me. Write about it. She didn’t say write it down. She said write it as you see it. And she never encouraged me to keep what I wrote. In fact, she positively encouraged me to throw it away, telling me that we didn’t have room for clutter. I must admit that thought struck me when I was clearing out her things and found that she had kept boxes and boxes of letters, birthday cards, Christmas cards and, latterly, orders of service from funerals. I suppose parents often tell children to do the things that they wish they could do themselves. Perhaps I shouldn’t have always done as I was told.”

Janet looked as though she was going to say something but, at that moment, Jasmine, who had been sleeping peacefully in her pram next to the table, started to fuss.

“She’s hungry,” said Janet. “I’d better get her home. Thank you for coffee. See you soon.” They parted with a hug and Hilary was left feeling afraid that she had made a mistake in not confiding in her friends.

She phoned Liz that afternoon. Liz was rushing out to collect Siobhan from school, but Hilary told her that she had something that she wanted to discuss, and Liz insisted that they talk later. Later, when Tobiasz had taken Hector for a walk, Hilary phoned again. She knew that Tobiasz would call in at the pub on his way home, so she would have time to have a long chat with Liz.

Liz was full of news but she surprised Hilary when she started to express some doubts.

"I do enjoy living by the sea," she said. "But I keep wondering if we should have waited until John retired. Life is good, it's a great community and the beach and the sea are so liberating. But it's all a bit at the edge of nowhere. John hasn't said anything and I don't think he's driving any more than he used to…he's certainly not doing any more hours, probably fewer miles on much more interesting roads. But I know that he misses his friends and it's an effort now to watch the rugby. He can't get into the local golf club and that's a blow."

"But wouldn't it be more difficult if he'd retired?" asked Hilary. "You'd have less money and, if you were older, you might be less mobile."

"Cheerful thought," said Liz.

"Anyway, what about you?"

"Oh, I absolutely love it," said Liz. "I've joined everything I possibly can. I'm even doing a life-drawing course."

"I didn't know you could draw."

"I can't. Can't draw for toffee, but it's very diverting." Liz laughed. "And I love all the space we've got. I can look out the bedroom window and just see the horizon and, apart from the occasional ship, there is nothing in the way. I miss all of you a lot, of course. But don't you think that, overall, we spend more time together? We don't meet up for ten minutes in town, or wave in the street. It has to be a planned event. I think it's great. I'm enjoying it. Siobhan loves having me here. Lisa seems to really appreciate me. And the baby is a dream.

"Anyway, you said that you'd got something you wanted to tell me. Something to talk about. Very mysterious. You haven't found another manuscript, have you?"

"No, nothing like that. Although it is related to Mum and her manuscript." Hilary stopped. She wasn't quite sure how to carry on. After Janet's reaction, she felt unsure of herself.

"Well?" asked Liz, when the silence went on.

"It seems unbelievable when I say it out loud," said Hilary. "But, the daughter of the man Mum spoke of in the manuscript—well, at least I think it is—came to see me. She wrote to me. The letter was waiting for me when I got back from not going to Poland."

"Oh wow," said Liz.

With frequent interruptions from Liz, Hilary repeated the story of the letter—Liz made her go get it and read it out—and of the bizarre meeting at the motorway service station and the afternoon at the house. She admitted to Liz that she really didn't like Gillian, that she couldn't warm to her, even though she wanted to because of the association with Phyllis.

"I really liked her daughter, though," she said. "She was really sweet and obviously very clever. She's doing a PhD. I'm sure she'll keep in touch with Sarah. Did I tell you that Tobiasz had secretly invited Sarah around to dilute the effect of Gillian? He's so thoughtful."

Liz smiled.

"At least you got some answers," she said. "And you know there's nothing else to find out. There aren't going to be any more surprises, no half-sisters or -brothers coming out of the woodwork."

"Yes, that was a huge relief," Hilary agreed. "The thought hadn't even crossed my mind until I got this letter making the man in the book real. Now that I know a bit more, I do wonder if I should get rid of the manuscript. I really don't think Mum meant to keep it..."

"I wouldn't do anything rash like getting rid of the manuscript," said Liz, "Not just yet. Gillian's daughter..."

"Marianne," put in Hilary.

"...might have second thoughts. She might change her mind. Of course, the manuscript is yours to do with as you like but it is about her granddad. So, perhaps she does have a bit of a say in it too. I suppose what I'm saying is, don't do anything rash. It's been hidden all this time. It can stay hidden for a bit longer."

"But what if I die?" said Hilary.

"I don't think that's likely any time soon," Liz said, laughing reassuringly. "But you could always put something in your will about it, even if it was just to say that it must be destroyed on your death."

"Just when I thought everything was sorted." Hilary sighed. "Anyway, what are your plans for the next few weeks?"

"Busy, busy, busy. Pearl is coming down for the weekend, which seems to have coincided with me having Siobhan and the baby for the weekend. Lisa's going to a wedding and children aren't invited. So, we've got a busy weekend coming up. Siobhan is very excited because Pearl is having her bedroom and Siobhan will sleep in a sleeping bag in the dining room. I have a feeling that she might end up in our room but, for the moment, she's saying that's what she wants to do. So, when are you and Tobiasz going to visit us? I bet there are still some photographs of your trip that I haven't seen."

"I don't think so," said Hilary with a wry laugh. "But we must arrange something soon. We could stay in a hotel. We don't have to stay at yours. I think that might be nice. Is there a hotel or guesthouse nearby?"

"There is a guesthouse within walking distance. I'll check it out, make sure it doesn't smell of cabbage—do you remember what seaside B&Bs used to be like? Ugh! In fact, now that I think about it, if it turns out to be okay, I wonder if Pearl would be happier there. John and I could pay. Now, that's an option. That might solve all our problems this weekend. You're a genius, Hilary. I'll let you know how it goes and get back to you with some dates."

TWELVE

The Proposal

Tobiasz wanted to treat Hilary to Sunday lunch. They set off at midday, leaving Hector sulking in his basket. Tobiasz was wearing a new navy-blue shirt with a buttoned-down collar, which Hilary thought looked very like the one she had admired on Paul Hollywood one evening on *Bake Off.*

They drove for miles, stopping at likely pubs and restaurants, but everywhere was fully booked. It became more of an effort to remain positive and finally, in desperation, Tobiasz parked in front of a hotel on the high street of a small, neglected market town. The hotel had obviously once been an imposing coaching inn but now looked sad, squashed as it was between an Age UK charity shop and a Paddy Power bookmaker.

"It will be fine," said Hilary, hunger getting the better of her. "If we don't stop here, everywhere will have stopped serving."

"I should have booked," Tobiasz said dejectedly.

They looked at the menu trapped behind glass at the side of the front door.

"Oh, they've got belly pork on. I love that," said Hilary. "Let's see if they have a table."

They did, quite a few in fact. Hilary's excitement over belly pork was short lived. The tired looking but very upright waiter recited a considerable list of unavailable items.

"Shall we…" asked Tobiasz, as the waiter walked away, "…go somewhere else?"

"No, it'll be fine." Hilary opened the leather-bound menu and glanced up as two Sunday roasts topped with unfeasibly huge Yorkshire puddings wafted past. "It'll definitely be fine. That's me decided."

The dinner was good even if it reminded Hilary of school dinners. The old-fashioned dining room with its white table cloths and whispered conversations made Hilary think of the black and white films she and her mother used to watch on Sunday afternoons; the smell of roast meat and the sliver of overcooked cabbage stuck in her back teeth completed the illusion.

The rarefied atmosphere in the dining room, Hilary's hunger and Tobiasz's sense of failure could have put a dampener on conversation, but the food, wine and the other diners—who all seemed to be caricatures of themselves—ensured that conversation flowed. Hilary couldn't stop herself from laughing when a sweet trolley, complete with sherry trifle, appeared at her side.

"I wanted to talk to you about something, but it doesn't seem right now," Tobiasz said, laughing with her.

"I've had such fun," said Hilary, not really taking in what he had said. "But we'd better get back to let Hector out."

They shared the bill and gave an excessive tip. "Entertainment value," said Hilary.

Not wanting to be caught out again, a few days later, Tobiasz cornered Suzanne and quizzed her about suitable restaurants. He managed to field her questions about why he was on the hunt for a nice place to eat and went home. He booked a table for two, so that he could present Hilary with a fait accompli.

The next weekend, they found themselves in a brightly lit modern restaurant, busy with smart, affluent people.

"Oh dear," said Hilary, as she stepped in. As she took off her old fawn mac it was whisked away by a smiling girl in an impossibly short skirt.

"You look perfect," said Tobiasz, looking around at the designer-clad women.

They were shown to the table and handed menus—plasticised and huge with pale typescript and no capital letters. Hilary tried not to let it matter and tried to figure out what some of the descriptions meant. She smiled at Tobiasz.

"This is amazing. I can't believe you've brought me here. The others will be so jealous." She caught sight of the shoes that the woman at the neighbouring table was wearing and longed for the floor-length tablecloths of old to hide her own.

"Can I get you some drinks?" the waiter asked with a smile.

Flustered, she looked down at the menu.

"A bottle of the house champagne, please," said Tobiasz.

"What are we celebrating?" asked Hilary, as the waiter went to get it.

"Being out together… Now, what will you have?"

They chose, they ate, they marvelled—at the flavours, the presentation, the whole theatre of the moment—and they talked.

After the waiter had cleared the dessert plates and they refused coffee, Tobiasz reached across the table and took Hilary's hand.

"You are the love of my life," he said. "Will you marry me?" He looked down at their joined hands and then lifted his eyes to hers. "We belong together."

Hilary extricated her hand.

"You know I love you," she said. She picked up her glass and put it down again. "I want to be with you always. But I won't marry you."

Tobiasz moved his hand from the table to his lap. He looked down, twisting the corner of the stiff napkin in his fingers.

"I don't need to belong to someone," said Hilary. "I don't want to belong to someone. I want to be with you forever but I don't want to marry you. This is all too soon. I am only just finding my feet. I want to be with you. I want to be part of a couple. But I want to learn how to be my own self before anything else."

"I do not understand. I did not mean that I want to own you."

"I used the wrong word."

"No, you didn't. Your words are perfect."

"I twisted the meaning to suit what I wanted to say. I don't want anything to change. I want us to carry on exactly as we are. I hope that you can see that is the best option. If we marry, everything will change, money will form barriers between us. Now, I feel that I can share everything with you. If we were married, I would feel forced to share everything with you. Do you see the difference? Am I making sense?"

"You make sense. But you make me feel very sad. I thought it would give you security."

"I have security. I just want love."

Thinking about it later, Hilary realised that Tobiasz hadn't looked upset. Hurt, perhaps, but her overall impression was that he had looked thoughtful. She wasn't sure why she had refused him, or why she had given that self-righteous speech about not wanting to be owned. She had always wanted to be married and at various stages of her life she had imagined her wedding day—in a big white dress on her father's arm, in a smart suit in a registry office surrounded by friends, on an exotic beach—but she realised that Tobiasz didn't fit into any of those pictures. As she had said, she didn't need to be married; she wanted things to carry on as they were.

They mentioned the restaurant many times in the days that followed but neither of them spoke about their conversation at the end of the meal. A palpable politeness rested between them.

Then, one morning a few days later, as they both ate breakfast before going to work, Tobiasz said, "I will go to Poland." Hilary was dumbstruck. Without another word, he gathered up his things, kissed Hilary on the forehead and went out the door. Hilary cleared away the breakfast things, made sure there was water in Hector's bowl, said goodbye to him and went to work herself.

She staggered through the day, hardly acknowledging her colleagues or customers. The words *I will go to Poland* kept flashing through her mind like a neon sign, impossible to ignore. She couldn't wait to get home, but when she got there, only Hector was there to greet her. But then she remembered that Tobiasz would be late home anyway. He'd taken another job, gardening for an old lady whose husband had recently died. She persuaded herself that he wouldn't have gone to Poland today; surely, he wouldn't want to let the old lady down. She thought about checking whether his passport was still in his desk. She knew that she should text and ask him, but she felt paralysed.

As ever, Hector came to her rescue. She took him out on a two-hour walk and, when they arrived home, one hungry, both very tired, Tobiasz was still not home. She fed Hector, made herself a mug of chamomile tea and sat in front of the television. Her mind refused to focus on the banal quiz show in front of her and her thoughts swirled around in her head.

She woke with a start when she heard Hector skittering along the wooden floor in the hall. The front door lock clicked and a warm smell of curry wafted towards her.

Tobiasz put his head round the living room door. "I have bought a takeaway," he said. "I did not think you would have got anything from the freezer this morning, so I bought a takeaway."

"Thank you," said Hilary. "Very thoughtful. But let's have it in the kitchen, not in here."

She pushed herself up from her chair and followed him through to the kitchen. When they were sitting on their familiar stools at the breakfast bar, dinner in front of them, knife and fork on either side of their plates, Hilary asked, "Well?"

Tobiasz spooned curry and rice onto their plates, tore the naan in half and got up to fetch a jar of mango chutney from the fridge.

"Well?" she asked again as he sat down next to her and proffered the mango chutney. She waved it away. "You can't drop a bombshell like that…"

"I realised that you were right," Tobiasz interrupted her. "That we don't need to marry. I have done a lot of thinking. We have done a lot of talking and I have done a lot of talking with Dan. I thought what I wanted was to put everything right, to get married again to rectify some of the mistakes of the past, to get things right with you."

"But you already get things right," said Hilary.

Tobiasz smiled at her. "We are very good together. I do not want to lose you and I now realise that by asking you to marry me I risked losing you. I do not want things to change between us. You are right. But…" He paused. "I must go back to Poland and I must go alone. I will go for five days. I will see my mother's grave, my grandmother's grave and, another day, Krystyna's grave. If they will agree to see me, I will speak to her family. But I will respect if they do not wish to. There is no one else living that I want to see but I want to see some places and I want to make my peace with Krystyna. I need to see the place where she died and then I will come back to you. Just four nights and then I will come back to you."

"When?" Hilary asked with tears in her eyes.

"Beginning of August. My mother's birthday was the fourth. I will go to her grave on her birthday." He put his hand on hers. "Come on, eat your dinner."

Hilary looked down at the now cooling curry and took a forkful to her mouth. "I'm sorry, I can't eat," she said.

"It's okay." Tobiasz pushed the plates towards the sink. Neither of them knew what to say.

THIRTEEN

A Day Out in Barwell

Liz found Mondays hard to fill. John invariably left early and Jason did Siobhan's school runs. Liz had given up the life-drawing class and taken up beach yoga instead. But it was raining today, so yoga was cancelled. She mooched about the house, hunting for something to do. The rain had dampened her spirits and hidden the sea from view.

I know, she thought, *I'll go to Barwell. I'll go shopping. Proper shopping, not for food or presents for others, but shopping for clothes that I want and probably don't need.*

Unless you were a tourist, there weren't many shops of interest in Debden-on-Sea. There was a sportswear shop where she had bought her yoga outfit and there was one dress shop. It was a gentleman's outfitters that had been updated, to a degree. The ladies' wear section was tucked upstairs in what had once been the store room. The display in the window—which looked like it hadn't been changed for years—was protected from the sun by peeling orange film over the windows. Liz had ventured in once when John wanted a new jumper but she was pretty certain that there would be nothing to tempt her upstairs again.

She'd tipped a pile of underwear onto her bed to sort. Now that she'd decided on a plan of action, she pushed it back into the drawer again. She changed from her tracksuit bottoms and sloppy Joe jumper into a mauve shift dress and low-heeled pumps. She pushed two combs into her hair to hold it back and, for the first time in weeks, applied makeup to her tanned face.

She stopped at the garage to fill up with fuel, then turned on the radio and sang along, as the miles whizzed past in a wet blur.

She pulled into the multi-storey car park and breathed a sigh of pleasure as she stepped out of the lift into the dry familiarity of the shopping centre. In John Lewis, she was surprised to find Hilary helping a nervous young woman choose a set of cake forks as a wedding gift.

"You don't work on a Monday," Liz said in a stage whisper, as the customer dithered over her task.

"I won't be a moment," Hilary said to the customer when she'd overcome her surprise at seeing Liz standing in front of her.

"What a lovely surprise," she said. "I wish I'd known you were coming. I wouldn't have swapped."

"Can you get off for coffee?"

Hilary looked at her watch. "I'll be finishing at 1.30. I'll meet you then."

They decided on a meeting place and Hilary turned back to find the customer wondering whether a cake slice might be a better gift after all.

While Hilary worked, Liz shopped. She bought two cotton jumpers, jeans that she knew Lisa would condemn as old lady jeans, and a pair of yellow and navy deck shoes. Just as she was wondering whether she should contact any of the others, she spotted Janet on the escalator. Her shout made several people look up. Janet was delighted and shifted her bags into one hand, to give Liz a hug.

After a brief discussion, they sent texts to Carol, Suzanne and Chahna, hoping that at least one of them might be in the vicinity. Sadly, all three were busy and sent apologetic texts with multiple emojis.

"There's something different about you, Janet," said Liz. "Is your hair different?"

Janet laughed.

"The only thing that's different about me is I'm getting more sleep! Claire has her own flat now; moved out a couple of weeks ago. Jasmine is a very good baby, but all babies wake at night, even the good ones. I could easily fall asleep again, if it wasn't for Richard, harrumphing, twisting and turning, tangling himself in the bed clothes, exaggeratedly trying to show that he'd been disturbed. Once Mum and Dad are settled, I shall be sleeping like the proverbial baby."

"What date are they moving?" asked Liz.

"July 5th," said Janet, as they arrived at the coffee bar to find Hilary waiting outside.

"Look who I found on my travels." Liz smiled.

"Perfect," said Hilary as she gave Janet a hug.

They found a table and organised drinks.

"It's as if I never went away," said Liz, as they chatted nineteen to the dozen. "But I have felt out of the loop. It's been like reading the headlines and I always hear after the event, and without the benefit of the full story. Do you know I still can't get my head around you not going to Poland?"

"Nor me, really," said Hilary. "Tobiasz is going to go on his own. He proposed, I turned him down; now he's going to Poland."

Janet was speechless, transfixed, her coffee halfway to her mouth.

"*What?*" Liz's cry turned several heads.

"Tobiasz is going to Poland…"

"Not that," said Janet, putting her coffee down. "He proposed?"

"And you refused?" added Liz.

"Mmm." Hilary drank her coffee without looking at the others.

"But you two belong together," said Janet.

"That's what he said. But we are together. I don't want to belong to anyone. I've only just started being me."

"You just do what you want to do," said Liz. "I still don't understand why he's going to Poland when he couldn't go with you."

"I don't really know either," said Hilary. "When we got back, I was afraid to admit to anyone that the whole purpose of the journey had gone out of the window because we hadn't gone to Poland. I thought that you would think badly of Tobiasz, although I don't know why. He couldn't explain it at the time but, oddly enough, he did seem at peace with his decision. He has a lot to sort out and, not knowing the full story, I feel at a loss to help him. Perhaps he would have carried on if I hadn't been with him. Anyway, he is going, but on his own this time. It annoyed me a bit that he made the decision again without any discussion. Just out of the blue, he told me he's going."

"I'd have been more than a bit annoyed," said Liz.

"It must make you feel very shut out," Janet said, in a gentler tone than Liz. "These are important decisions."

"I think he feels the need to protect me," said Hilary. "Anyway, we've talked about it now, he's not going straightaway—he needs time to sort out the finances. He'll go at the beginning of August and he's only going away for five days."

"And I bet I'm going to need you an awful lot while he's away. Once Mum and Dad move down, I'm sure there'll be loads to do."

Hilary smiled. "You're only saying that, but thank you anyway. It's not that I can't occupy myself but, of course, I'll help out."

"Actually," said Janet. "I don't know if this is a good time to ask, Hilary, but would you be able to come with me to pick them up? It's the 5th of July. Richard can't take any more time off. I could go on my own but Dad suggested asking you. And he suggested Hector come too. Mum loves Hector."

"Absolutely, I'm off that week and I have nothing planned," replied Hilary, touched to be asked. "I'd be glad to help with your mum and dad. Since Tobiasz decided to go to Poland alone I've been thinking a lot about our trip that didn't quite get there. Do you know, the best thing about the trip that we took together was that it made me feel closer to Mum and Dad. Tobiasz and I walked and explored. I had time to think. Driving in Germany, I think I recognised some of the places from my trip with them all those years ago. I'm not even sure that I was recognising the right places but the feelings it evoked were very special." Hilary looked thoughtful. She couldn't explain how repeating that trip had made her realise how happy her parents had been with each other; not exciting and joyous, but comfortable in each other's company.

"I hadn't thought so deeply about Dad in years," continued Hilary. "He was such a kind, gentle man. Talking to Tobiasz about him brought him back to life, and I think I started to understand him. A bit late, I suppose."

A lot of things had become clearer to her during the trip. She thought about things that she hadn't thought about in years. Her mother had completely overshadowed her dad, and that had seemed to be where he wanted to be, in the background, in her shadow.

When her father died, Hilary had stepped into his shoes. Phyllis had only been in her late 50s and Hilary had subconsciously felt that she had to take her dad's place and be there for her mother. The situation was never discussed and Hilary wasn't offered an alternative.

Talking to Tobiasz about her father as they travelled about had forced her to recall how much he had stood up for her. At school, when she had felt homesick, when the bullies got to her, he had responded with love and support.

"Tobiasz suggested that him insisting that I go to boarding school might have been to remove some of Mum's influence, to allow me to grow. It certainly could have been."

"I agree," said Janet.

"Whenever I was struggling at school, Mum would be quick to point that out that it had all been Dad's idea. But when I said that to Tobiasz, it brought back all the time that Dad had spent with me, reassuring me, encouraging me. He showed me that there will always be people who treat you badly and are determined to put you down. Tobiasz said that it sounded as though he wanted me to learn to deal with them while I was young. He was right. I understand now that Dad was trying to understand, help me see them in a different light."

"He sounds like a very caring dad," said Janet.

"He was," said Hilary. "I found out, long after I'd left the school, that Dad had a friend who was a teacher there. He would phone him to check how I was getting on. I like to think that he was always ready to rescue me if it all got too much. I didn't find out until after I left school. I can't remember how I found out. I suppose Mum must have told me, but…"

"Probably just as well you didn't know while you were still at the school," said Liz.

"I know," replied Hilary. "I would have felt spied on, been constantly on my guard. In fact, I'd have been mortified that he felt he needed to check up on me. Now I understand. I'm just grateful that he was there for me and understood me well enough to know how to protect me.

"I suppose after he died, I had no one to fight my corner," she continued. "And Mum needed me. She had lost her best friend. I was at work a lot of the time and I think that's why she took on all her committee stuff. I don't think there was ever another man. I never went out much, so we sort of settled into a dull routine. Comfortable but dull."

"Your life is anything but dull now." Liz smiled.

"I know! Fancy me going on a month-long trip! I got a bit homesick at first. It surprised me, but cooped up in the car, not knowing the language, not having any time to myself, I even wondered if we'd done the right thing. It just shows that I'm not very used to going away. Even practical things threw me. It hadn't occurred to me that we'd need to do washing. Well, I had thought about it. I remember saying to Tobiasz, when we were planning what to pack, that we wouldn't need any more than you would for a fortnight's holiday because we'd be able to do washing as we went along. But I hadn't thought of the practicalities.

"I don't know whether I imagined launderettes on every corner or hotel laundries but the reality is I didn't think about it properly at all. We had to do some washing in a launderette when we had both almost run out of clean underwear. An English launderette would be a complete mystery to me but, with all the instructions in another language, I was completely lost. Of course, we managed, but you wouldn't believe how excited I got when we arrived at Peta's flat and discovered not only a washing machine but also an airer on a sunny balcony. You would have thought I had found the Holy Grail."

"Oh, Hilary, you are priceless," said Liz, wiping tears from her eyes.

Hilary smiled.

"Have you got time for another coffee?" asked Janet.

"Definitely," said Hilary. "I want to hear how the preparations were going for your mum and dad."

"It's all a bit tough at the moment. Mum's upset. I don't think it's the packing particularly. It's more that her routine has all gone to pot," said Janet.

"She keeps saying, 'No, no, no, no'. It reminds me of Claire sitting in her high chair when she went through a phase of refusing everything except pasta, and it's just as frustrating. I know Mum has no idea what she's refusing—as everyone keeps pointing out—but that doesn't make it any easier. Dad keeps telling me that she'll be fine, she'll get used to it. He says it isn't up to me. He'll be there to help her through. The trouble is that makes me feel even more helpless."

"It must be really difficult," said Hilary.

"I can't imagine," said Liz.

"I will get through it because I know there is an end. Richard has been a huge help."

Richard was firmly on George's side. He was aware of his father-in-law's struggle over the last few months, was witness to the vulnerability that George refused to show to his wife or daughters. Beryl needed care and George needed help. To Richard, it was as simple as that.

"I did think," continued Janet, "that once the decision had been made, that it would be easy. I wish Julia and I had a better relationship. She just says, 'Dad knows best', which, of course, he does, but I'm just finding it a bit hard. Dad takes no notice of Mum's objections. He doesn't seem to hear them but then, he never has." She smiled ruefully. "Dad knows what's best for everyone, always has. So, it will all be okay, I know it will."

Liz and Hilary, not sure how to respond, murmured agreement.

"Are you sure about helping with the move, Hilary?" said Janet. "It's a Friday, but I think it will be a long day, so I'd prefer to go down the day before."

"Of course I am. I should have thought to offer," said Hilary. "I'll make a note." She wiped her hands on a serviette and extracted her diary from her bag.

"I had no idea they still made those diaries with a little pencil slotted down the spine," said Liz. "Don't you use your phone?"

"Not for important things," said Hilary. Her seriousness made the others laugh.

"This has done me so much good," Liz said, as they reluctantly parted company. "What a great way to spend a Monday."

"You must come back and visit Chahna's shop," said Janet. "I think Carol is prouder of it than Chahna herself."

"Definitely," said Liz.

She left feeling happy and relieved, her equilibrium restored, full of news to tell John.

I wish I'd done this before, she thought as she drove home. *Why have I been living in some sort of self-imposed exile?*

FOURTEEN

Growing Apart

Suzanne found Chahna's shop irresistible and visited frequently.

"I'm going to bring Betty next time. She'd love all these beautiful fabrics," she told Carol, watching as she expertly measured a length of turquoise cloth for Suzanne to make cushion covers.

"She is amazing for her age, isn't she?" said Carol.

"Yes, she is and she does really well. I don't know how she does it."

"She's got you on her doorstep."

"But she's pretty independent. We don't do much," said Suzanne, taking her carefully wrapped purchase. "How's your mum doing?"

"Not great. Not great."

Not wanting to upset Carol at work, Suzanne changed the subject. "Jag was singing the praises of the shop the other day, but I think the main thing for him is that Chahna is around so much more," she said. "In a way, she is much busier now that she works for herself but he says her stress levels are much lower. Much easier to live with."

Carol smiled. "I absolutely love working here. I can't believe how different I feel but…" She trailed off.

"What is it?" asked Suzanne.

"Oh nothing."

"It's obviously not nothing."

"I don't like moaning. It feels like I'm telling tales." Carol looked up gratefully when a customer came in to collect an order. Suzanne stepped to one side.

When the customer had left, Suzanne said, "We're eating out tonight, so I won't have lunch. But why don't we go and get a coffee somewhere? You shut for lunch soon, don't you?" Carol agreed but without her usual enthusiasm. She felt cornered.

In spite of her reluctance, she found herself telling Suzanne about Jonathan's recent behaviour.

"He is so negative about everything to do with the shop. Doesn't want to hear anything about it. He says I've changed. Doesn't even like the fact that I've lost weight," she said.

"I think you look great, if that's any consolation," said Suzanne.

Carol shuffled forwards in the queue and Suzanne passed her a tray.

"I hadn't planned to lose weight," said Carol. "I'm just doing more. We eat the same, exactly the same. I tried to introduce some of the lovely recipes that Chahna told me about, the ones that she learned in India. That was a disaster. You'd have thought I was trying to poison him. I can't understand it—he loves the meat madras and pilau rice from the Tandoori King after the rugby."

"A regular cappuccino please," she said to the barista as she placed a chicken wrap and a flapjack on the tray.

"I didn't know that I wanted change," she continued when they had found a table and had removed the plates and cups from their trays. "He's drinking more than he ever used to as well. He seems to be on a path of self-destruction. It's as if he hates the fact that I am happy." Carol looked near to tears. "I hadn't complained about my life or sought a new job. All I did was grab the opportunity with open arms. I was just a bit dissatisfied with life, with the way I looked, and I did feel as though everyone was taking me for granted. My fault, I know. I volunteered for everything, never said no. But, perhaps subconsciously, I wanted a change. So, when I heard about Chahna's new venture at the New Year party, I was ready to dive in. I don't know why Jonathan can't see that I'm the same person underneath. I just have a bit more confidence."

"Perhaps that's it," replied Suzanne. "The newfound confidence.

Perhaps he doesn't feel as needed as he did."

"But he's being really babyish about it," said Carol.

"It seems that he is somehow feeling threatened by the new lovely you," said Suzanne. Carol gave a weak smile.

"I've always been happy with him. I still am. But I feel more alive now, more like I used to when I was younger."

"And poor Jonathan doesn't want to change and he's just getting older!"

"I don't want him to change, except to stop being so miserable over this. I love working at the shop and I think—no, I know—I'm good at it."

"Have you tried talking about it?"

"I've tried. He keeps saying that we don't need the money. He refuses to understand that I don't do the job for the money," said Carol. "I know we don't need the money. I just don't understand. We have never stood in each other's way. He has always been happy to let me do what I wanted. He never complained when I worked at the charity shop."

Carol stirred her coffee thoughtfully.

"Do you know, you're right. It isn't me working in the shop that has upset him or is a threat to him. It's the change in me, the fact that I have lost weight, that I take care of my appearance. Have stopped being so mumsy. I'm not doing any less at home. I'm not working any more hours. In fact, in real terms, his life hasn't changed at all. He just doesn't like the fact that I look (and feel) better."

"I think you've hit the nail on the head," said Suzanne.

"Although that doesn't help me find a solution."

They drank their coffee in silence, letting the noise of the busy café surround them.

"Anyway, enough of me," said Carol as she placed her cup in the saucer. "What's happening in your life? How's the beauty therapy going?"

"I'm really enjoying it," said Suzanne. "When I plucked up courage to tell Jag, he was really enthusiastic and suggested that I go to India to learn massage techniques there. But I'm quite happy at the local tech. I find that I don't want to be involved with collagen injections and Botox. Apart from anything else, I'm not sure I agree with them, both are so temporary and the collagen in particular can be quite disfiguring.

"It's much more my thing just to make people feel better and massage does that every time. I'm learning so much about skin, creams, lotions and potions. In fact, you know, I think what I'm really enjoying is that I'm learning something new."

"That's exactly how I feel," agreed Carol.

"I've no intention of leaving nursing. Well, not at the moment anyway," continued Suzanne. "I've talked about it with David and Betty. Betty suggested turning the garage into a consulting room—she does love a project. It would give me a side line and an insurance policy; in case I became really fed up and decide I want to leave nursing. The NHS has become so money orientated that we seem to be losing the whole purpose of being here. Jag has even noticed a difference since he came back; there are so many more rules and regulations about referrals––referrals being returned if the correct hoops haven't been jumped through, treatments being delayed simply in the interest of saving money and keeping GP budgets on track. To many of the staff now, the patients are just a bit of a nuisance that get in the way of getting to the end of your day. All the negativity gets a bit wearing."

"I know Mum's GP is always a bit more harassed these days," said Carol. "And now that you mention it, before all her tablets were stopped, several of them had been changed to cheaper. Katie complained about the same thing with her contraceptive."

"I know that the money is finite and it has to go around evenly," said Suzanne. "But it doesn't seem fair any more. Decisions depend on where you live and money seems to be the most important thing in all decision-making."

"Thinking about it, that's probably why the doctor didn't refer Jonathan about his knee pain. I just thought that the doctor agreed with me that Jonathan was making something out of nothing."

"That's not like you." Suzanne looked shocked.

"No, it's not. What on earth is he turning me into?"

"Don't be silly," said Suzanne. "Let's face it, you might be right. If he saw Jag, he's pretty good and will refer if at all possible and, if not, he'd have explained why to Jonathan."

"He did see Jag but he didn't tell me what he said apart from that he has to keep taking the painkillers and exercise as much as he can."

"So, he probably didn't need a referral, as you suspected."

"Oh, I don't know. We just don't talk to each other properly anymore," said Carol. "It can't all be my fault."

"Nothing is your fault. Come on, Carol. You're losing your sense of reality."

"He makes me so cross. He sometimes makes me feel as if I am going mad."

"Now you are being dramatic. Come on, let's walk back across the square. It's the long way round, but you'll be back in plenty of time and I promise not to get het up about the NHS if you promise to not mention Jonathan."

"Deal," said Carol.

FIFTEEN

Jonathan Feels Bad

"What is it about women and their weight?" asked Jonathan.

"It's about looking good, feeling good," replied David.

"But I liked Carol how she was, cuddly, motherly," said Jonathan. "Now she's always preening in front of the mirror. She's started wearing makeup every day, jewellery when we're not going out. She keeps asking me if I like this dress or that, if things suit her, make her look fat! As if. I'm terrified of saying the wrong thing. I can't relax." Jonathan picked up his drink and leaned back in his chair with a weary sigh.

"I suppose she has to look smart to work in the shop," said Richard. "I went in once with Janet to look at some curtain material. Never again. I'll leave her to it. It's a very impressive shop though."

"Carol's lost weight, hasn't she?" said David. "I saw her the other day unloading her car outside the shop. I almost didn't recognise her. She's a real stunner."

Jonathan stared miserably into his pint.

Tactlessly, David blundered on.

"It must be because she's happy and of course she'll lose weight with all that running about. She has to. I'm sure the stairs up to the storeroom are a workout for anyone."

"But now she's lost weight, she wants me to cut down, drink less, do more exercise…" complained Jonathan.

"Is that what all this is about?" joked Richard. The others laughed but Jonathan was not to be deflected from his misery.

"I liked things the way they were. I liked Carol as she was. This job has changed her."

"For the better," David muttered into his pint.

"But I liked her how she was," Jonathan almost whined. "We fit together better. She was happy. I think the children wonder what is going on, although Lucy seems very happy with the remnants that Carol gets her from the shop," he added grudgingly.

"But, surely, now she's happier," said David, "or more fulfilled, as a life coach would say, that's got to be better for her, your relationship and the rest of the family." David finished his pint with a flourish and put his glass down on the table.

"I can't keep up," muttered Jonathan. "I don't want to keep up. I don't want to change." He stood up. "I'm having another drink. I'll have to walk home tonight. I came straight from work. Only planning to have a couple of halves. That didn't work!"

"I'll give you a lift," said Richard. "I'm only having a half."

"No thanks," said Jonathan. "This way I can annoy her and please her at the same time. More drink and more exercise."

As he walked towards the bar, he heard Richard say, "It's a shame he can't just be happy for her."

The words made Jonathan feel worse. The truth was that he was jealous of Carol, of her newfound youth and enthusiasm for life. Jealous of the shop that excluded him, made her less reliant on him, less available for him. He knew that this was selfish and it made him wonder if he had held her back all these years, if her life had all been dedicated to him and the family. But she had never expressed any wish to change, had seemed perfectly happy with their way of life. But, worst of all, he felt angry with himself for letting these feelings crowd in on him and take over his thoughts.

He walked home past the familiar landmarks—the bus shelter empty except for litter, the stone facade of the library hiding its underfunded interior, the roundabout planted in a neat patchwork of evergreen shrubs. A light rain was falling that lifted the sweet smell of damp earth from the grass verges and mixed with the sour scent of dog urine. Everything was reassuringly unchanged.

As he walked, he unsuccessfully tried to push all thoughts of Carol from his mind. He was embarrassed by his outpouring in the pub and ashamed of the thoughts that he had kept to himself.

He could not voice the realisation that he might have taken Carol for granted all these years, taken their whole life together for granted, expected that nothing would change, that things would forever be the same. The changes in her were so dramatic, they had taken him by surprise and left him feeling that he was losing her. He couldn't face that. They had bumbled along together for so long. He couldn't admit to his friends that he didn't like the fact that other people were noticing how lovely she looked, that she was good at her job, that she seemed to be getting younger and leaving him behind.

Why can't I just be pleased for her? he mused. Richard's words came back to him, as if written in a bubble above his head.

He trudged home, his hands in his pockets, the collar of his jacket up against the rain, unable to latch on to the jumbled thoughts that wound round and round in his mind.

Why did I have so much to drink? he thought as he turned into the road to the house, and almost tripped when he didn't lift his foot high enough at the kerb. Station Road stretched out in front of him. It always seemed the longest part of a journey, from whichever direction he approached it. In reality, he only had to walk past twenty-seven almost identical terraced houses.

The gate of number fifty-five, which had dropped on its hinges and tended to get stuck on the brick path, was wedged open——another job on his never-ending list of things to do. In spite of this reminder, he felt the comfort of home as he put the key in the lock on the second attempt.

He stepped into the narrow hall and, although he failed to notice the new mirror with its intricately inlaid frame hanging by the door, he was immediately aware of the welcoming smell of slow-cooked beef and onions. He hung his damp jacket on one of the hooks.

"I'm home," he called as he opened the door to the kitchen, trying to rearrange his face into a smile. "Sorry I'm a bit later than I said."

"That's okay," replied Carol. "There's nothing to spoil. I made a casserole. I've had mine. All you've got to do is reheat the mash. I said I'd nip round to see Janet for an hour. I think she's a bit worried about her mum and dad. She's moving them in a few days into that posh new home, James Place." She squeezed past him into the hall, put on her coat, picked up an umbrella and went out.

"Richard didn't say anything," muttered Jonathan, as Carol closed the front door with exaggerated care. He went upstairs to change into an old tracksuit.

He sat in front of the television, watching a programme he despised, trying to find fault with his plateful of casserole, knowing that he couldn't blame Carol for the lukewarm mashed potato. An unwanted bottle of beer sat open next to his chair.

SIXTEEN

Moving Day

Janet was troubled by sleepless nights, as the day of her parents' move to James Place approached. She had wanted Richard to take over, to do the driving and settle them in, but she knew that she had to do it. Richard had taken too many days off already and given up weekends to help with the packing, so work had to take precedence. Julia was in Guatemala but had at least sent a good luck card and offered to come home (even though Janet knew that she had only made the offer in the sure knowledge that it would be refused). In the end, it had been her father who had suggested asking Hilary and Hector to join her.

She and Hilary had travelled up the day before and stayed in the nearby Travelodge. In the evening they went out to an Indian restaurant while Hector, having enjoyed the attentions of the reception staff, waited in the room for them. The restaurant hadn't changed much since Janet's teenage years when it had been the only Indian for miles. The flock wallpaper had been replaced with fake marbling and a chrome bar, but the food took her back to the years when an Indian meal was only ever eaten after the pubs shut.

On moving day, Janet almost faltered when she looked around her childhood home emptied of all its treasures, its walls stripped bare. The carers had settled Beryl in her usual chair in the living room.

"They gave her a hug; seemed really upset that she was going," reported George, when Janet and Hilary arrived. "Everyone loves her."

Beryl touched Hector's back as he sniffed around her chair for dropped food, but she was seemingly unaware of the removal men noisily working around her, carrying out George's clear, precise instructions. Janet smiled as she watched him check the labels against the list on his clipboard, making sure that the small items of furniture that he would be able to have in his room would be delivered the next day. Most of the stuff was destined for a storage facility just outside Barwell, where it would remain until Janet could bear to sort it.

"Come on now, my love, we are going in the car," said George. Beryl, who rarely recognised George any more, seemed to know, on some level, that his voice was to be obeyed. She had always followed his wishes, and even from the depths of dementia, she continued to do as he wanted.

Janet and Hilary helped her to her feet and, between them, moved her slowly towards the door, as two of the removal men dodged behind them and picked up her chair. They shuffled in a slow procession, with George murmuring encouragement, until they reached the doorstep, something they hadn't factored into their plans. It proved too great an obstacle to overcome.

"We should have borrowed a wheelchair," Janet said, almost in tears. "I didn't think. She hasn't been out in months. She manages with help to get around the house, and of course the stair lift. I didn't think…"

George appeared diminished as he stood on the drive holding his arms out to Beryl.

Hilary didn't say anything but she looked over her shoulder at the removal men and nodded towards the chair.

"No prob," said the scrawny lad, his acne-laden cheeks red with exertion.

"Oh, I don't know, looks a bit too 'eavy to me," his burly mate replied, eyeing Beryl's tiny frame.

"C'mon, we can do it."

"The wife'll kill me if I can't tek 'er shoppin'."

"I'll k…"

Their wise cracks continued as Beryl was gently lowered into the chair and the unwieldy recliner lifted down the step. Beryl's hands gripped the arms but something like a giggle escaped from her as she was carried past the removal lorry to the waiting car.

Janet and Hilary once more helped her to her feet and manoeuvred her towards the car door. The clunk of the car door opening startled Beryl. Her body went rigid. She stood with her hands against the car, resisting all attempts to get her in, until Hector pushed past her legs and leaped onto the seat. Beryl bent forwards to pat Hector. Seeing an opportunity, Janet and George managed to manhandle her in. Hilary, who had dashed around to the other side, took the seat belt from Janet and secured Beryl in her seat. Hector was supposed to be travelling in the luggage space behind the seats but he settled himself in the middle of the back seat with his head on Beryl's lap. Hilary squeezed in next to him and strapped herself in.

George shook hands with his neighbour who would oversee the last of the clearance of the house and keep a spare set of keys until the new people moved in. He climbed stiffly into the passenger seat and didn't look back when Janet stopped at the bottom of the road to take one last look.

It all seemed very final as Janet pulled up outside the solicitor's office. George insisted on going in himself to hand over the keys.

Looking around as they drove beyond the end of the High Street, George said, "This was fields when we moved in. Used to get eggs from Wagg's Farm across there. Remember, Beryl?" The place was now a sprawling housing estate.

Beryl said nothing.

"I remember it being fields," said Janet. "And I remember town when the only shops were the ones on the High Street, no shopping centre, no retail park. And the cinema was still a cinema," she added as they drove past the semi-derelict art deco style building. "We used to go there, didn't we, Mum? And you let Julia and me go to Saturday morning cinema, didn't you? All gone now."

Beryl stared at the seat in front of her and picked at the stitching on Hector's collar.

"Sad," said Hilary.

Within minutes of leaving town, they were on the motorway. The road noise made conversation between the front and back of the car more difficult but Hilary heard snatches as George reassured Janet that although the house had been sold to pay for his room and her mum's care, she could still rely on some sort of inheritance. It felt as though it was something she should not be listening to and was relieved when Janet turned on the radio.

Beryl was alarmed by the lorries thundering past. She fidgeted, tried to release herself from her seat belt, pushed at the seat in front of her, plucked at her clothes. Hilary leaned across Hector, took her hand; she spoke softly to her. Quickly running out of things to say, she described what they were passing. George and Janet joined in with her the sixth time she said, "Under the bridge we go."

Beryl finally fell asleep. Hilary reassured George with a smile each time he twisted awkwardly in his seat to check that Beryl was alright. Hector kept up his vigil, his head never moving from Beryl's lap.

They had not planned a stop, agreeing that it would be too disruptive for all concerned. But George's prostate had other ideas. Janet turned off the motorway at the next services and parked as close to the building as she could. Beryl stirred as Janet switched off the engine, but didn't wake. Janet followed her dad into the service station, leaving Hilary strapped into her seat, her hand resting on Hector's back, gently willing him not to move, as she waited anxiously for the journey to resume.

Beryl slept until they reached the outskirts of Barwell, but then sprang awake at the sound of a siren. She screamed and strained against her seat belt, battering the back of George's seat. Then she turned and banged on her window as they stopped at traffic lights, scaring a cyclist who had pulled up on the inside.

Hector sat up in alarm. Hilary saw Janet's eyes in the rear-view mirror looking strained and frightened. She undid her seat belt, reached across Hector and tried to take Beryl's hands. Her fingers were gripped painfully. George twisted round and patted Beryl's knee.

"Nearly there, my love," he said. "We'll get out soon."

"Should I stop?" asked Janet.

"No. Keep going. It will be okay." He managed to keep his hand on Beryl's knee until she faded back into her normal torpor and Hilary was able to ease her hands out of their vice-like grip.

Tension filled the car. Janet silently railed at traffic lights and other drivers who slowed their progress. Hilary's eyes never left Beryl, willing her to stay calm. It was as if they all held their breath until Janet turned the car into the drive and James Place—brightly lit and boldly modern—came into view.

A welcoming committee comprising the manager and a carer with a wheelchair eased Beryl's transition from car to bed. A volunteer provided tea and cakes, which revived the others sufficiently to unload the car.

Janet had made up a bed for George, and Richard was expecting them both home once Beryl was settled in. But George had other ideas and was adamant that he would remain at James Place.

"Apart from under orders," he said, "we have never been apart for even one night."

When Hilary and Janet had finished unloading the car, Hilary left Janet to unpack George's case and went to phone Tobiasz and give Hector a bit of a walk.

"You are not putting that on there," George said, as Janet lifted up the case to put it on the bed.

He smoothed his hand across the cotton bedspread stretched over the neatly made bed.

She balanced the suitcase on the chair and, under his scrutiny, started to unpack. A carer came in to ask how they were getting on and Janet found herself almost begging the woman to take George up to see Beryl.

"I only agree because she sleep," the carer said in heavily accented English. "It is best she has no visitors until she settles in." George, who looked as though he had other ideas, eagerly followed her out of the room.

Janet put the suitcase back on the bed and rapidly unpacked the rest of his things. A lump came into her throat as she placed George's badger hair shaving brush next to the bowl of shaving soap on the shelf above the basin, just as it had been at home. The top of the chest of drawers looked a little bare, with just his comb and two tortoiseshell-backed brushes.

She had stowed the suitcase at the top of the wardrobe and straightened the bed before George came back.

Hilary followed him in. "All okay?" she asked.

"All okay," he replied.

"I think I've finished for today," Janet said. "I'll come back tomorrow,

Dad. It's time I got Hilary and Hector home."

George saw them to the door. As Janet turned to wave, he was already talking to another resident.

"They'll be fine," said Hilary, climbing into the car.

"I think they will," replied Janet.

SEVENTEEN

Time for a Get-Together

Suzanne had hardly seen Hilary in the two weeks since Hilary had helped with Janet's parents. She hadn't seen Janet at all and hadn't wanted to phone, sure that Janet would be busy helping George and Beryl to settle in. She had seen Carol briefly when she'd taken Betty to have a look around the shop. It had been a successful shopping trip but Carol had been too busy with other customers to talk for long.

Right, she thought, as she ended a chat on the phone with Liz. *It can't just be me that's missing seeing everyone. We seem to be all over the place this year.*

She thought about her friends. Liz was pleased that she and John had moved but things were not going as smoothly as she had hoped. Janet would be more relaxed now that her parents were nearer, but the process must have been difficult and visiting them would still take its toll. And, of course, Claire had moved out. Janet would miss having her and Jasmine around all the time. Carol's life was being torn in two and Chahna was both exhilarated and exhausted by the new business. Hilary...well, Suzanne didn't know what was going on with Hilary; it was as if she was going through a teenage rebellion rather than a midlife crisis as, in reality, her life was only just beginning.

"Right," she said aloud. "Everyone has got too much going on, too many changes. I think that we need to arrange something. A get-together. All of us. We need to make sure that we can all be together. I'll see if Chahna can get us a bit of a discount at the spa now that she is supplying all the candles. Yes, that's what I'll do."

"What will you do?" asked Betty, putting her head around the kitchen door.

"Arrange a trip to the spa for the six of us," she said. She pushed a chair out for Betty and reached behind her for a coffee cup. She poured the coffee and pushed the cup and milk towards Betty. "You can come if you like."

"Oh, no," she replied. "I'm too old for all that. I'll stay here and relax in my chair. I don't want to be exposing this old body to anyone other than the doctor and the undertaker."

Suzanne laughed. "Well, you can always change your mind."

"I won't," said Betty, changing the subject to the building project that was nearing completion on the land where her family home had once been.

As soon as Betty went back up to her flat, Suzanne emailed Chahna and was surprised to receive a reply within seconds.

I'll look into it.

Suzanne replied that she would start canvassing the troops to find a date that suited them all.

Within a few days the date was set, a special rate had been arranged for a mid-week overnight stay, work rotas were swapped and Chahna had cajoled one of her daughters into looking after the shop for two days.

EIGHTEEN

Spa Break

"I like that swimming costume, Hilary," said Liz as they took off their bathrobes to go into the sauna. "But it still makes me chuckle, thinking of you stuck in that old one."

"If I ever get a new one, I shall always have to bring this one here," said Hilary, pulling up her strap. She felt a bubble of laughter inside her. "It was so funny, I thought I was going to wet myself."

"You'd been in such a state, all anxious and upset and then the laughter just burst out of you."

"I was such a misery at that time, I'd thought I'd never laugh again," said Hilary.

"Heavens above, you'd just lost your mum…"

They settled down on the benches to relax in the steam. The door opened and Carol and Suzanne came in.

"Move up a bit," said Carol.

"I can only stand a few minutes of this," said Suzanne. "And don't even suggest a cold shower."

"Where are the other two?" asked Hilary, wiping the sweat from her very red face.

"Janet has a treatment booked and I bet Chahna is talking business with the manager, knowing her," replied Suzanne.

"No, she isn't," said Chahna, squeezing herself in. "Today, I'm spoiling myself."

"It's no good," said Hilary. "I can't stand any more. I'm going in the pool. Although that might be a bit cold after this. Perhaps I'll get there via the jacuzzi." She opened the door. Suzanne went with her, leaving the others to continue steaming.

Later, feeling relaxed after a day of gentle exercise and pampering treatments, and having eaten a healthy dinner accompanied by a couple of bottles of wine, the friends gathered on two settees, angled to take advantage of the view of the grounds and the countryside beyond.

Liz called a waiter over and ordered another bottle of wine.

"To celebrate getting together," she said when Suzanne looked at her questioningly. "Thank you for organising everything. And we can do it all again tomorrow!"

"I've missed our get-togethers," said Hilary. "I feel a bit guilty for not having had a lunch for my birthday."

"We'll forgive you." Liz smiled.

"I can totally understand you wanting to have time with your lovely Tobiasz," added Janet.

"I think I got a bit selfish for a while," said Hilary.

"We all have to be selfish sometimes, have to look after ourselves a bit," said Suzanne.

"Look at me," said Chahna. "In India for a year and now I've given up a well-paid job to indulge a fantasy. It could have gone so wrong."

"Yes, but me trying to do what I want to do seems to have backfired," said Carol, looking glum.

"Don't you dare think of leaving me or the shop," said Chahna, sitting up straight in her chair. "You hold it all together. How could I go off on my buying trips without you?"

Carol flushed with pleasure at the compliment.

"I'm not thinking of leaving," she said. "I love the shop, working there, being among all those beautiful things, learning loads. No, I won't be leaving, but Jonathan is going to have to buck up a bit, or..." She stopped. "Or I don't know what will happen."

"Good for you, Carol," said Janet, quietly.

Afraid that she was being disloyal to Jonathan, and not wanting to say more, Carol quickly shifted the focus back to Chahna, encouraging her to tell them all about the new fabrics she was importing from India.

"Enough about curtain material," said Chahna after fifteen minutes. "You should have shut me up."

"No," chorused the others.

"I for one will be in to see the new stock," said Suzanne. "Make sure you tell me as soon as it arrives."

"I'll let you know," said Carol. "I'll make a note, otherwise I'll forget. Memory like a sieve." She got out her phone and made herself a reminder.

"Are your mum and dad doing okay?" asked Liz.

Janet smiled. Any mention of memory brought the conversation around to her mum.

"They've settled in so well," she said. "It's lovely to see Dad so relaxed. Mum is deteriorating but the care is excellent. I can't fault it. Even I feel cared for."

"I've heard really good reports about it," said Suzanne.

"When it was being built, Jag thought that it was all for show," said Chahna. "But he's had to eat his words. He's so impressed with the manager and the staff seem excellent."

"They are," said Janet. "I am still a bit worried that things might not be so good when they are fully occupied, when they no longer have to sell themselves. But Dad's got himself onto the residents committee. I'm sure he'll keep them in line."

The others laughed.

"It certainly seems better than where Mum is," said Carol. "But I would never move her now. And I'm not sure we could afford it anyway."

"Pearl has said I'm to shoot her if ever she needs to go in a home," said Liz. "I'd better get some target practice in."

"Liz!" the others shouted in laughter.

"Changing the subject," said Suzanne. "Did I tell you David and I are off to South Africa for three weeks before Christmas?"

The friends expressed their envy and amazement at this announcement.

"I don't feel so bad telling you that Jag and I are taking the girls for three weeks' trekking in Nepal next February."

"My trip that didn't quite get to Poland can't compete with any of that," Hilary said, laughing.

"But I don't suppose they'll come back to such momentous news as you did," said Liz.

"It was a bit of a shock!" said Hilary. "I wish I could introduce you to Gillian. Before I met her, I had this fantasy of introducing her to you all, including her in things like this."

"Why can't you?" asked Carol.

Hilary looked down, moving her glass further on to the table. "I don't like her. She isn't a nice person. I don't know what makes her so prickly. Her letter was quite encouraging and she was lovely with Luke, playing peekaboo but… It terrified me to think that we could be related. We're not, thank goodness. Her daughter's lovely, though––heaven knows how."

"It's a shame that your mum never got to meet Lance again, though," said Liz.

"I really don't think that she would have wanted to," replied Hilary. "I don't know, but she was always very decisive and that letter saying that she had lost the baby very definitely ended all contact. I'll never know, but I like to think that although I didn't know everything about Mum's history, I did know her personality."

"Well," said Chahna, "you certainly lived with her for long enough."

"I agree," said Suzanne. "You must have known her better than anyone. You lived with her for longer than anyone else."

"Mmmm," said Hilary. "I did. It seems a bit silly now that I got myself in such a state about a manuscript from years ago."

"Not silly," said Carol. "But you perhaps were wrong to think that she wasn't the woman that you knew."

"I suppose it was because the manuscript was so explicit and she had always seemed so strait-laced to me. I couldn't reconcile the two. I've been influenced by the wrong side of her." Hilary hiccupped as she laughed.

"Whatever influenced you," said Janet, also feeling the effect of the wine, "turned you into a lovely, kind person. Don't change."

"I think I was more like my dad," continued Hilary, not acknowledging Janet's words. "I just wanted to please everybody. If I'd been like Mum, we'd have fought and I'd have left home long ago. There wouldn't have been room for two people like Mum in the house."

"I'll second that, Hilary," said Liz. "But I, for one, think I had better call it a night, if I want to make the most of everything I've booked for tomorrow."

There were murmurs of agreement and slowly they got off the settees, said goodnight and went to their rooms.

The next day, Chahna, true to form, left early for a meeting with her wallpaper people.

"Her commitment is amazing," said Carol, when Liz complained about her absence yet again at breakfast.

"Whatever she does she puts her whole self into it," continued Carol. "Although she has come unstuck sometimes when she tries to drag her daughters along with her. Daisy flatly refuses to help in the shop. I was a bit surprised to hear that the girls are going to Nepal but apparently it was their idea."

"Odd names, aren't they, for an Indian child?" said Liz. "Daisy and Rose."

"They suit them though, don't they?" said Carol. "Chahna said they made a deliberate choice. She remembered being teased at school about her name."

"You've got to know her better in the last few months than the rest of us in all these years," said Suzanne.

"She does hide behind her work a bit. Believe it or not, I think she's a bit insecure."

The others looked unconvinced.

"Well, perhaps she'll be able to join us more now you're working together," said Liz. "Is there any more coffee in that pot?"

After a leisurely breakfast, they draped themselves on loungers in the relaxation room. Carol was delighted when, Ashley, the girl who had bought all the candles, greeted her and took her for a neck massage. Suzanne and Liz were also soon whisked away, leaving Hilary and Janet waiting for their final treatment—a manicure for Hilary and a pedicure for Janet.

"You haven't said much about Tobiasz," Janet said. "Is everything okay?"

"Definitely," said Hilary. "I suppose you're right. I haven't said much. It doesn't mean he's not on my mind, though. It's funny. I don't feel the need to talk about him like I did when we first met. He's just there. He's always there."

"You are lucky to have found someone like him," said Janet. "He's so kind. He has been so good for you. You are like two halves of a whole."

"We are very like each other in some ways but he has much more confidence than me. I feel…"

"Hilary Walton," a quiet voice gently called.

"Yes, that's me." Hilary pulled herself upright.

"I am Celine. I will be doing your treatment. Come with me."

"See you later," Hilary said to Janet as she was led to her treatment room.

Hilary thought about what Janet had said while her hands were being pampered. *She is right. He is like part of me. I wonder if I should have said yes when he asked me to marry him? Have I missed my chance?*

"What a lovely colour you've chosen," Celine said as she started to apply the polish to Hilary's nails.

"Coral," said Hilary. "It's an old-fashioned colour. My mum always wore coral lipstick. It doesn't suit my face but I do love the colour."

"Your nails are a nice shape. And they're in good condition. You're lucky," said Celine.

"Thank you," said Hilary, hoping that the compliment was genuine and she wasn't just being buttered up for a tip.

When she and Janet got together for a final herbal tea before they went home, Hilary asked, "Do you think I was wrong to turn down Tobiasz's proposal?"

"Where did that come from?" asked Janet. "You must do whatever you think is right at the time. Maybe if he proposed tomorrow, you would give a different answer."

"Who knows?" said Hilary.

Carol, Suzanne and Liz met them at reception with their suitcases.

"We must try and make sure that we meet up regularly," said Hilary. "Time just goes. Time with you lot does me so much good. You have no idea."

"Of course we do," said Liz. "It does us all good, doesn't it?"

There were nods of agreement.

"I still go swimming on Mondays," said Hilary. "If anyone wants to join me. I kept on going. When you get out of the habit, it's very difficult to pick it up again, isn't it?"

"I might go," said Carol. "Sometimes."

"You never know, I might too," said Suzanne.

"I should have more time now," said Janet. "If I know you're going to be there, I'll come."

"I am," said Hilary, "because Sarah goes with Luke."

"I could perhaps see if Claire would let me bring Jasmine."

"There's an idea," said Hilary.

"Well, I'll just have to put up with swimming in the sea, won't I?" said Liz, smiling. "When it's warm enough."

"Anyway," said Suzanne. "Must be off. Let's not leave it so long next time."

NINETEEN

Homecoming

Jag, Daisy and Rose listened with amazement, as Chahna told them about the spa break later that evening. Jag was pleased that she had enjoyed herself but she had spent many hours at the spa and had never shown such enthusiasm.

"I don't think I've ever really had time to relax with the others," she said to Jag when Daisy and Rose had gone to their rooms, after eliciting a promise from her that she would take them soon. "I've always been a bit on the edge, dropping in when they get together but never having time to get involved. I wish I'd gone on my own sooner."

"So do I," said Jag, wistfully.

"Everyone was very excited and very jealous when I told them about our trip to South Africa," Suzanne told David when they sat down to dinner that evening.

"I bet they were," said David. "But I thought you weren't going to tell anyone until we'd told Mum."

"Sorry. It just came out and no one will say anything," said Suzanne. "I'll just mention to Hilary, as she's the only one likely to see Betty before we have a chance to tell her."

"It doesn't matter. I'll tell her tomorrow when we drive to the meeting. I don't know why it had to be a secret anyway."

"I just felt a bit guilty about leaving her around Christmas again."

"We'll be back the week before. She'll manage."

"Of course she will," said Suzanne. David didn't ask about her spa break, so they ate their meal quietly and companionably, and discussed what he'd done while she was away.

Carol had dinner ready for Jonathan when he got home from work. She didn't mention the trip, knowing that he wouldn't be interested, but she made the mistake of saying, "You'll never guess where Suzanne and David are off to in December."

"Somewhere exotic, I suppose."

"South Africa. Wouldn't that be amazing? You'd love it, the safaris and everything."

"Another place I've always wanted to go, but there's no way we could afford it and I don't suppose you'd want to leave the precious shop to make it worthwhile going."

Carol didn't say anything, knowing that whatever she said would be wrong. She concentrated on eating her dinner until she felt calm enough to ask how he had got on while she was away.

"Same as I always do when you're not here."

Carol gave up. She put her knife and fork down and said, "I'm quite tired. Think I'll have an early night. I'll do the washing up in the morning."

Liz got home to an empty house. She was on the phone to Lisa, arranging a mother–daughter day at the spa, when John arrived home. Liz was less successful when she tried to persuade John to book a couple's day.

Richard was delighted to see how relaxed and happy Janet was on her return. He listened as she described the treatments they'd all had, the food, the rooms. He hadn't seen her this animated in a long time and it was the next day before she asked about her parents or phoned Claire. That evening, he had her all to himself.

*

The greeting that Hilary received from Tobiasz was almost as exuberant as the one from Hector. They were both delighted to have her back. Tobiasz carried her case in and made her sit down while he made coffee.

"I'm not ill," she said, laughing.

"I just want to show that I miss you."

"I've missed you too. Yes, and you too, Hector," she added when Hector pushed his nose under her hand. She stroked him. "But I bet you've had loads of walks and lots of treats."

"I have had walks but no treats," said Tobiasz with mock seriousness.

"You are silly, but I do love you." Hilary laughed, getting up from her chair.

"No," she said, when he tried to push her down again. "I want to unpack, get changed. Do you want me to do anything for dinner?"

"No. It is done."

The evening was as special as their first. Tobiasz had prepared an extravagant meal and bought an expensive bottle of wine. He insisted she tell him all about the spa and the treatments that she had had. He loved the colour of her nails and told her that she was not to do housework in case she chipped it. He was as excited as she had been to hear about Suzanne's and David's proposed trip and, to Hilary's delight, immediately said that they must keep an eye on Betty, perhaps invite her around for lunch. Tobiasz's behaviour was flawless; he even loaded the dishwasher.

"If I didn't know you better, I'd wonder if you were up to something," Hilary said. She took his hand as he sat down next to her on the settee. Tobiasz put on a hurt look.

"I just wanted to have everything right for you," he said.

"It couldn't be more right," she replied, snuggling up to him. "Shall I put the telly on?"

He took the remote control from her hand and put his arms around her.

TWENTY

An Unexpected Invitation

A week later, Hilary called in at Chaja Bazaar. Before the shop had opened, Hilary hadn't fully realised the joy of buying things simply to decorate her home; now her bedroom was beginning to look like a harem. Today, as well as browsing, she was keen to talk to Carol about the wonderful time they'd had at the spa. Although Carol spoke enthusiastically about the trip, Hilary found herself commiserating when she heard about Jonathan's attitude. She'd wanted to tell Carol about the meal that Tobiasz had cooked upon her return, but instead she remained quiet and hugged her own good fortune to herself.

On Saturday afternoon, she went with Janet to visit her mum and dad at James Place. She told Janet about her conversation with Carol but neither of them had a solution to their friend's troubles. Hilary played dominoes with George, while Janet dealt with one of the many administrative tasks that seemed to require her attention. Later, she sat with Janet and George in Beryl's room. Hilary felt more comfortable with George there, as Beryl seemed more at ease and, at the same time, more alert. Janet described the trip to the spa to her parents and Hilary chipped in. George laughed at their description of the treatments.

"You wouldn't catch us going to a place like that, would you, Beryl?" He squeezed Beryl's hand. Beryl lifted her head and rewarded him with a look.

Hilary was happy to see Janet looking so relaxed.

When she got home, she phoned Liz to tell her about the visit, and about how much better Janet seemed.

"I noticed a change in her last week," said Liz. "Less like a frightened rabbit."

"Don't be mean," said Hilary. "She's had a lot on her plate."

"I know, and I'm really pleased. Finally, a solution's been found that seems to suit everyone. Anyway, you seemed to enjoy yourself at the spa."

"It was great. I love it when we all get together."

"Did Tobiasz and Hector manage without you?"

"Of course," she replied.

Hilary didn't want the conversation to be about Tobiasz, so she asked Liz about Siobhan and Sonny. Liz, not one to be diverted, repeatedly asked when she and Tobiasz were going to visit.

"I can't think about that," Hilary finally felt the need to admit. "Not until after Tobiasz has been to Poland. We will come. Definitely. But let us get through this first."

Tobiasz's visit to Poland was the only blot on Hilary's horizon.

"It's a couple of weeks yet," said Tobiasz. "And I'm only going for four days. But I have to go."

"I know. I know," said Hilary. "I just wish I was going too."

"I must do this alone."

Hilary knew that her fear that he would not return was unfounded and Tobiasz could not adequately explain his feelings about Poland; he just knew that he needed to go back in order to move forwards.

Over lunch, they talked in circles about it; the quiche that Hilary had lovingly made, aided by several phone calls to Sarah, was eaten without comment.

As usual, to put them back on track, they took Hector for a walk.

Hilary was feeling better when they returned, the fresh air and exercise—together with watching Hector as he did his 'glad to be alive' run the moment he was off his lead—had put her fears and anxieties into perspective. Tobiasz took Hector and his muddy paws around the back and Hilary went in through the front door. She removed her coat, changed her shoes and tutted as she picked up what she thought was yet another takeaway menu that had been pushed through the letterbox. She put it on the counter in the kitchen. Hector was already lying in his basket.

"I'll put the kettle on," she said and picked up the piece of card to put it into the recycling bin.

"Oh," she said, taking a closer look.

"What?" asked Tobiasz.

"The neighbours have invited us round for a party. They are celebrating their tenth wedding anniversary," she said, holding the brightly coloured piece of card out to him.

"That's nice," he replied.

"I'm not sure I could go. I don't know them very well," Hilary said. "Sarah knows them. I think she's even babysat. After the barbecue last year, I thought we'd see a lot of them but we don't seem to have done. I don't know."

"Well, then it would be a good thing to go to get to know them more."

"Mmmmm," said Hilary.

"You could see if Sarah and Tom are invited, or even Suzanne and David. After all, they are neighbours too."

"I could, I suppose," said Hilary.

"Where is the party?"

"At the house."

"So, what is the problem?"

"I don't know. I'll think about it."

She put the invitation on the noticeboard in the kitchen, where she could have a think about it.

When she next saw Suzanne, she asked if she and David had been invited to the party.

"We were," said Suzanne. "I was quite surprised. I hardly know them but it was nice of them to ask.

"We can't go," she continued. "It's the Sunday of the weekend of Esmée and Erik's wedding, so we'll be away in Amsterdam. We're staying for a week. I've always wanted to go to the Rijksmuseum. I can't say David's keen on that idea but I'm sure he'll come along."

"Oh," said Hilary. "I hadn't realised it was so soon. I'll have to get them a card. Do you mind taking it?"

"Of course not. I'm sorry we'll miss the party. It's about time we got to know them better. I'll perhaps invite them around when we get back."

"I was hoping for some moral support. I hardly know them either," said Hilary, having difficulty imagining Sharon and all her children in Suzanne's immaculate home.

"Tobiasz'll be with you, won't he?"

"He will, but he does like to go off and talk to other people. I can't glue him to my side."

"I suppose not. What about Sarah? I've seen her and Luke coming to the house a few times."

"I'll ask her. Tobiasz suggested that too."

It took several attempts to get hold of Sarah, but when she finally spoke to her, Hilary was relieved to hear that Sarah and Tom—and of course Luke—had been invited.

"I'm taking Luke," she said. "Tom won't be there."

"Oh, I am glad," said Hilary. "Not about Tom, but that you and Luke will be there. I didn't want to go if I wasn't going to know anyone except Tobiasz. I shall definitely accept, then. I'll see you there. And I'll see you at the pool on Monday, won't I?"

"Probably," said Sarah, with less enthusiasm than usual. "Sorry, I have to go now."

"Yes, I won't keep you. I know how busy you are. Take care. Love to Luke and Tom. Bye."

Sarah ended the call without saying goodbye.

She sounded tired, Hilary thought, looking down at her phone. *These young people try to fit so much into their lives. I don't know how she manages, juggling work and Luke.* Sarah had recently called on Hilary on a couple of occasions to take care of Luke. Hilary loved to be asked, loved to feel needed.

"Well," she said to Hector, who looked up from his basket in the hope of another walk. "I had better find a card to accept this invitation." He tucked his head back under his paw.

Tobiasz was pleased when she told him that Sarah was going and she was going to accept the invitation. He offered to go round to tell the neighbours.

"It's okay. I've written a note. It's on the hall table."

"I will put it through the door on my way to work tomorrow," he said.

Hilary was in the supermarket, picking up the things that Tobiasz had forgotten, when she saw their neighbour Sharon walking down the aisle with her youngest, Ewen, imprisoned in the trolley. He was leaning sideways trying to reach things on the shelves. Hilary was staring at the shelves, wondering why supermarkets felt the need to continually rearrange the stock. The two trolleys almost bumped into each other.

"Oh, hello," said Hilary.

"I'm so sorry," said Sharon, steering out of the way. "If I'm anywhere near the shelves, he's pulling things onto the floor or I end up with a trolley full of items that I don't want."

Hilary smiled down at Ewen, as he grabbed the side of her trolley. "I'm sorry, I didn't see you. I was miles away, looking for something. Pesto, of all things."

"It's in the next aisle," said Sharon, pointing with one hand and undoing Ewen's grasp with the other.

"Joe and I are really pleased that you and Tobiasz are coming to the party."

"Yes, we're looking forward to it," said Hilary. "I'm sorry if the reply took a long time but I wasn't sure we'd know anyone."

"Well, you know me, Joe and the children, so that's quite a crowd! But, anyway, I'm really glad you're coming."

While they talked, Ewen managed to grab a packet of ginger nuts, releasing several packets from the pile behind. They rolled onto the floor with a clatter.

"Naughty boy." Sharon sounded exasperated. "I better go." She bent down to retrieve the packets of biscuits.

"Can I bring anything? Do anything?" asked Hilary.

"I can't think at the moment. I'll let you know." Sharon broke off the end of the baguette in her trolley and gave it to Ewen to distract him. She started to walk towards the tills and then turned. "Would it be possible to use your drive for parking?"

"Of course," said Hilary. "Suzanne and David are away, so perhaps you could use their drive too. I'm sure they wouldn't mind, but you'd better ask."

"Great, thank you," Sharon said. "Well, I'm sure we'll meet up before but, otherwise, see you on the day."

TWENTY-ONE

Surprising News

On the day of the party, Hilary and Tobiasz followed the noise and let themselves in through the side gate, as instructed on the invitation. Tobiasz soon found his way to the barbecue where Joe was cooking burgers and sausages, while drinking a steady supply of lager, surrounded by the male contingent of the party. Hilary wandered into the kitchen. "Happy anniversary," she said to Sharon.

"Oh, thank you. Wonderful, you came," Sharon enthused. "Are you on your own?"

"No. Tobiasz got side-tracked by the beer and the barbecue. Can I help?"

Sharon was busy tearing open packets of ready-made party food and pouring the contents onto baking trays, which she then crowded into the oven. She decanted anything that didn't require heating into bowls of various sizes, which she handed to the children to put on the table, reminding them to leave space for "Dad's sausages and burgers."

She waved away Hilary's offer to help with entreaties to enjoy herself. Hilary went to find a drink and realised she was still holding a gift bag containing a card and a bottle of champagne. She had wanted to buy an ornament or a candle from Chaja Bazaar but Carol had advised against it. "All those children and it's not a special anniversary like Silver or Golden. It sounds like just an excuse for a party. Alcohol would be better." Tobiasz agreed with Carol and settled on champagne. She spotted several other gifts and cards piled on a table just inside the living room, so she left hers there too.

She wandered into the garden with a glass of warm Prosecco and found herself smiling at the chaotic jolliness of the party. She talked to various relatives, friends, and teachers from school. She spotted Sarah and Luke, waved and was just about to make her way through the throng when Joe pushed past her with a plate piled high with meat and, a few seconds later, Sharon appeared on the patio banging the bottom of a mixing bowl with a metal spoon and shouting, "Food's ready. Come and get it."

Hilary lost sight of Sarah, as Sharon hustled her and the people around her into the dining room. She filled her paper plate with a burger and savoury pastries, some more soggy than others. She added a tomato and then helped the elderly lady behind her who was struggling to hold a plate, serviette, glass and cutlery. They sat down together on two dining chairs that had been pushed into the corner of the room. Unfortunately, the woman was deaf and, with the noise of the chatter, the music and the children shouting, couldn't hear any of Hilary's questions. Hilary never did find out who she was.

It wasn't until much later that Hilary found Sarah sitting on a chair in the now empty dining room, with Luke asleep on her lap. Darkness had fallen and the party had shifted to the living room. Music and shouts of laughter seeped through the wall.

"How come Tom isn't here?" asked Hilary. She picked up a lone vol-au-vent and pulled a chair across to sit next to Sarah. "Why are you on your own?"

"He's left me," she said, holding Luke to her. "He's left us both. I wanted to tell you, but how could I? I feel such a failure."

"Oh, Sarah." Hilary put her arms around them both. "Why didn't you tell me? I wish you'd said something. I didn't even realise there was a problem."

"Neither did I," Sarah whispered. "He's found someone else. He was very nice about it. It was all very calm. I was too shocked to say anything. He had it all planned out. He must have practised his lines. Luke was playing in the corner, piling up blocks and knocking them down. Tom didn't take any notice of him. I didn't even think to say, 'What about Luke?'" Tears slid quietly down her cheeks.

"But what about Luke?" asked Hilary.

"I don't know. He's with me at the moment. I suppose we'll have to sort something out. I suppose we'll have to share him. He's the only reason I have to carry on."

"Oh, Sarah," said Hilary again. "I do wish you'd told me."

"I couldn't. I feel so ashamed. It hasn't been long. Feels like forever. He only moved out properly last weekend. You were so happy, so full of your trip and then all the business with Gillian and stuff about your mum. You seemed so busy. I couldn't tell you. I didn't want to spoil things for you."

"So full of my trip and other things, that I didn't even notice," said Hilary. "Is that why you needed me to have Luke? Has Tom's mother deserted you both too?"

"It's only right. I suppose she has to side with her son." Sarah sounded defeated.

"No, she doesn't," said Hilary with unusual force. "Not only is Tom in the wrong, it means that she is also willing to desert her grandson. And I thought the two of you got on so well."

"So did I. But she has to support her son. She's seen Luke the couple of times when Tom has had him. I feel as though I have been deceived by her too."

"You poor thing. People can be so nasty," said Hilary. She squeezed her shoulder and handed her a serviette to blow her nose. "Anyway, you mustn't hide yourself away. People will be wondering where we've got to. Tobiasz will have sent out a search party. He gets quite twitchy when he doesn't know where I am."

Sarah stood up awkwardly, shifting the still sleeping Luke onto her shoulder. "I can imagine that," she said. "He thinks the world of you. Do I look alright?" she added.

"You do," said Hilary, taking her arm. Together they went to re-join the party.

They looked at each other and smiled when Tobiasz, true to form, asked, "Where have you two been? I was thinking of sending out a search party."

Hilary found it hard to sleep that night. She lay next to Tobiasz, staying very still, not wanting to disturb him, going over and over in her mind how it was that she had not seen that something was amiss with Sarah. As she looked back over the last few weeks, she realised that the signs had been there, if only she hadn't been so wrapped up in herself.

Simply the fact that Sarah had asked her—twice in the last week— to look after Luke should have alerted her, at the very least made her question whether one of the grandmas might have been ill. But it hadn't even occurred to her.

She'd also cancelled swimming one week. She had been working at the Bistro one day when Hilary and Carol called in for a coffee, but hadn't come out of the kitchen to say hello. So many things should have alerted her.

Sarah's appearance at the party distressed Hilary beyond words. Although she looked as tidy as ever with her hair pulled back off her face, it was no longer shiny and it didn't look clean. Her clothes hung off her. Even dressed for today's party, she had an uncared-for look about her.

Hilary turned onto her side. The clock with its bright green 2.03 mocked her. She turned the other way. Tobiasz stirred but didn't wake. If he had been awake, he would have told her it was no good trying to fall asleep; you had to just wait for sleep to come. But however hard she tried to trick her mind into relaxing, sleep eluded her. She carefully got out of bed, put on her dressing gown, went through to the kitchen and switched the kettle on, to make a cup of camomile tea. Hector looked up from his basket and padded after her when she took the steaming mug through to the living room.

She sat down on the settee and tucked her legs under her. Hector jumped onto the settee next to her. He looked unsure for a moment, waiting to be told to get down. When the order didn't come, he curled up next to her.

I used to be a nicer person, she thought, *did things for others, never put myself first. I should have been here for Sarah. All that nonsense I spouted about feeling as though Sarah was my daughter. Fine mother substitute I turned out to be. I knew where I stood before. Before Mum died, before I met Tobiasz, started going off on trips, altering my home, updating myself, rebelling. I was dull, in the background, but I would have noticed if a friend was in trouble.*

She twisted around to pick up her mug. Hector took the opportunity to snuggle into her side more closely. Cradling her mug, she admitted to herself that if her mother were still alive, she wouldn't have met Sarah and wouldn't have developed this close relationship that meant so much to her. She acknowledged that, since her mother's death, all her relationships with her friends were stronger.

"I've grown up a bit late," she whispered to Hector. "I could have broken away, left home years ago. When Dad died, I realised that it was too late. I couldn't leave Mum then. She needed me. I allowed myself to live the life she wanted. Just lazy, I suppose, Hector." She put her arm across him as she bent to put her drink, which was still too hot, on the floor in front of her. She wondered if she had let Tobiasz take over too much. She had allowed herself to slot into his life, although, from the outside, it looked as though he had slotted into hers. She wondered if they really were equal partners, or if her habit of subservience was too ingrained.

Is that the price I have to pay to ensure that there is someone there if I need them? she wondered, as she drifted towards sleep. *I've always just done as I'm told. A bit like Hector, I fit into someone else's life, live by someone else's rules. I lived as Mum expected me to, not exploring, not experimenting. Is Tobiasz now calling the shots? I have lived other people's lives long enough. I must now live my own.*

She was woken by the loud clanking of the refuse lorry as her wheelie bin was emptied. Cold and stiff-limbed, she pushed Hector down from the settee and narrowly avoided knocking over the mug of cold camomile tea.

"Bed," she said. "We've got an hour before I need to get up." Hector went obediently to his basket.

She emptied the tea down the sink and put the mug into the dishwasher before going back to her warm bed with Tobiasz at her side.

TWENTY-TWO

Another Piece of the Puzzle

Tobiasz didn't ask why Tom wasn't with Sarah at the party and, for a reason that she couldn't fathom, Hilary didn't tell him that the pair had split up. She was aware that it was yet another secret between them, but she told herself that it was more a matter of timing than secrecy. She decided that she would tell him after she next talked to Sarah.

She could hear shouted instructions coming from the garden next door as they cleared up after the party. At Joe's request, Tobiasz had gone around to help and, as he went out the door, Hilary reminded him to make sure that he retrieved their garden furniture that had been requisitioned when, at the last minute, Sharon realised she didn't have enough chairs.

Hilary closed the patio doors to shut out the noise. She was feeling a bit jaded after Sarah's revelation and her disturbed night, not to mention the wine from the party. She suspected that Tobiasz would not be back before lunch—he and Joe seemed to have a lot to talk about—especially if there was any beer left from the night before. She decided to take Hector for a walk.

"I always think better when I'm walking," she said to Hector, as she clipped on his lead. Her main concern was how she could help Sarah, how she could be there for her.

She felt that she needed to see Sarah, but the week ahead was already full up. Apart from work, there was nothing that couldn't be cancelled, but she had something on every day. She'd arranged a meeting with Marianne towards the end of the week; perhaps that would be the best thing to cancel. It seemed so wrong to be dwelling on the past, when the present needed her attention.

Hilary had wanted to hold on to any link with her mother, however tenuous, and, soon after the awkward afternoon at the bungalow, had suggested another meeting with Gillian and Marianne. At first, Gillian accepted, but then, twenty-four hours later, cancelled. Marianne then emailed to say that she would still like to come, adding that she had more information that might be of interest to Hilary. Unable to resist the implications of that final sentence, Hilary had replied to say she would be delighted to see Marianne (and her mother, if she should change her mind). She had been secretly pleased that Gillian didn't want to come and was excited about the promised information. But now things had changed and she felt that Sarah must be her priority.

It started to rain. She called Hector back from his explorations and started to head for home. A couple of young girls rushed past her, their heads together under an umbrella, chattering and laughing. They reminded Hilary of Sarah and Marianne sitting on the settee chatting, comfortable in each other's company.

I wonder if Sarah would come too, she thought. *It might take her mind off things.*

She phoned Sarah as soon as she got home.

"Just checking you're okay," she said.

"I'm okay."

"And Luke?"

"He's fine." Hilary could hear the smile in her voice.

"I was wondering…" Hilary paused.

"What?"

"Whether you're free Friday lunchtime."

Hilary told her about Marianne's proposed visit and asked if she'd like to come too. Sarah said she'd love to but she might have to work. She'd have to check her diary. Hilary didn't press her. Instead, she asked if she minded if she told Tobiasz about Tom leaving. Sarah sounded genuinely surprised that Hilary hadn't already told him everything.

"I'm not sure why I haven't," Hilary said. "I suppose sometimes I just have to process things and get them right in my own mind before I share them with anyone else."

They chatted for a little longer. Sarah interrupted Hilary as she was saying goodbye.

"I'd love to see Marianne again, thank you," she said. "I knew I wasn't working. I just needed to think about it a bit, work out if I could cope with it. It seems shameful to admit it but I'm not sure who my friends are anymore. I keep in touch with a few people from school but all my recent friends are mine and Tom's. Those who have said anything have said all the right things, said that they won't take sides, but I don't know anymore. You are my friend, of course, and Marianne has never met Tom, so I don't feel that I need to apologise or explain."

"You certainly don't need to apologise. Would you like me to tell her about Tom?"

"No, there's no need. If it comes up, I'll tell her. But the meeting is about Marianne's research, so I can't imagine that it will."

"Okay," said Hilary. "Take care. Keep in touch. See you Friday."

"See you then."

Later, over dinner, Hilary told Tobiasz about Tom.

"I thought something must be very wrong but I did not like to ask," he said. "She look so sad. Even when she was smiling, she look sad. And, at the party, I came to look for you. I saw you two sitting in the dining room talking. She looked upset. So, I went away again without you seeing me. I knew that you will tell me when you are ready."

"I had no idea that you'd seen us," said Hilary. "She was very upset."

"And she needed you."

"Thank you for being so understanding."

Tobiasz bowed his head towards her.

"Anyway, I've asked Sarah to come round on Friday when Marianne comes," said Hilary. "You remember that she's coming?"

"Of course. I am going to work to be out of your way."

Hilary poked him in the ribs and got up to load the dishwasher.

On the day of the visit, Tobiasz let Sarah in. "I am very sorry to hear about…"

"Thank you," Sarah interrupted. "It's okay. We're getting through. Aren't we, Luke?"

"That is good," Tobiasz said, giving Luke a smile and a gentle pinch on his cheek. "Well, I am actually going to work now. I leave you ladies to lunch in peace."

"Sarah is here. See you later," he shouted to Hilary. She came out of the kitchen, drying her hands on a tea towel. She accepted a peck on the cheek from Tobiasz and gave Sarah and Luke a hug. Tobiasz went out the front door.

"Where's Hector?" Sarah asked.

"In the garden, I think. I'm surprised he didn't hear you come." As if on command, Hector shot into the hall and slithered on the wooden floor as he tried to round them up. "Enough!" said Hilary. "Enough!"

"Let's go through to the kitchen," she said.

"You take Luke. I'll go get the food from the car," Sarah said as she passed Luke into Hilary's willing arms.

"Let's see what we can find in here," she said, carrying Luke through to the kitchen.

"You didn't have to do all this," said Hilary when Sarah came in laden with bags and a quiche balanced on top of one. "I invited you."

"I really enjoyed it. At least when I'm cooking, I'm not thinking of other things. I'll just go and get his chair."

"I'll look into getting a high chair here, if I'm looking after him more," Hilary said when Sarah came back in from the car.

"I'll look on the notice board at toddler group," said Sarah, putting the high chair together. "There are always baby things going spare."

Marianne arrived a few minutes later. Hilary sent Sarah to open the front door, while she occupied Luke with a wooden spoon and a saucepan and sent Hector to his basket, where he obediently sat trembling, struggling to control his instinct to give a rapturous welcome to all visitors.

Lunch went well. Luke kept the three women entertained and busy, as he spread his food far and wide—Hilary was glad that she had suggested they eat outside. Hector was in his element hoovering up around Luke's chair.

After lunch they went through to the living room and Marianne took a folder out of her backpack and began to explain to Sarah and Hilary how she had gone about gathering the information for her dissertation. "I started with the V&A's theatre and performance archives and extended my search from there," she said. Even Hector looked interested as she explained the process of following leads, just like a detective.

"I concentrated on the performers and the people who worked backstage, like Granddad. But then, after talking to you, I extended the search a bit. Look who I found," she said. "I remembered you saying that your dad was called Gordon. There can't have been two accountants called Gordon Walton. That would be too much of a coincidence." Hilary looked over her shoulder as she pointed to the page.

"It must be Dad," Hilary exclaimed. "He worked at the theatre too."

"No," said Marianne. "But he worked for the accountancy company that covered several theatres and chances are he will have visited. I checked and, in the past, one of the more junior accountants would have visited the theatre to pick up the books. It could have been him, his name certainly appeared on the accounts. Perhaps he was given tickets to the show. Accepting perks was more acceptable then."

"Golly," said Hilary. She stared at her father's name on the page. She didn't know what to say.

"Wow, I wish I was clever like you, Marianne," Sarah said. "I didn't even stay on to do A Levels."

"Huh," said Marianne. "And I didn't make that delicious quiche or the divine salad." Sarah started to interrupt, but Marianne continued, "And don't say you could give me the recipe. You could, but it would never be the same."

"We all have different skills," said Hilary, finding her voice. "I wonder if that's how he met Mum."

Hilary was thoughtful for a moment.

"So, if that is Dad, that could have been how they met," she said. "No one ever talked about how they got together and it never crossed my mind to ask."

"I wonder if he knew about the pregnancy," said Sarah.

"He definitely did. I don't think you saw the letter that Mum brought last time," said Marianne.

"She lost the baby," said Hilary. "After they were married."

"How very sad," said Sarah. She hugged the now sleeping Luke to her chest.

Hilary went to make some more coffee and was not surprised when she got back to find Sarah telling Marianne about Tom's desertion. Hilary put the cups down and listened silently as Sarah finished her sorry tale.

"I don't know where I'd be without Hilary," she said.

Hilary smiled and tried to say that anyone would have done the same but Marianne interrupted her with, "But they didn't. Sarah is lucky to have you."

At her strident tone Luke woke and cried briefly. There was a feeling of relief in the room as talk turned to more general things.

Later, after they had gone, Hilary wanted to tell Tobiasz about Marianne discovering that Gordon had connections with the theatre but the opportunity didn't arise. He came in late from work, washed and changed and went out again to meet Dan for an early drink.

"When I get back," he said, as he was going out the door, "you must tell me all about this afternoon."

But when he got back, he seemed to have forgotten all about it. He told her about the flat that Dan had found—bigger, less basic, better in every way—and about the job interview that he'd secured—more money, more prestige and, best of all, for a rival company to his old firm.

"Things are certainly looking up for Dan," said Hilary, genuinely happy for him but struggling to sound enthusiastic.

The comment sent Tobiasz off on a monologue about Dan's good fortune that took up the duration of their meal.

Hilary decided that now wasn't the time to talk to Tobiasz about her discovery and she sent him into the living room to find a film they could watch, while she loaded the dishwasher.

Later, as Hilary watched the closing credits of the film, she realised that she had absolutely no idea what it had been about. She looked over at Tobiasz lying on the settee. He had not even made a pretence of watching it and had been gently snoring for at least the past half hour. He woke when Hilary switched the television off.

"We might as well go to bed," she said.

"Mmmmm," said Tobiasz, stretching.

He made the transition from settee to bed via the kitchen, to let Hector out and to pour a glass of water, and the bathroom, without seeming to return to full wakefulness.

Hilary lay next to Tobiasz, wide awake. She thought about her mum. She wondered how Phyllis felt when she had found out that she was pregnant. Hilary couldn't imagine that she would have been happy. Pregnancy out of wedlock—such an old-fashioned phrase that sounded so binding—was frowned upon in the 1950s. Was that why her father and mother had married? To protect her? Hilary had difficulty imagining her mother in a position of such vulnerability but she now felt that maybe she understood why her mother had been overprotective, why she had tried to prevent Hilary from getting hurt, from making the same mistakes she had.

Dad must have loved Mum very much, to have married her when she was carrying someone else's child, she thought. *I wonder what would have happened if that baby had been me? If I hadn't grown to be like my dad? If I'd have been brash and bossy like Gillian?* Hilary smiled to herself in the darkness. Her life story would have been very different if that were the case. But there was no denying her likeness to her father, not only in her looks, but in her behaviour towards her mother. She could see why her dad had gently overruled her mother to allow Hilary some freedom to grow, but Hilary's nature was too similar to his, too passive for her to take full advantage of the opportunities he offered her.

"I am who I am, and if my life hadn't followed this path, I would never have met Tobiasz." Hilary realised that she must have said the words aloud, because Tobiasz turned over and sleepily asked, "What?"

"Nothing. Just talking in my sleep."

Tobiasz accepted this incongruous statement and settled back into a deep sleep.

Hilary touched his shoulder and snuggled down next to him, hopeful that sleep would come to her soon.

The next day, she had Tobiasz's full attention. They took Hector for a walk and stopped for lunch at a pub on the canal just outside Barwell. It was busy but they found a table in the corner of the garden. Hector stretched out in the shade under the table.

As soon as they had drinks and had ordered food, Tobiasz listened as Hilary told him all that she had discovered.

"It's all falling into place," he said. "You have a better picture of your mother's life. I hope that when I go to Poland, I will get answers too."

"Oh, golly," said Hilary. "It's not long now, is it?"

"No, but I will only be gone a few days."

"I know. I'm being silly," said Hilary. "I know that you have to go and I know that you have to go alone, but…"

The food arrived and Hilary was, for the moment, prevented from saying more. However, they both avoided the subject of Poland for the rest of the afternoon.

TWENTY-THREE

A Day on the Beach

Hilary phoned Liz a couple of days later.

"We had a lovely time with Marianne," she said. "Sarah prepared a great lunch."

"Sarah?" asked Liz. "How come?"

"I invited her too. She and Marianne got on so well when they first met and, with her problems…"

"What problems?" interrupted Liz.

Hilary told her about Sarah's predicament and Liz immediately suggested that Hilary bring Sarah and Luke for a day on the beach with Siobhan.

"Do it while Tobiasz is away," she said. "It will stop you moping."

Hilary put the idea to Sarah. She emphasised the benefits of the seaside for Luke and confided that Siobhan was having some problems since the arrival of the new baby.

"Liz is trying to arrange as many different activities as possible. And," she added as an afterthought, "it would really help me. I need some things to occupy me while Tobiasz is in Poland."

Hearing that Tobiasz was going to be away, Sarah immediately agreed. "The sea air will do us both good and I know how much you miss seeing Liz," she said.

On the day that Tobiasz left for Poland, Hilary dropped him off at the train station on her way to work, from where he would catch a train to the airport. In the chaos of morning rush hour, there was nowhere to park and he had to hurriedly get out and retrieve his bag from the boot with impatient drivers queuing behind.

"Safe journey," said Hilary.

"I'll let you know when I land."

An angry honk from the car behind precluded any more words and forced Hilary to drive away with an apologetic wave in her mirror to the irate driver. As she turned the corner, Tobiasz reached the station entrance, turned, smiled and waved. She waved back and headed for work.

Hilary was relieved that she had the seaside trip the next day to keep her occupied; she didn't want to think of Tobiasz in Poland without her. She couldn't believe how much she missed him. She'd been glad of work on the day he left, but the evening had seemed endless and the bungalow was unnaturally quiet the next morning. She and Hector were waiting on the doorstep when Sarah arrived. Sarah insisted on driving—it was easier than moving the car seat to Hilary's car—and had made lots of good things to eat. All Hilary had to do was sit back and enjoy herself. The journey passed quickly. Hilary amused Luke and made Sarah smile, singing along to a CD of nursery rhymes. Hector slept, undisturbed by the racket.

Sarah pulled into the clifftop car park where Liz and Siobhan were waiting. She and Hilary transferred the picnic and their beach paraphernalia into Liz's recently purchased trolley.

"Luke can go in it," said Siobhan. "He won't be too heavy, will he, Granny?"

"No, sweetheart, he won't."

Sarah wedged Luke on the picnic rug between the buckets and plastic containers of food and Liz picked up the wooden handle. Hector ran ahead and Luke giggled as they trundled down the steep path to the beach. Siobhan took hold of Hilary's hand and held it solicitously as they negotiated the path behind the trolley.

When they had found the perfect spot, in the lee of the cliff, they set out the rug. The women settled into three ancient camping chairs that Liz had found in the shed, left behind by the previous owners. Away from the promenade with its shops and cafés, and with the exception of a few dog walkers, they had the beach to themselves.

Siobhan took her baby-minding duties very seriously. She showed Luke how to make sandcastles, letting him pat the sand in the bucket before tipping it out. Granny had shown her how to do it. She wanted Granny to see how well she was doing it, but Granny was busy talking to Hilary and Luke's mummy. Hector, who had been mooching about turning seaweed and shells over with his nose, wandered across the sand to Siobhan and Luke. He sniffed Luke's bottom with interest.

"Naughty boy! Dirty boy!" said Siobhan, batting Hector away with sandy hands. She gave him a self-righteous, indignant look, as only a five-year-old can. Unabashed, Hector wandered back to the more interesting smells of the beach.

Siobhan stood up, and brushed her hands on her pink shorts.

"Come on," she said, pulling Luke up beside her. "Let's find some shells."

They started to walk towards the base of the cliffs. As she bent down to pick up a cockle shell, Luke slipped his hand from her grasp and toddled off at a pace in the direction of the sea. Siobhan ran after him.

Liz jumped up and cut off Luke's escape route. She scooped him up and delivered him back to Sarah.

"You can't take your eyes off them for a moment," she said.

Siobhan looked as though she was going to cry.

"It wasn't your fault. He's very quick," said Liz, pulling Siobhan towards her. "I was watching you both. I saw you make all those sandcastles. Let's go back and make some more."

"Did you really see me do it?"

"We all did," said Hilary.

"I wanted to put some shells on them…"

"What if I help you get some shells, while Luke stays with his mummy?" Hilary took Siobhan's hand.

"Is that okay, Granny?"

"Of course," said Liz, lowering herself into her chair. Sarah took

Luke's bricks and trucks from the trolley and sat him on the picnic rug.

"I was really sorry to hear about Tom leaving," said Liz. "Really sorry."

Sarah absentmindedly piled Luke's bricks so he could knock them down.

"I don't know how anyone could bear to leave this little man," continued Liz.

"He said he knew how Hector must have felt, usurped by Luke," muttered Sarah.

"Oh, for heaven's sake!" said Liz. "He needs to grow up."

"Luke was planned," said Sarah. "We both wanted him. I thought he loved him. Tom was great when Luke was tiny. He took time off just after he was born, encouraged me to go back to work, even facilitated it. His mum was very helpful, seemed to understand how difficult my relationship with my own mum is. It was Tom who suggested we get rid of Hector. He said we'd have more time for Luke. Well, that was one of the reasons he gave. Perhaps even then he felt he was being pushed out. Perhaps I was supposed to understand the subtext."

"Why should you? You're not a mind reader," said Liz. Out of the corner of her eye she saw Hilary distract Siobhan as she started to head back to show off her shells.

Sarah went on as if Liz hadn't spoken. "It definitely was easier with Hector out of the way but now I have no idea if Tom was off with this other woman, when I thought that he was being kind by giving me space. He bought Luke things, he bought me things, we went on outings supposedly to try to cheer me up. The trouble is, now I don't know if any of that was genuine or if it was simply guilt. It's funny how bits of conversations come back to you, arguments, discussions, little bits that were glossed over at the time. I'm sure if we had worked at it, we could have kept Hector." She patted him as he came over at the sound of his name. "I suppose it was difficult with us both working, but other people manage to get through difficult times with pets and stuff. You just have to be willing to put in the time. But then others take the time to sort out their own relationships. They don't just give up and go and find someone else…"

"You poor love," said Liz.

"I had no idea what was going on," continued Sarah. "I knew that things weren't right between us but I had no inkling that there was someone else, and for all those months. I even thought about trying for another baby. Imagine what a disaster that would have been!" She leaped up to grab Luke who had abandoned the bricks and was heading rapidly towards Siobhan who was returning with her pink bucket half full of shells.

"Lunch, I think," said Hilary. "I'll get everything out while you show Granny and Luke what you've found."

After they had eaten, Liz sat on her chair as Hilary and Sarah chased after Luke and Hector who seemed to be competing to see who could snaffle the most food scraps.

"What has your mum said about Tom leaving?" Hilary asked when calm was restored. Hector had gone to investigate some seaweed and Luke was sitting on the edge of the rug running sand through his fingers.

"I haven't really given her a chance. I didn't phone her when he went. I couldn't face her. She's always so judgemental. I actually wondered if she would side with him. Honestly, I did," she said when Hilary looked disbelieving. "I didn't tell anyone and the one person who bothered to ask, who bothered to try to find out, was you, Hilary, not my mum."

Hilary took her hand as Luke toddled towards them. Sarah took a shell from his hand before he put it in his mouth. She took her hand from Hilary's and pulled Luke onto her lap.

"I feel in such a muddle. The trouble is," she said, "when something like this happens, you start rewriting history. You doubt your own memory, even the good times, because there are always questions that will never be answered."

"Look at me when John left," said Liz. "He was only gone three days and he left a note which, had I bothered to read it properly, explained things. But it literally turned my head. I couldn't think straight. I doubted myself. I doubted him. I was convinced there must be someone else. I went on the rampage, checking up on him, looking for…" She was interrupted by an anguished shout from Siobhan.

"Hector! No, don't, Hector."

Liz pushed herself up from the chair and went to gather up Siobhan from the ruins of her sandcastles, while Hilary grabbed Hector who was digging as if to find the way to Australia.

"Look what he's done," wailed Siobhan.

"I'm sorry," said Hilary. "I'll help you build some more."

"They won't be the same," Siobhan said, sobbing.

"Don't be silly," said Liz. "He's a dog. Sand is sand."

"I told him not to."

"Stop it now! Don't spoil the day," said Liz, taking Siobhan's hand firmly in hers. "I think it's time for a paddle in the sea," said Liz. "Enough talking and sitting for now, come on…"

Hector excitedly ran back and forth into the water as they gathered together the buckets, spades and toys that were scattered around and put them higgledy-piggledy in the trolley. Sarah carried Luke, not even attempting to keep up with Hilary and Liz as they ran to keep up with Siobhan and the almost forgiven Hector.

"What happens now?" asked Liz, as Sarah gave up the battle of keeping Luke dry and allowed him to sit in the shallow water at her feet.

"I don't know," said Sarah. "I just don't know. I suppose I'll get divorce papers through. I suppose we'll have to sort out access. I feel as though everything, my whole life, has been taken out of my hands."

"It most definitely hasn't," said Liz. "If you don't feel that you can talk to him, email him, write him a letter, but somehow set out how you would like things to look in the future."

"Mmmmm. That might work," said Sarah. "I'm not sure. One thing I am sure of is that I can't face the thought of meeting her, his woman."

"You don't have to meet her, or certainly not now, anyway."

"No, but I will if she's going to be an important person in Luke's life."

"Just make sure you do it on your terms."

"I'll try," said Sarah.

"You must," said Liz. "For your sake and Luke's, you must."

"It's all so difficult," said Sarah.

"One step at a time," said Hilary, who had been quietly standing beside them.

Liz opened her mouth to say more but a rogue wave knocked Luke sideways. Sarah scooped him up and pressed him against her chest as the three of them jumped backwards in alarm. Liz windmilled her arms as she unsuccessfully tried to stop herself falling into the hole that Siobhan had been quietly digging at the water's edge. Siobhan collapsed in a fit of the giggles.

"Oh, Granny…you…did…look…funny," she said, gasping.

Sarah, partly from relief, couldn't stop laughing too and Hilary soon joined them.

Liz, sitting in an unladylike tangle, tried unsuccessfully to look cross with them all and soon they were all rolling around on the beach laughing uncontrollably.

"She's quite bossy, isn't she?" said Sarah, when she and Hilary were sitting in the car, driving home. Luke was fast asleep in his seat.

"Yes, I suppose she is," said Hilary. "To me, she's just Liz. She's never any different. Well, rarely. But her suggestion to put this in writing was a good one," she continued. "It's always a good idea to write things down. Helps you organise your thoughts."

"I know," Sarah replied. "I'll definitely try emailing him. At least I'll have a record of what I've said. I hate it when he phones and I dread phoning him. I get so upset; I can't think straight. I can't think what to say. I end up saying something I regret or I get so angry that I just put the phone down and then it's worse the next time. It's awful." She took her hand from the steering wheel to wipe a tear from her eye. "So, perhaps I will email him and see if we can do it through emails."

"And, of course," said Hilary, "as you say, if it's written down, neither of you can dispute what has been said."

"Absolutely. And if it's written down, I might actually be able to see how it can all work."

"I suppose my one piece of advice in all of this," said Hilary, "is don't expect to get everything your own way."

"Well, before today, I didn't think I was getting anything my own way. Nothing at all."

"No. I can understand that. If it was me, I think my instinct would be to gather Luke up and go and hide somewhere. But you can't because Tom is his dad and whatever he's done he has to have his say."

"I know," said Sarah. "I know and we will work it out, but can we talk about something else now? Please."

After a few desultory attempts at conversation, they both fell silent and Sarah put the radio on for the remaining miles.

TWENTY-FOUR

Ghosts Laid to Rest

Suzanne and David were in Scotland, attending yet another wedding. Hilary was visiting Betty for coffee.

She carried the cups through after Betty had made the coffee and they sat in their customary seats in the window overlooking the drive and Hilary's bungalow across the street.

"We are both on our own," said Betty. "Suzanne didn't want to go, you know. The wedding is an old girlfriend of David's getting married for the umpteenth time. She's convinced that this woman is still after David. David is completely clueless and thinks that she's just being kind. Men are so dense sometimes."

Hilary looked shocked. "Poor Suzanne," she said.

"She'll be fine," said Betty. "This woman will have to throw herself at David's feet for him to notice and I can't imagine her doing it on her wedding day."

Hilary laughed. "Do you know her?"

"Not really, but I know who she is. Brash thing, no shame."

"I haven't heard you talk like this before," said Hilary, smiling.

"No, well…" Betty replied. "Anyway, have you heard how Tobiasz is getting on in Poland?"

"Not really, only that he's arrived," said Hilary. "To tell you the truth, I didn't think that he would go. I hoped he wouldn't, but I knew he had to. I just wish that we had talked more about it. He thought it all through before he told me," said Hilary.

"But surely it's just something that he has to do to feel comfortable about committing to you?" said Betty.

"But he wanted to marry me, so how does that make sense?"

"I suppose it doesn't," said Betty, picking up her cup. "Perhaps he didn't want you persuading him not to go or trying to convince him to take you with him."

"Mmmmm," said Hilary.

"I'm not sure you're going to make any sense of it but I think you just have to trust him, let him do whatever he has to do to come to terms with the past."

"It's just so difficult…"

"He'll be back before you know it, and I bet I'm going to need you an awful lot, with Suzanne and David away."

Hilary laughed.

"Janet offered to keep me busy too, helping with her mum and dad. But I seem to be filling the time. I had a day at the seaside yesterday. Sarah and Luke came with me. We spent the day with Liz.

"Well, that will have taken your mind off things. You had to let him do this."

"I know. But it is a bit strange, him not being around."

Twelve hundred miles away, Tobiasz was laying some ghosts to rest. On his first day in Poland, he had knelt in front of the granite headstone that marked his mother's grave. The graveyard—adjacent to the church that she had attended, where she had wanted his wedding to Krystyna to take place—was deserted and quiet. Her grave was near the boundary wall, shaded by an old oak tree, her parents' graves just a few steps away. He arranged a small bunch of anemones in the stone urn and began to talk, slipping without thought into his native Polish. Unselfconsciously, he told her all about Hilary—how they had met, their life together, his love for her. He described how fearful he had become on their trip and how ashamed he had felt when he was unable to go through with their plans to visit his homeland together. He found himself describing the marriage proposal, and Hilary's response. "The best thing about it," he said, "was that her refusal brought me up short, made me think. Sent me here, to talk to you. I will bring her next time…" A sudden breeze moved the branches of the tree, throwing dappled light across the headstone. Tobiasz leaned forwards and kissed it.

"I will go to Krystyna's grave tomorrow," Tobiasz had told Hilary later. She looked uncomfortable as she stared at him from the screen. "I went past the family hotel after I had been to visit my mother's grave. It looked different, but it is twenty years after all. I did not go in. I don't know if Krystyna's parents are still alive…"

"I miss you," said Hilary. She had wanted to say something supportive, to show that she understood what he must be going through, but they were the only words that came to her.

They were the only words Tobiasz wanted to hear as he lay on top of the bed in a featureless room at the impersonal hotel where he had chosen to stay.

"I miss you too. I will be back soon."

The cemetery where Krystyna was buried was extensive, with broad pathways and ostentatious tombs showily proclaiming their occupants. Tobiasz had difficulty finding her grave. He thought he'd remembered precisely the route they had taken on the day of her funeral but either his memory was playing tricks on him or he had come into the cemetery through a different entrance. He came upon it almost by accident, just as he was wondering whether to give up and return to the hotel.

It wasn't the white marble headstone decorated with heavy scrolls that he recognised. He had never seen it. Rather, it was a stooped grey-haired vision of his father-in-law, Jakub. Tobiasz watched from a distance as a younger man placed a folding chair at the side of the grave and his father-in-law sat on it, his hands together, head bowed.

After a few minutes, Tobiasz watched the young man move towards Jakub and hold his hand out to help him to his feet. Tobiasz stepped forwards. His father-in-law didn't show any surprise. He beckoned Tobiasz closer. Together they looked at the tombstone.

"Anna joined Krystyna eight years ago," said Jakub, pointing to his wife's name inscribed in the marble.

"I am sorry," said Tobiasz. Jakub inclined his head.

Then, with some of his old formality, his father-in-law said, "This is my nephew, the youngest of Anna's sister's children. They all fuss round me, now that I am alone." After he had shaken Tobiasz's hand, the nephew retreated to a bench a few yards away and took his phone from his pocket.

"How I have longed for this day," said Jakub. He felt for the chair behind him and allowed Tobiasz to ease him down onto it. "You disappeared. We understood your grief and sadness, even though we were lost in our own anguish. We did not look for you. You had made that choice." Tobiasz lowered himself to the ground and knelt beside Jakub.

"I felt guilty," he said. "I thought the accident was my fault. I thought you blamed me."

"For a time, we did. We couldn't be angry with the one we had lost, so we turned our anger on you. It was easy to blame you because you weren't there, we couldn't see your hurt. We were angry. Angry at everything––the loss of our daughter, the loss of our dreams, the loss of you. We had such high hopes for you and Krystyna." He stared at Tobiasz as if trying to remember the young man he had been.

"Then we found out who Krystyna had been going to see that night, that fateful night…"

Tobiasz waited for him to continue.

"A friend, a cruel friend, told Anna that Krystyna had been on the way to meet her lover. Of course, we did not believe her, but we found out that it was true… I am sorry." He squeezed Tobiasz's shoulder.

Tobiasz stared silently into the distance.

"As Anna said—after many agonising weeks, maybe months, I don't know—at least it gave a proper focus for our anger. We did not blame Krystyna. She paid the highest price. And we did not blame you. Anna wanted to try and get in touch with you and tell you but, knowing how it had made me feel, I could not imagine that you would want to know. We knew nothing about your new life in England but we knew that we did not want to disturb it."

Tears ran down Tobiasz's face.

"Thank you. Thank you for telling me. Thank you."

"Let us not talk of it further. I will leave you now to say your own goodbye to Krystyna and then we will go to my home together."

"The hotel—I drove past it yesterday," said Tobiasz. He wiped his nose on a crisp white handkerchief, comforted by the laundered smell.

"We sold the hotel ten years ago. Our dream died with Krystyna."

"So, where are you now?"

"We bought a small flat, manageable as we got older. Now I am alone but I have family around me, although fewer and fewer every year. I would like to offer you a meal. My sister-in-law, his mother," he nodded towards his nephew, "feeds me well. There will be enough to share. I want to hear what you have done since you left. Will you join me?"

"I would be honoured to," said Tobiasz.

Jakub beckoned to his nephew, who came over, helped the old man out of the chair, collapsed it and put it under his arm. They walked away slowly.

When Tobiasz was admitted, by a smiling Jakub, into the utilitarian flat on the ground floor of a faceless block, he recognised some pieces from the hotel. An incongruously bright rug lay under a faded three-piece suite. The small square dining table sat, as it had in their rooms at the back of the hotel, covered with a felt cloth, with a high-backed wooden chair at either end. The brass gong, used in the hotel to summon diners three times a day, stood silent on the floor next to the electric fire. There was a photograph of Krystyna next to her parents' wedding photo.

Jakub's sister-in-law, Bernadeta, was an older, rounder version of Anna. She lived next door, with her children and grandchildren scattered in apartments throughout the block. She let herself into the flat, greeting Tobiasz as if she had seen him only yesterday, and placed a lidded metal pot on the thick mat in the centre of the table. A child who followed her in with a bowl of potatoes was shooed out of the room once he had put the bowl down.

"Smacznego," said Bernadeta, as she left them to their meal.

Tobiasz and Jakub sat opposite each other, the food and a bottle of vodka between them. When Jakub removed the lid from the pan, steam rose and a rich meaty smell took Tobiasz back fifty years to his boyhood.

They ate. They talked.

They drank a toast to Anna and another to Krystyna.

"Even if you had stayed and Krystyna had not died," Jakub said, his eyes filling with tears. "I know now that it would not have worked.

You and Krystyna, your relationship would not have lasted, as ours did. Your mother recognised this. She was more perceptive than all of us. At the time, I thought she was very rude to doubt my beautiful Krystyna. You were very shy. You did not realise how much we thought of you, how much we valued you, as a son-in-law. We wanted you and Krystyna to take over the business from Anna and me but, of course, like many parents, we made the mistake of foisting our dreams on our children."

They drank a toast to Tobiasz's mother.

"I wish my mother could have met Hilary. I was dazzled by Krystyna, her energy, her confidence, her beauty. I think my mother thought that she would be too much for me. Hilary is different… We understand each other."

"We must drink a toast to Hilary," said Jakub. "I hope that I live long enough to meet her. Perhaps now you will not be afraid to come back."

"To Hilary!" they both said, and drained the shot glasses.

TWENTY-FIVE

Doubts

Hilary found Tobiasz's call that night very unsatisfactory. They both blamed the Wi-Fi, but it wasn't the connection that was at fault.

Hilary took a rather disconsolate Hector for a walk before work the next morning and promised, as she left, that she wouldn't be late and that they would have another walk when she got home. Hector lay in his bed, his head on his paws, as she hurried out.

She didn't want to eat her lunchtime sandwich in the noise of the canteen; nor did she want to have to make polite conversation. So, she took a brisk walk to Chaja Bazaar in the hope that Carol would be free for a chat. Carol was just putting the CLOSED FOR LUNCH sign on the door when Hilary got to the shop.

"Can I join you for lunch?" she asked a little breathlessly. "I've got my sandwiches."

"Of course," said Carol. "I'll buy a sandwich and get us both a coffee on the way. I was going to go and sit in the square and watch the world go by."

"Perfect," said Hilary.

They chatted about this and that as they walked. Hilary was

saddened to hear Carol complaining about Jonathan again.

"I can't seem to talk about anything else," she admitted. "I just don't know what to do. Sometimes, I have to walk away from him. He makes me so angry and frustrated I want to shake him."

"I don't understand. I thought he would have got used to it by now," said Hilary.

"We seem to be going from bad to worse," muttered Carol.

They found a bench in the sun and Hilary took a ham and mustard sandwich out of her Tupperware. She shut the lid quickly, ashamed of the pang of sadness she felt at missing the heart-shaped serviette that Tobiasz always added when he made her packed lunch. They ate in silence for a few moments.

"Suzanne told me about how angry Jonathan became when David mentioned how good you look since you've lost weight. She said that David was quite taken aback," said Hilary, picking up her coffee.

"I don't know whether to be cross that we're being talked about or pleased at the compliment."

"Take the compliment," said Hilary. "You are looking good. You always looked good, but now you look even better," said Hilary, flustered.

Carol smiled.

"Thank you," she said.

"I had no idea things had got this bad for you," said Hilary. "I feel as though I've been going around with my eyes shut." She told Carol about Sarah and Tom, admitting that she had missed all the signs that anything was wrong there too.

"We all seem to have been wrapped up in ourselves lately, don't we?" said Carol. "And the bigger the problem, the harder it is to share."

That should have given Hilary the opening to tell Carol about her fears about Tobiasz and what was happening while he was in Poland. But she found that she couldn't say anything. She took a large bite of her sandwich and told herself that it was because Carol was upset and had enough on her plate without burdening her with more.

Instead, they sat, lost in their own thoughts, watching the world go by. When it was time to get back to work, Carol stood up and shook the crumbs from her skirt.

"We ought to do this more often," she said. "Just text next time, save you a bit of a walk."

"I will," said Hilary. "I hope you and Jonathan sort things out."

"I'm sure we will," said Carol, sounding anything but sure.

They were both thoughtful as they went their separate ways.

Hilary got through the afternoon and raced home to Hector, who greeted her exuberantly and accepted the affection, walk and treats as his due.

The phone call that evening was a little less fraught but afterwards Hilary wondered if that was simply because they had mostly discussed practicalities, such as the time of Tobiasz's flight.

"But," she said to Hector, "he is coming back. I'm not sure I'll believe it until I see him at the airport, though. It's a shame you can't come into the terminal and greet him—that would show him how much he is loved."

TWENTY-SIX

Hilary Speaks Her Mind

Hilary forgot about her conversation with Carol the next day as she drove to the airport to pick up Tobiasz. She gave in to Hector's sad face as she was about to walk out the door and decided to take him with her—a decision she regretted when she arrived at the airport early and had to leave him in the car in the short stay car park. She met Tobiasz at the gate and they self-consciously greeted each other.

Hector, aware of Tobiasz as soon as he stepped out of the car park lift, barked and scrabbled at the window trying to get to him, scaring half to death a couple wheeling their cases past the car.

"Hello, boy," said Tobiasz, as they reached the car. With his customary calmness, he opened the door and put his arm across the space to prevent Hector leaping out. Hector gradually calmed as Tobiasz fussed over him.

"He's excited to see us," he said, turning to Hilary.

"To see you, not us," she replied. "He's missed you. He's been really fed up. Quiet, almost sulking. Kept looking at your bedroom door. I had to let him sniff around to convince him that you weren't under the bed."

"Daft thing," said Tobiasz, patting Hector's head.

"Come on, get your case in the car. Let's get home," said Hilary, suddenly feeling tired.

Hilary listened quietly as Tobiasz talked of how the scenery had changed, how the country had become more European, more modern. He said nothing about his reason for the trip, his mother, his grandmother, his wife.

The next day he was solicitous and loving towards Hilary. She accepted his gifts, but didn't ask any questions—being too afraid of the answers. They circled around one another with extra care and attention. Hilary, on tenterhooks, wished that she could be as obvious, lavish and accepting in her affections as Hector.

Tobiasz's silence lasted until after they had finished dinner. Hilary watched as he loaded the dishwasher. As he straightened up, he seemed to come to a decision. He poured them each another glass of wine before putting the bottle back in the fridge.

"Let's go and sit in the living room," he said as he picked up the glasses. Hilary followed, with Hector on her heels. They sat down on the settee, and Hector lay down on the rug in front of them. When Tobiasz spoke, she realised that she had been holding her breath.

"I want to tell you about Poland," he said.

"I hope you managed to do everything that you wanted to do, see everyone you needed to, sort everything out," Hilary chattered nervously, as if to delay whatever he was going to say.

"Yes. I did everything," he replied, gently. "I put flowers on my mother's grave and my grandmother's grave. Then I drove to the place where Krystyna's accident happened and then I went to her grave." Tobiasz paused. "Her father was there," he said. He told Hilary everything that he had learned from Jakub.

Hilary remained silent as she tried to imagine how she would have felt in his shoes.

"We talked and talked. I went to dinner with him. He has mellowed. He was interested in what I am doing now," he said. "He was interested in you. His wife has died. When his daughter should step in and look after him, she is not there. He has family but the people who meant all to him have gone. He is a lonely old man. I should have gone before. I will go again before it is too late. I will take you. He wants to meet you."

Hilary leaned against him. Hector lay in sleepy watchfulness, lifting his head every time Tobiasz moved, not allowing him out of his sight.

"Before you had told me the whole story, I would have thought it very odd to meet your dead wife's father, but now I think I would like to meet him. Poor man, to have lost his only daughter and now his wife, he has had more than his fair share of sadness. You are one of the last links with his daughter. It is very generous of him to want to meet me and there's certainly no chance of me letting you go on your own again, so…" Any more words were smothered as Tobiasz held her to him.

"Thank you," he whispered into her hair.

Hilary could think of nothing else. Her understanding didn't take away her anxiety about meeting this man from Tobiasz's past. Always calm, Tobiasz seemed more at peace with himself since his return; she thought she might be a little in awe of this man who had such power over Tobiasz.

One morning, after a night disturbed by her thoughts, as soon as Tobiasz had set out to work, she drove out of town to walk Hector. She chose a country park that she and Tobiasz had not visited together, so the place had no associations. She and Hector had a wonderful walk but she missed Tobiasz's company and realised that the only way she was going to allay her fears was by talking to him and in the end just going and meeting Jakub.

"I must just stop thinking about it," she said to Hector, who was resting his head on the back of her seat. "We will sort it out. Come on, let's get home." Hector lay down as she pulled out of the car park.

Driving back into Barwell, she spotted Jonathan's car parked in a gateway. Jonathan was in the driver's seat, staring into the distance. He didn't stir as she approached. She stopped the car, got out and knocked on his window. He looked up, smiled and opened the window.

"Hello…er…Hilary," he said. "You caught me. What are you doing out here?"

"We've just been to Catcombe," she replied. "Can I have a quick word?"

Jonathan looked puzzled but unlocked the passenger door.

"Of course. Get in."

"What are you doing here?" she asked.

"Just having my lunch," he said, pointing at the half-eaten sandwich that he'd put on the dashboard as she got in. "Why?"

"Do you always have your lunch here?"

"Yes, most days. I used to go home, but it's peaceful here."

"It's lovely," agreed Hilary, looking across the gently sloping farm land. "Anyway, I want to talk to you about Carol."

"Oh?"

Hilary leaned back in the seat and fixed her eye on the distant trees that formed a wind break at the edge of the field. "When I found out about Mum," she said, "I thought that she had betrayed me, hidden her true self from me. But it was just another phase in her life. She wasn't pretending. Her past made her much more protective of me than was healthy perhaps, and then she lost the person who had rescued her from that life. I was there when Dad died but I can't imagine what that must have been like for her. She didn't talk about it. She never allowed me to see her vulnerability. Perhaps she never wanted to admit it to herself."

"What's that got to do with Carol?" asked Jonathan, a trace of aggression in his voice.

Hilary paused. She smoothed her skirt and turned towards him. He had turned his face towards her, challenging her. His hands rested on the steering wheel. She tentatively reached her hand towards him but withdrew it abruptly. He gripped the steering wheel and stared straight ahead.

"We all change, all the time," Hilary continued. "Circumstances change us, we make conscious decisions to change. Look at me, I may look different. I may be less frightened by people and situations, more likely to speak, but I'm just as afraid of getting it wrong, of hurting people. In fact, I'm wondering if I should have approached you at all. I hardly know you, really, but I do know Carol. I know that she is happy in what she's doing but she is unhappy about how you feel. She has found her niche and all she wants is for you to feel happy for her, to support her."

Hilary turned in her seat and put her hand on his arm, forcing him to look at her. "She is still there for you. She didn't plan this. She hasn't left you, gone off with someone else. She's just..." Hilary trailed off, turned towards the door and started to open it.

"I've said too much, haven't I? I'm sorry. Take no notice." She returned to her own car and drove away without a backwards glance.

Jonathan re-wrapped his abandoned sandwich and drove back to work.

Later that afternoon, when he got home, he sent a text to Carol. *Are you still at the shop?*

I won't be long, was her immediate reply.

Can I come and see you?

There was a delay before the reply came. *Of course.*

Carol was serving a customer when he arrived. She looked at ease as she guided the woman through the process of ordering curtains. Jonathan wandered around the unfamiliar surroundings, picking things up, marvelling at the prices. He had had no idea that people spent this sort of money on useless objects. When the customer left, he went to the counter and gave Carol a kiss on the cheek. He placed a carved wooden fish on the counter. He hadn't realised that he had picked it up.

"How come you wanted to come here?" Carol asked. "I thought it didn't interest you."

"It doesn't, although I can see the appeal of some things." He ran his finger along the smooth grain of the fish and fitted it into his palm again. "I think I've just had a dressing down from Hilary."

"Hilary??"

"I know."

"Hang on a minute," said Carol. "I'll just lock up. Where is your car?"

"I walked."

"You walked?"

"I needed to think."

"Right," said Carol. "Five minutes. I'm parked just around the corner. You can buy me a drink. I want to hear everything she said."

"I shouldn't have said anything," Hilary said to Tobiasz at breakfast the next morning. "Carol will hate me." She had been saying the same thing to herself over and over since her meeting with Jonathan the day before. Tobiasz had been unable to reassure her.

"She won't hate you," he said, for the umpteenth time.

Then he added, "Others have said the same to Jonathan, but perhaps he listened to you."

"Why would he listen to me?"

"Because," said Tobiasz.

"Because what?"

"Because you don't often say anything, so when you do, people listen."

"Huh?"

"It is true."

"Anyway, I wish I hadn't said anything. I want to hide under a stone."

"You are being silly." Tobiasz took her into his arms and she relaxed against him.

"I'll apologise to her tomorrow," she said into his jumper.

"No. It had to be said. He is behaving badly. He is not being kind to Carol."

"Well, we'll see."

Hilary almost didn't answer when she saw Carol's number on her phone later that day. She let it ring and ring. But hearing her mother telling her to face up to her mistakes, she touched the green answer icon.

"Hello," she said cautiously.

"Oh, Hilary, thank you," said Carol. "I don't know what you said to Jonathan exactly but, for the first time in weeks, we actually talked last night. Actually talked. He didn't apologise. I don't think that he sees anything wrong in his behaviour but somehow you made him want to make things better between us, understand what I'm doing. I didn't want my marriage to fall apart, but I didn't want to give up something that made me so happy either."

"I thought I might have made things worse, interfering like that, interrupting his lunch break."

"You couldn't have made things worse than they were. Things might not sort themselves out but we are talking, which is a start. He even paid me a compliment: said I look gorgeous like when we first met. I couldn't believe my ears." She giggled. "So, thank you."

"I couldn't see you suffer for something that wasn't your fault. I didn't let him get a word in or even answer me. I just told him what I thought."

"Good. Someone needed to. You are a treasure. Anyway, got to go, customer just coming in. See you soon." She blew a kiss down the phone, leaving Hilary staring at the handset.

"See," said Tobiasz, who was sitting on the settee beside her. "I told you."

For a moment, Hilary remained silent.

"Let's take Hector for a walk. I think I need some fresh air."

TWENTY-SEVEN

Time for a Pint

"Is Jonathan joining us tonight?" David asked as he sat down with his beer.

"I don't know," Richard replied. "If he is, I hope he's a bit more cheerful. I'm getting fed up with his continual moaning."

"Can I join you?" asked Tobiasz.

"Of course, mate," said David. "Take a pew."

"Did I hear you talking about Jonathan?" Tobiasz asked.

"Yes," said Richard. "Just wondering if he is going to join us."

"Oh," said Tobiasz. "I don't know that, but I do know that Hilary had a word with him and he has almost apologised to Carol."

"Hilary!" said David. "The woman never ceases to amaze. What will she get up to next?"

Tobiasz didn't reply, unsure whether David was impressed or shocked.

Richard rescued him by asking about his recent trip to Poland.

"All sorted now, then?" he asked when Tobiasz had finished telling them what had happened.

"I hope so," he replied. "A lot of time wasted."

"Funny old thing, life," said David. "We do get ourselves into some muddles, waste a lot of time worrying about things."

"As they say, life is too short…"

"Well, in that case, we had better get another beer, then," said David, getting up, gathering the glasses and going to the bar.

Tobiasz turned to Richard.

"It must be much better for you now Janet has her parents near," he said.

"It is. It's better for everyone, especially George."

"That's Janet's father?"

"Yes," said Richard. "I don't know how he has coped as long as he has. Janet and I have been talking about it. Neither of us wants to put the other through what he has been through. And Janet definitely doesn't want Claire to have to go through what she has had to."

"We cannot prevent getting old."

"No. But we can put things in place to confirm our wishes about end-of-life care while we still have the capacity to make those choices."

"Wow. What on earth are you two talking about?" asked David as he put the beers on the table.

"Making decisions now, in case we lose capacity later," said Richard.

"Not something I want to think about," said David, always uncomfortable around discussions concerning death and illness.

"No. But I don't like the thought of other people having control over my life without having any say in the matter," said Richard.

Tobiasz, who now regretted inadvertently bringing the subject up, steered the conversation to happier topics.

TWENTY-EIGHT

Difficult Discussions

The dementia ward was the top floor of James Place. Janet felt disorientated as she came out of her mother's room and started the wrong way down the seemingly endless corridor in search of the lift. She wondered if this was a deliberate ploy to prevent the residents from escaping should they take it upon themselves to go wandering at night.

She had left her mother sleeping, something that Beryl spent more and more of her time doing since moving here. Janet asked the staff if they were medicating her but was reassured from several quarters that Beryl was not being drugged.

George met her at the lift on the ground floor. He was dressed as smartly as ever in a jacket and tie and she had to admit that he looked happier and more relaxed than he had for quite some time. She had enjoyed helping him move into his ground floor room with its tiny patio. He had already populated the patio with pots and garden ornaments and had transformed the once featureless room. The shelves were now full of books, a small desk held wobbly piles of papers, and his beloved train pictures had been mounted on the walls. He had begun to badger the manager to organise more trips, coffee mornings and talks. Initially, she had been slightly irritated by his persistence, but when she recognised his ability to organise and motivate people, she enlisted his help.

He tried to include Beryl in as many events as possible, holding her hand or leaving her to doze in a corner, depending on her needs, always watchful in case she woke and was frightened.

Unaccountably, he had accepted that his visits to Beryl would have to be limited until she had settled in. "As long as she knows I am here," he told one of the managers, "I will abide by your rules."

"Your picture is by her bed," the manager assured him. "So, even when you're not in the room she will be able to see you."

Janet knew these gestures were futile, but also that they were important to her father. Beryl, who now needed help with the simplest of tasks, possibly would have accepted anyone's reassurance or hand to hold, but Janet knew that it was important to George that it was his hand and his voice.

On more than one occasion Richard told Janet that he would hate it if she gave up her life for him as George had for Beryl. As much as she loved Richard, she could not see herself doing what her father had done or imagine making the sacrifices he had made over the years. The thought of Richard and Claire being in the position that she had been in didn't bear thinking about. She and Richard discussed writing a living will, in case such a situation should arise, so that some of the more difficult decisions could be made, perhaps easing the pressure on those tasked with caring. Janet wanted Richard to draw the documents up but his legal mind raised all sorts of possible complications. Instead, he asked a colleague, who had more experience in this area, to draw something up.

Janet was terrified by the sight of her mother dissolving before her eyes. She was filled with dread that her own life might end the same way. Her fear was such that she hoped that euthanasia would be legalised in time to be included in an advance directive while she still had the capacity to decide. She kept these thoughts to herself, not wanting to upset Richard or Claire.

"What a horrid conversation," said Claire, as she walked into her parents' kitchen one afternoon, the paperwork pertaining to the living will on the table in front of them. "I wish you wouldn't talk like that. I can't bear it."

"But…" started Janet.

"Please, don't," said Claire. "If everything is written down and it is in my power, I will try to follow your wishes. But, whatever happens, I don't think I could ever help someone to die."

"I would never ask you to. How could I?" replied Janet. She wanted to say that she would never ask either of them to help her die, but that she also didn't want them to stand in her way if she made that decision.

"No, love," said Richard, pointing to the papers. "This is not about helping people to die. This is just setting down what treatments we will accept if for any reason we can't communicate our wants and needs for ourselves in the future."

"In a way, it will help you," said Janet. "You won't have to make those difficult decisions. We will have made them for you."

"But I thought I heard you talking about euthanasia when I came in."

"We were, but only in general terms and, I have to say, sometimes I can see a case for it. It's more difficult when you're young."

"Mmmmm," said Claire.

"I never thought," said Richard, sensing her distress, "that I would have this conversation with your mum, never in a million years. I don't want to think about getting old and useless, but it's all about choice. As you become more dependent, for whatever reason, your choices become more limited."

"No one knows how they will react," said Janet. "Until a situation arises. I never thought that I would be happy if my mother were to die but I can't bear to see her like this. To see her distressed or lost because so much of the world is beyond her comprehension. I felt more comfortable with yesterday's visit because she slept through most of it.

"Dad is very special," she continued. "Very strong and he is dealing with it in his own way, but I wouldn't want Richard or you to have to go through that. If there is anything I can put in place to prevent that, I will. Heaven forbid, if I develop Alzheimer's, I may think completely differently. I only know how I feel now. Anyway, that's enough on that topic for now. I've said my piece."

Jasmine chose that moment to wake and cry for her feed. Richard gathered up the signed documents and decided he suddenly had to get them back to the office. Janet and Claire smiled at each other as he left. Claire sighed, relieved to be released from such difficult thoughts.

As she walked home later, her thoughts turned to her parents' discussion. She thought they were over-reacting, and didn't really understand why they had to talk about it now. *Grandma's old*, she thought, *so you sort of expect it. When people get old, they lose their memory a bit and in the worst cases get Alzheimer's. But Mum and Dad don't need to be thinking about it now. They've got plenty of time.*

She couldn't understand why her mum worried so much about everything. She was sure that it was her, not Richard, who had sparked all this discussion and form filling. She would never say so to her mum, and would always support her mum in everything, do anything for her, but Claire had some sympathy with her Aunt Julia. Much maligned for not helping out, Julia seemed to have a much healthier approach to life. Claire admitted to herself that Aunt Julia could be selfish and had left an awful lot of the care of her parents to her sister, but they had had a long chat when she came over to meet Jasmine. She had brought lots of things for the baby and helped out no end while she was there. Claire enjoyed her company and remembered her saying, "Janet likes to do everything herself, she worries even more if other people try and interfere, so it's best if I stay out of the way and leave her to it."

"I hope that I don't end up being a worrier like Mum. I certainly hope that Mum doesn't pass her anxieties on to you," she said, looking down at Jasmine asleep in the pram. "It's so difficult getting things right."

She had been relieved to find a flat to live in, quite near to Dan, who was handy for a bit of support. She found the flat just before it became too easy to stay at her parents' and too difficult to leave. She appreciated all they had done for her but she needed her independence. *Life shouldn't be too easy*, she thought philosophically. *Better to have a bit of a struggle.*

"You're looking very thoughtful." Dan made her jump as she came to the entrance to the flats.

"Just been to Mum and Dad's. All doom and gloom there. What are you doing here?"

"Just came to see if you fancied coming round for supper. I've been cooking and made far too much, as usual. Don't worry if you don't want to come. I can have it three days running."

Claire laughed and Jasmine woke with a start. "We'd love to come, if you can stand the noise. I was going to have a microwave meal with my feet up."

"Well, you can have chilli with your feet up. Come round whenever you're ready."

TWENTY-NINE

Last-Minute Celebration

"It's my birthday soon," said Janet. "I don't want to make a big thing of it. I don't usually take any notice of them at all, really. Well, I try not to, but I thought it would be a good excuse for us all to get together again. What do you think?"

"That would be lovely, Janet. Brilliant." Hilary had answered the phone while preparing Hector's dinner. She put the phone on speaker while she opened the can.

"Let's see what date suits everybody best. My birthday is mid-week, so either weekend would be fine, or mid-week, I suppose. Lunch should be better, I think, unless Liz can stay with one of us. Silly me, she can stay here. I keep forgetting we've got a spare room now that Claire has her own place. So, it could be dinner or lunch."

Before Hilary could say anything, Janet continued, "Oh, and as well as that, I wanted to ask if you would like to come with me to James Place and see Mum and Dad on my birthday. I thought I could take a cake for the residents."

"Is it a special birthday?"

"No. But the last few have really gone by without anyone noticing.

There's always been a disaster getting in the way of any sort of celebration and Richard and Claire keep saying that we ought to make something of this one to make up for it. But what I'd most like to do is have a meal out with my friends."

"What about the Chinese on the High Street? We could have one of their banquets, share everything and take home what we can't eat for the menfolk."

Janet laughed. "Don't get carried away. I'll get in touch with the others and see what I can organise."

Everyone was available, with the exception of Chahna, who had arranged a week away with Daisy and Rose. Janet hadn't realised that she shared a birthday with one of them. She had a long chat with Chahna on the phone, who was keen to quiz her about James Place.

"I've heard the medical opinion on it, but I want the view from the other side. She's a lovely lady but you hear such horror stories about some of these homes," she said. Jag's auntie had been in hospital for some time and they were looking for somewhere for her to go for respite and a little TLC before going home. Janet couldn't think of anything negative to say and convinced Chahna that it was the ideal choice. She was not deterred when Janet said that there might not be a room available, as word had spread about the good reputation of the place.

"I'll tell Jag to get onto them, see if he can pull a few strings and secure a bed," she said. "Enjoy your birthday meal. Love to all."

"Thank you. Enjoy your trip away."

While she had the phone in her hand, Janet made a reservation at the Chinese and phoned Liz to confirm the arrangements for her stay.

Claire was in her mother's kitchen when Hilary arrived ready for the trip to James Place. She placed the plant that she had bought as a birthday present on the table.

"She's changing Jasmine," Claire said. "I didn't ask her. She just did it. Anyway, I wanted to say that I'm really glad that you organised something for her."

"I didn't…" Hilary started to say.

"Well, it doesn't matter how it got organised. At least she is doing something. She's had such a raw deal the last few years. It's about time."

Janet came into the room carrying a smiling Jasmine.

"Happy birthday," said Hilary.

"Thank you. Oh, is that for me?" Janet said pointing to the azalea. Hilary nodded. "Lovely, thank you. Come on. Let's go and have cake. I can't wait for tonight. I keep waiting for something to happen."

"Don't be silly, Mum. We won't let anything spoil it," said Claire. "Give my love to Granny and Granddad."

"She wouldn't let Dad or me arrange anything," Claire said, turning to Hilary. "In case something went wrong."

"I think Dad is going to take you out on Saturday night," she told Janet. "And I'm going to treat you to lunch one day next week. And I won't take no for an answer." Janet wanted to say that there was no need, but she diplomatically remained silent.

The celebration went well. The family-run restaurant was busy but not crowded; the owner greeted them like honoured guests and seated them at a table near his little bar.

"So that I can keep an eye on you," he said, smiling.

Carol turned up a little late, dropped off by Jonathan. She came in flushed and flustered and full of apologies, but no explanation.

Liz was on fine form and kept them entertained with stories of the other members of the beach yoga club, which had moved to the cricket pavilion for the winter.

Janet sat at the end of the table, smiling, accepting birthday wishes and enjoying the good-hearted banter.

Hilary, who had driven Suzanne, was not drinking. However, she soon gave in to pressure from the others and decided to leave her car and get a taxi home.

"You should have got Tobiasz to drop you off," said Liz.

"I never thought," replied Hilary. "I didn't think it would be such a boozy night. If I asked him, he'd probably walk into town later and drive us home. He's daft like that."

"Besotted," Suzanne and Janet said in unison.

"Don't worry. Richard's picking us up. I'm sure he can fit two more in," Janet said, to save Hilary's blushes. She then suggested a photo to mark the occasion, and asked the waitress to take it when she came to clear their plates.

The waitress, the youngest daughter of the owner, readily agreed. When he saw what was happening, her father came over and insisted on being included. He stood behind Janet's chair and beamed as his daughter stood on a chair to take the photo.

"We don't have many occasions for photos. Do we?" commented Janet, once order had been restored.

"I've got a few from our walks in Debden this year," said Liz. "But you're right. I think we should have more get-togethers in Barwell. That way I'll get to try out everyone's spare rooms."

"No," said Hilary, feeling brave. "I think that we should all come and try out your spare rooms. I fancy sleeping in Siobhan's little princess bed."

"You'd be welcome," said Liz. "But you'd have to come on your own. There's no way Tobiasz would fit under that canopy."
Amid the laughter, Liz whispered to Hilary, "But I definitely want the two of you to come. Don't leave it too long. There's some decent B&Bs."

"We'd love to. We'll get something organised."

There was no further conversation, as the owner and his daughter brought out a cake that Hilary had sneaked in when they arrived, complete with a lit candle on top. They started to sing 'Happy Birthday to You' and, to Janet's embarrassment and pleasure, the other diners joined in and clapped and cheered at the end.

They paid the bill, and the leftover cake, back in its box, was placed in front of Janet. Wearily, they began to put their coats back on, say goodbye to each other and thank the restaurant owner and his family.

Jonathan was leaning into Richard's car when they stumbled out into the fresh air, shivering at the chill. He stood up and smiled, holding out his arm to Carol.

"Your carriage awaits," he said and, "See you later," he called over his shoulder to Richard and the women, as he led Carol towards the car.

With good grace, Richard accepted that he had been volunteered to drive everyone home and Hilary, Suzanne and Liz squeezed into the back seat.

"Those two seem to have sorted out their differences," Hilary observed as they drove past Jonathan opening the car door for Carol.

"All your doing, Hilary," said Liz, her words only slightly slurred.

"Carol told me all about it."

"I wondered what you two were talking about," said Janet, twisting round in her seat. "You two had your heads together for ages."

"Mmmmm," said Liz, resting her head on Hilary's shoulder as Richard turned off the High Street.

Hilary rested her head against the car window and allowed herself to hope that Tobiasz was still up.

THIRTY

Life by the Sea

Hilary and Tobiasz sat in the car, looking across the harbour through the windscreen. The rain was slowing a little, the early October sky becoming lighter. Hector sat in the back, patiently waiting for the promised walk.

After Janet's birthday meal, Liz had continued to badger Hilary to visit Debden. Tobiasz suggested that they combine a visit to Liz and John with a few days exploring the surrounding coast. Hilary was unsure. She wanted to see Liz but it was not a stretch of coast she knew very well and her mother had always been a bit scathing about some of the resorts and the hordes of twitchers who flocked there.

"We might have a different opinion from your mother," said Tobiasz. "And it will only be a few days."

"And, let's face it," said Hilary, deciding to give in, "if we don't like it, we can just come home."

They decided on a date.

Liz was delighted when Hilary told her the plan. She recommended Meadow View, the bed and breakfast that her mother, Pearl, had used when she visited. Liz sounded like an advert, enthusing over the comfortable rooms, reasonable cost and magnificent breakfast. She was able to describe the breakfast in great detail because the landlady had afforded her and John the honour of joining Pearl for breakfast one morning during her stay. Hilary checked it out online. It reminded her very much of the bed and breakfast places that she and her mother had stayed at on some of their holidays. Tobiasz thought it looked a bit like an old folks' home. Both of them were relieved when the only room available was very small and at the top of the house. It meant they could look elsewhere without offending Liz. They found a newly opened, spotlessly clean, dog-friendly, boutique hotel just a few minutes' walk from the beach.

Their day with Liz and John whizzed by. They ate lunch in the restaurant that Liz had taken her friends to earlier in the year.

"We did miss you that day," Liz said as they took their seats at the table, this time inside, out of the cold. "And Hector would have loved it."

Because they were eating inside, Hector had been taken for a long mid-morning walk, and was now alone at Liz and John's house. "He loves running in and out of the sea, but he won't swim," said Tobiasz. "If it wasn't so cold, I would go in with him and teach him."

John looked aghast. "The sea is always cold here. There are people who swim in the sea all year round. Must be mad!" he said. "Not me. Give me the Mediterranean any day."

"Wimp," said Liz, digging him in the ribs.

The waitress arrived with menus, saving Liz from John's response. Drinks ordered, Liz turned to Hilary and asked if she had seen anything of Janet since her birthday.

"You visited her parents with her a few times, didn't you?" Liz asked. "Before they moved."

"I did. And since then, too. It's always a bit distressing. Beryl's in bed a lot of the time now," said Hilary. "They get her up and, apparently, George gets the carers to bring her down to his room or the lounge and he sits with her, talks to her. It's really sweet. He's settled in really well, going on outings, helping organise things. He's a great ambassador for the place and Janet says he's made friends with residents and staff. It must be a great weight off Janet's mind, but she still visits several times a week. George has tried to discourage her, but she says she needs to. She takes Jasmine sometimes. That's always a great success."

"Jasmine came along just in the nick of time, didn't she?" said Liz. "Saved Janet from breaking down altogether."

"I suppose she did. She is a very sweet baby," said Hilary. She didn't feel comfortable with the conversation and thought that Liz ought not to be talking to her about Janet's parents. For some reason, it felt as though Liz was prying. She quickly changed the subject. "Speaking of which, how is Sonny?"

"Not so new now. Getting bigger and noisier every day but at least his feeding difficulties have been sorted," said Liz. "Lisa sometimes calls in on a Saturday, so you might see him this afternoon. And Siobhan, of course."

"Ooh, that would be lovely."

They were interrupted by the waiter bringing their drinks. He asked if they had already decided on what they would eat.

"Yes," John started to say, but Liz sent him away again, saying she needed more time. Hilary studied the menu, not wanting to see the looks that passed between John and Liz.

"We've got a lot to catch up on. Talking too much, weren't we?" said Liz.

"Yes," said Hilary, keeping her head down.

Once they'd ordered their food, Hilary asked John if he felt as though he had settled in Debden. She was surprised by his long, enthusiastic answer, with interjections from Liz, which lasted until their food arrived.

Feeling that he had held the floor for too long, John turned to Tobiasz to ask how he had got on in Poland.

"Friends of mine have been to Kraków. It sounds like a great place for a weekend break," he said.

"I think it is very popular to visit. But I know Warsaw better. I could recommend places to visit," said Tobiasz.

"You see a place with different eyes if you are a tourist," said Hilary.

"You do," said Tobiasz, looking at her. "When I went back recently, the main places I saw were cemeteries. It was not a holiday."

"Oh," said John, worried that he had put his foot in it.

"I needed to lay some ghosts to rest, I think you say." Tobiasz paused as the waitress put a plate of sea bass and couscous in front of him. "I don't know if Hilary told you but my wife died in a car crash. I thought the family blamed me. My mother did not like my wife. She is dead also. Very complicated, like all families. But I feel more settled now. I hope that Hilary will let me take her to see my homeland soon. I will not let you down again," he said. Hilary smiled at him.

"I had no idea," said John. He looked towards Liz who was concentrating on spooning soup from her mussel bowl. "Sorry, mate. I should not have brought it up."

"It is not a problem," said Tobiasz. "Not now."

There was an uncomfortable silence. Hilary racked her brain for something to say. Finally, Liz put her spoon down and looked up. "That was delicious," she said, wiping her chin with her napkin. "I do love mussels. How was the sea bass?" she asked Tobiasz.

"Superb!" he replied. "Superb."

There was a feeling of relief as talk turned to the food and other local restaurants that Liz and John had tried. After the waitress had cleared their plates, Liz proposed a toast to life and all its nonsense.

"To life," they chorused. The two couples clinked glasses and exchanged smiles.

Later, as they pulled into the drive, John saw that the neighbour across the road was working on one of his cars. He asked Tobiasz if he would like to meet him.

"He's really interesting. Very knowledgeable about vintage cars. He's got a vintage V8 Bentley somewhere."

"I'd love to," Tobiasz replied. He knew nothing about cars but felt that John was trying to make up for his imagined faux pas earlier.

"Do you mind if I go?" he asked Hilary.

"Of course not," she replied as she followed Liz into the house.

"Any excuse to go and inspect those old cars," said Liz, as she and Hilary were greeted by a very excited Hector.

"I don't know why he asked me if he could go," said Hilary.

"It's what comes with being part of a couple, consideration for your other half."

"Oh," said Hilary, still puzzled.

Within a few minutes, they had taken off their coats and Liz had switched on the log-effect fire in the living room.

"I can't wait to get this replaced with a proper log burner," she said as she adjusted the gas. "It's on the list."

"Won't that be a lot of hassle?" asked Hilary, imagining Liz splitting logs on the patio.

"No," said Liz. "And it'll be so much nicer." Warming her hands in the instant warmth of the fire, Hilary looked unconvinced.

They were soon ensconced in front to the fire with steaming cups of coffee. Hector settled in front of them, his back to the fire and his head resting on Hilary's foot.

Desultory conversation passed between them as the fire and large lunch made them drowsy. They had fallen into a companionable silence when they were jolted awake.

"*Hello, anyone in?*" Lisa shouted as she let herself in. Hilary sat up on the settee and patted her hair. Liz, without moving, shouted, "*In here.*"

"We're getting out of the way while Jason constructs a flat-pack chest of drawers," Lisa explained as she came into the room. She started to unstrap Sonny from her chest.

"Where's…?" Liz started to ask as Siobhan flew into the room.

"Granneeee," she said, flinging herself onto Liz's lap.

"Say hello to Hilary," Liz said as she tried to extricate herself from Siobhan's arms.

"Hilareeeee." Hilary was treated to the same greeting while trying to hold on to Hector's collar to stop him from adding to the chaos.

Siobhan made herself comfortable on the rug beside Hector and, seeing a gap, Lisa plonked Sonny down on Hilary's lap and went to the kitchen to make an herbal tea for herself and prepare a bottle for Sonny.

Sonny leaned against Hilary's hand and stared at her, unblinking. She smiled at him and he rewarded her with a gummy grin.

"What a big boy you are," she said.

"He's not as big as me," put in Siobhan. "He's a baby."

"Well," said Hilary, shifting her arms into a more comfortable position. "He's quite heavy."

"Do you want to feed him, Mum?" asked Lisa, as she came back into the room, put down her tea and took Sonny from Hilary with as little ceremony as she had passed him over to her in the first place. Sonny took it all in his stride and was happily transferred to Liz.

Liz couldn't get used to Lisa calling her 'Mum'; since she was a teenager she had always called her 'Liz'. She thought it must be Jason's influence, but whatever the reason, she liked it. It made her feel closer to Lisa. She realised from Hilary's quizzical look that she had noticed too.

She was grateful that Hilary didn't comment; perhaps, like Liz, she didn't want to jeopardise this welcome change.

Siobhan insisted that she take Hector into the garden.

"Don't get all dirty out there," Lisa called to her departing back.

"Is the garden secure?" Hilary asked. "Can Hector get out? I can go out with them."

"No need," said Liz as she lifted Sonny up to wind him. "It's all fenced in—just as important with children as with dogs."

Hilary relaxed back into her chair and asked Lisa when she was going back to work.

"In a couple of months," she replied. "I'm just having six months, can't afford any more and I think I'd go mad anyway."

They sat and chatted until Siobhan and Hector came back in, cold and wet.

"I'm not dirty," said Siobhan. "I'm wet. It's raining. But Hector's got dirty feet. He went on the garden."

Liz gave Sonny to Lisa.

Hilary took Hector back to the kitchen, apologising all the way.

"It really doesn't matter. He's a dog," Liz said, giving Hilary a towel to dry his paws. "I bet Siobhan threw a ball on the garden."

"I didn't," came the reply from an indignant Siobhan. "He just found a ball that was already there."

Liz laughed and found another towel to dry Siobhan's hair before sending her upstairs to find some dry clothes from her room.

"Do you want to see my room, Hilary?"

"Perhaps another day," Hilary said, still getting the mud off Hector's paws.

By the time John and Tobiasz returned, laughing and talking like old friends, all was calm in the house again. Sonny was asleep on Lisa's lap, Siobhan was once again lying on the rug with Hector, and Hilary and Liz, despite the early hour, each had a glass of wine in hand.

Tired, Siobhan made a fuss when it was time to leave, trying to persuade her granny to let her stay. When that failed, she asked her mummy if they could take Hector home to meet Daddy.

"Tell you what," said Hilary, before the day could be spoiled by a scene. "I could bring Hector again, another day. And if your mummy will let me, we'll take you for another walk on the beach."

Siobhan let go of Hector's lead and, putting on her best smile, said, "Pleeeeeease, Mummy."

With a grateful smile at Hilary, Lisa readily agreed and calm was restored.

THIRTY-ONE

Change Is in the Air

Tobiasz and Hilary had booked a few places to stay along the coast, so they could explore a little and spend time together.

"Wouldn't it be lovely to have a place by the sea, so that we could come here when we liked?" said Hilary.

"We could do the same as Liz and John and sell your bungalow," said Tobiasz, half joking.

Hilary didn't reply.

"I'm sorry. Of course you would not want to sell your mother's home."

"It's not that," said Hilary. "It's not that at all. It's just what about work? My friends? I think I'm too old to find pastures new. Even Liz has struggled a bit."

"Of course you are not too old to move," said Tobiasz. "I did and I am older."

"But you had to. You had no choice."

"I could have stayed in the same area. I could have rented a small flat or shared a cottage. I could have found work like I do now, where I was. But I chose to move."

Hilary looked thoughtful.

When they returned to Barwell and the normal routine, Hilary said nothing, but she couldn't stop thinking that there was no reason not to sell the bungalow. Her mother had always thought it too big for just the two of them. But sentimentality and associations with Gordon, or simply sheer laziness, had stopped her from doing anything about it. Hilary loved it now that she'd had it done up, but she knew that it would be more suitable for a family than for an older couple such as herself and Tobiasz.

She needed to talk to someone. So, she went round to Janet's and, over coffee, confided that she was thinking of selling the bungalow.

Janet hid her surprise and agreed that the property would be ideal for a family.

"But we are a family of sorts," Hilary said, backtracking. "And I'd definitely miss having a garden."

"Other properties have gardens," Janet reminded her. "Or you could always get yourself onto a waiting list for one of the allotments by the railway line."

"I could, couldn't I?" mused Hilary.

"I was joking," said Janet. "But, yes, you could. I can see you cycling up to the allotment with your trug on the handlebars."

"It might work…if I had a bike," Hilary said, laughing.

"Are you really serious about selling?"

"I don't know. But since Tobiasz mentioned it, I know that I haven't been able to stop thinking about the possibilities it could open up. Don't say anything to the others yet, though, please. I need to be clear in my own mind before I get everyone else's opinion."

"I certainly won't say anything to anyone. But please don't think about moving too far away."

"We've talked about the possibility of buying a smaller place in Barwell and somewhere on the coast," said Hilary.

She immediately regretted sharing these thoughts, as Janet responded with a list of reasons why they shouldn't do that—the cost of upkeep of two properties, one property lying empty—what if a pipe burst while they weren't there, what if there was a power cut, burglars, vandals? Janet's imagination ran away with her.

"But," said Hilary, "any one of those things could happen while I was at work or away on holiday."

"I suppose so," Janet agreed. "But there's still the cost of running two properties!"

"Well," said Hilary. "We'd have to work it all out. And I haven't yet decided definitely whether I'm going to sell. Don't worry, I'll keep you informed."

The following Tuesday, on an impulse, and during her lunch hour, Hilary went to one of the many estate agents in town to book an appointment for a valuation. The estate agent, confident in his sharp suit, had to change his snap judgement of Hilary when she told him the address of the bungalow. His manner came close to obsequious as he held a chair for her to sit in for the thirty seconds it took to book the appointment.

"I shall come myself," he said, as if bestowing a great honour. Hilary took his card with the appointment written on the back and hurried back to work. She hoped that Tobiasz would be in when Mr Cracken of Cracken & Bold came to call.

Hilary could hear Tobiasz speaking in Polish when she got in from work. She took off her anorak, hung it up and sat down on the hall chair to pull off her boots, before going into the living room to find out what was going on. Hector, tired from a long walk, lay on the rug and beat a greeting with his tail. Tobiasz was sitting on the settee staring down at his phone.

"What was that all about?" she asked. "You talking in Polish made it sound very mysterious. What are you plotting?"

"It was Jakub, Krystyna's father," he said. He explained that his father-in-law had called because he had received a letter addressed to Tobiasz. It had been delivered to the old family hotel, Tobiasz's last address in Poland. Jakub's family no longer owned the hotel, but an astute employee had forwarded it to Jakub by chance. It had arrived a couple of weeks after Tobiasz's visit to Krystyna's grave.

"Why was it sent there? Why not here?"

"It is from a solicitor."

"A solicitor…? Why?" Hilary sounded worried.

"Come and sit down." Tobiasz put his hand out. Hilary sat down next to him.

"Is it bad news?"

"I asked Jakub to open the letter, while I was on the phone. He read it out to me. It was from a solicitor in Kraków. The solicitor of my father's brother. They have been trying to find me for some time. I am his only relative. My father's brother died four years ago. He was ninety-five. They want to talk to me about his will."

"You've never mentioned an uncle," said Hilary.

"No," said Tobiasz.

"Did you know him?"

"No."

"I'll make a cup of coffee and feed Hector," said Hilary. "Then you can tell me what you do know." Hector followed her out to the kitchen, leaving Tobiasz to his thoughts.

When she returned a few minutes later with two mugs of coffee, Tobiasz was sitting exactly as she had left him.

She put the mugs down and took a KitKat from her cardigan pocket. She broke it and handed half to him, batting away Hector's enquiring nose.

"I knew of him," Tobiasz said, taking a bite of the KitKat. "My mother told me of him, he was a war hero. I think she wanted me to be proud. He was in the Polish air force. When Poland fell, he fled to Britain and fought in the RAF. I never met him. I did not know he had survived the war. He was not real to me. He was like someone in a book."

Hilary remained silent by his side.

"I understand what you told me better now," he said, turning to look at Hilary. "How you felt when you learned about your mother's other life. I thought I understand but now I know that I didn't know the force of what you felt… I feel like I have had an electric shock. My mind is a mess. As you say, all seven and sixes."

"Sixes and sevens," Hilary gently corrected him.

"What happens now?" she asked.

"I will contact the solicitor. I may have to go to Poland. Will you come with me? If I have to go, will you come with me?"

"Of course," she said.

The next day, before work, Tobiasz contacted the solicitor and was on the phone for what seemed to Hilary a very long time, considering that the only outcome was that Tobiasz had to write to the solicitor and send certified copies of various documents. Once these were received, Tobiasz would learn the contents of the will. He looked tired when he put the phone down and went to work with less enthusiasm than usual.

It really has affected him badly, thought Hilary.

However, the true reason for Tobiasz's tired and dejected demeanour was revealed later when he returned from work coughing and sneezing, his face flushed and generally looking very sorry for himself. Hilary fussed around him, settling him on the settee with tissues and the TV remote before going into the kitchen to prepare him a hot lemon drink.

"Thank you," he croaked.

They both went to bed early, each to their own room, Tobiasz not wanting to disturb Hilary with his coughing. He was worse the next morning and Hilary insisted that he stay in bed. She made sure that he had everything he needed before she set off for work.

It worried Hilary that he was still ill at the weekend. They had been invited to Suzanne and David's for lunch to celebrate Betty's birthday, but Hilary phoned Suzanne to explain that Tobiasz couldn't make it and to ask if they still wanted her on her own.

"Of course," said Suzanne. "Betty will be upset that Tobiasz can't come but she'll understand. You must come."

Hilary reassured her that she would be there.

"Are you sure you will be okay?" Hilary fussed as she was about to leave.

"Hilary, I only have bad cold," said Tobiasz. "I feel terrible but I will be okay. You are only going over the road. Go!"

Hilary kissed his damp forehead and pulled the duvet up to his chin. "I'll see you later. I won't wake you if you are asleep." She went out the door but was back thirty seconds later with a glass of water for beside his bed. "Have you taken any paracetamol?"

"Please stop fussing and go for your lunch. They will wonder where you are. Say 'happy birthday' to Betty for me."

"I will." She smoothed the duvet, stepped round Hector, who lay by the side of the bed, and went out, picking up a bottle of wine and Betty's gift from the hall table and gently closing the front door behind her.

*

After lunch, Hilary sat in the centre of the cream leather settee between Suzanne and Betty, holding court. She was telling them about getting the bungalow valued.

Tobiasz wouldn't allow her to cancel Mr Cracken's appointment and when the estate agent had turned up at the appointed time, Tobiasz was ensconced on Hilary's chair looking pale but upright, pretending to read a book. Mr Cracken was too busy with his laser measure and exaggerated delight in the dimensions of the property to even notice Tobiasz.

"He could probably have stayed in bed," Hilary said, as she finished relaying the story of the exhausting meeting to Suzanne and Betty.

"I can't believe how much he said it would make, though." Hilary named an astronomical sum of money. "Way beyond anything I would have imagined."

"It's worth at least that and it will make a lovely family home for someone," said Suzanne.

"I'm still not sure," Hilary admitted, emboldened by the wine she'd had with lunch. "It seemed such a good idea but now that it's becoming real, I'm not sure."

"Where are you thinking of looking?" Betty asked. "Not too far away, I hope."

"We don't know where to look. I certainly don't want to move away from my friends, but the idea came when we went to stay near Liz…there is something about living by the coast."

David appeared with a tray laden with a cafetière, cups and a plate of petits fours. He had heard most of the conversation from the kitchen. He couldn't believe that someone could live in a house for that long and not know its value.

"Why don't you rent it out?" he suggested as, under Suzanne's eagle eye, he placed the tray on the coffee table and started to distribute the drinks. "Rent somewhere, anywhere, until you decide where you want to buy."

"But what about the garden?"

"Employ a gardener."

"What about damage?" asked Hilary. "What if whoever rents it sets up a cannabis farm? It's all so beautiful since I've had it done up."

"Rent it through an agency. There will be damage but nothing that can't be repaired. There's always wear and tear. Even you must break things, Hilary, get stains on the carpet, marks on the walls."

Hilary laughed.

"I bet if Hilary does spill things on the carpets, she cleans them up straight away," said Betty. Talk turned to the best remedies for cleaning carpets and fabrics and David retreated to his chair with a cup of coffee and two petits fours.

Tobiasz's chesty cold lingered for another week. Hilary wanted to call the doctor but he was adamant that it was unnecessary. He tried to reassure her but, until the cough began to ease and he began to look like his normal self, she was not convinced. It had seemed to Hilary that he understood her fears, but as soon as he started to feel better, he went back to work and refused to listen to her pleas to slow down and give his body time to recuperate. She continued to worry and fuss over him. Her feeling of relief that he was better was out of all proportion to the illness that he had suffered. She was terrified that if he did too much, he would have a relapse. She couldn't believe how worried she had been about a cold. She had never seen him ill before. It hadn't crossed her mind that he might ever get ill, but this simple cold had exposed all her fears…of loss, of being alone again, fears so deep that she didn't dare admit to them. She tried unsuccessfully to make light of it when Liz told her off for making a fuss of him. "He's a man," Liz said. "That only prolongs it. Sad thing is, they like to make the most of illness."

I don't think Tobiasz did, Hilary thought. *How could he have made up that hacking cough and horrible runny nose?*

Hilary thought a lot about the future, during the wakeful nights when, despite the separate rooms, Tobiasz's cough disturbed them both. David's pragmatic view of her property and his suggestion of renting out the bungalow, while she and Tobiasz considered their options, opened her mind to the possibilities before her. Until now, the bungalow had just been home, somewhere to live. More importantly, she had always thought of it as her mother's. She had taken her absent mother's wishes into consideration during the renovation work, even if she later rejected them. The realisation that this valuable asset was now hers alone liberated her. She could do with it as she wished.

*

194

"I've considered all the options," Hilary said to Liz, when she phoned to share the news. "Although David's idea of renting has a lot to recommend it and is probably safer, I have decided to sell the bungalow and start again."

"Are you sure it's not a reaction to losing your mum?" said Liz. "Tobiasz isn't pressurising you, is he?"

"You know Tobiasz. Of course he isn't pressurising me. And he's been too poorly to discuss it properly anyway," Hilary replied, ignoring the first question.

"Sorry. I hope he's on the mend, now. Send him my love. What I meant was, you're not just doing this to please him?"

"That thought has gone through my mind," Hilary admitted. "But no, I think it was just that his suggestion started a chain reaction in my head. And what you said just now about it being a reaction to Mum's death—I think it's my chance to finally cut the apron strings, gain my freedom."

Liz laughed. "You make that sound dramatic, but I know what you mean. As long as it's something you are doing for yourself and not to please others."

"No, I think that this is the best thing that I could do for myself. I have allowed myself to drift, take the easy way, for too long. I'm going to take a risk."

"Another risk."

"What?"

"Tobiasz?"

"Another risk. After all, the first one paid off!"

"Well, let's hope you get an offer on the bungalow."

"And we find somewhere to move to."

"Well, yes, there is that. I'm keeping my eyes open down here. You don't want a flat, do you?"

"No. Perhaps in Barwell. But I fancy a little house by the sea."

Before ringing off, Hilary promised to keep Liz up to date with developments.

A few days later, Hilary met Carol in town at lunchtime. She could find nothing negative to say about Hilary's plans.

"Brilliant! Go for it," she said. "What an adventure. Can I tell Chahna? Well, can I tell everyone?"

"Tell anyone you like," said Hilary, giving her a hug.

Sarah, the person who Hilary had worried most about telling, was also very positive and excited about the idea, once she realised that Hilary didn't plan to move very far.

When Tobiasz was fully recovered, Hilary finally felt able to discuss the possibilities with him. She shared the doubts and fears that her friends had raised and they talked about their options.

"The valuation was far more than I imagined," she said as they walked slowly, hand-in-hand across the edge of the golf course, Hector charging ahead of them. "I've been thinking…"

"Yes?"

"You know we talked about buying here in Barwell and on the coast."

"Yes," said Tobiasz. "Best of both worlds, you said."

"Well, with the amount that the bungalow is worth, we'd definitely be able to do that," said Hilary. "I've worked it all out. We'd have enough money to run both properties."

"I have been thinking too," said Tobiasz. "If my uncle has left me a large amount in his will—and I think it's possible, otherwise why would the solicitor take the trouble to find me?—then I would like to buy the houses with you. So that we are equal partners."

"Oh, wow. That would be wonderful. It feels as though everything is falling into place."

"If you wanted to, you could give up work. If we bought a property by the sea, we could rent it out some of the time for income."

"And if it's somewhere near Debden-on-Sea," put in Hilary, "Liz and John could keep a neighbourly eye on it for us."

As ideas flowed between them, a plan started to take shape.

THIRTY-TWO

Worries

Janet couldn't help but feel concerned when she read the estate agent particulars for the cottage that Hilary had just emailed to her. She was feeling a bit out of the loop since Beryl died, quietly in her sleep, with George by her side. The funeral, which had taken place a week ago, had been a blur and she couldn't remember talking to any of her friends, all of whom had attended. She phoned Carol.

"How lovely to hear from you," said Carol. "How are you?"

"I'm okay, really okay," Janet replied slowly. "I know its early days. It probably hasn't sunk in properly. But I just know that Mum's in a better place. And it was all so peaceful in the end. No drama, and Dad was with her. A good death, as they say these days. Thank you for coming to the funeral. It meant a lot that you were all there."

"It was a lovely service. Your dad held up really well. I was impressed that there were people from the home. They've not been there very long— shows what an impression he's made."

Janet smiled.

"I imagine Christmas will be difficult for you," Carol continued. "What will you do?"

"We'll be at home," replied Janet. "Dad is coming—just for the day. Of course, Claire and Jasmine will be here—it's hard to be maudlin with a baby around. I doubt that Julia will come again so soon after the funeral, but she said she'd try and make it."

"A bit of a houseful, then?"

"Yes, I'm better if I'm busy," replied Janet. "Anyway, I was phoning about this email from Hilary. I feel a bit anxious about it all."

"I know what you mean," Carol agreed. "I can understand why she wants to sell that great big bungalow. Even all done up, it must still feel like her mother's."

"I understand too but it's all been so quick. I couldn't believe it when she put an offer in on one of those gorgeous flats in Barwell Grange. It's a lovely building. Even when it was part of the college, it had style. There was a write-up in the paper about the conversion. I can see why she would want one but I don't think they even looked at any other properties. And now this cottage."

"I know. The flat is amazing and the little cottage is quaint, but…" replied Carol. "One minute she doesn't want to marry Tobiasz, the next she's buying two properties with him."

"Richard is doing all the conveyancing for the flat and I presume he'll deal with the cottage too. It's reassuring that he'll be the one to draw up any agreements. I'm not allowed to know anything but I'm sure he won't let her do anything too stupid. I don't want to interfere and she is an adult, but I'm just worried. I emailed back, saying how lovely it looked. I couldn't say any of this. I didn't want her to think that I don't trust her— or Tobiasz—or that she doesn't know her own mind."

"I know," said Carol. "And it is all a bit silly because I think if they were married, we wouldn't be having this conversation."

"That's true."

"Hopefully, at some point, we'll find out all the details. I don't want to think that she is making a mistake but, for now, we have to leave her to it."

"I suppose you're right," Janet tentatively agreed.

Hilary could not have guessed that her email would cause such a flurry of concern among her friends. Suzanne mentioned it to David over breakfast and later talked to Liz on the phone. Liz phoned Carol when John had been unable to see any problem with it. Carol discussed it with Chahna over coffee. The consensus was not to interfere.

Tobiasz had been swept along by Hilary's enthusiasm when they had gone to view the flat, and could not stop her putting in an offer as soon as they got back home, but he had misgivings. He was worried what people would think and, until his inheritance became a reality, he didn't want to look at properties on the coast.

His relief was obvious when the letter arrived from the solicitor confirming the amount that he would receive from his uncle's will. "I'm pleased that I will be able to contribute," he said. "I didn't want people to think that I am living off you, taking advantage."

"The people who know me, love you," said Hilary. "With the money from the bungalow we would have done everything we want and more, but I understand why this is important to you."

Free to explore the possibility of a house by the sea, it had been Tobiasz who had fallen in love with the tiny mid-terrace cottage opposite the harbour in Debden-on-Sea. They had gone into the estate agent after seeing it in the window and, as Hilary said later, it was as if he was trying to put them off. It had been on the market for nearly two years, was unmortgageable, had no heating and only a basic kitchen. He begrudgingly took them to see it. Tobiasz was obviously enamoured, full of plans. To Hilary, the position was perfect, the view ever changing, she could find no fault with it. To the estate agent's amazement, they made an offer there and then.

Hilary felt completely comfortable with her decision to buy the properties with Tobiasz. She could easily afford both properties, but as Tobiasz wanted to contribute, they worked out a scheme that suited them both. Tobiasz insisted that they have a formal agreement that would provide the necessary protection if anything should go wrong. Hilary didn't think it was necessary but decided to go along with it.

THIRTY-THREE

Starting Over

Early in December, Hilary and Tobiasz received a Christmas card from Gillian and Marianne. Hilary was not surprised. In fact, her card to them was written and waiting in the pile to be posted on the hall table. But the letter inside, addressed only to her, stopped her in her tracks.

She showed it to Tobiasz as they ate breakfast.

Dear Hilary,
I hope that you are both well.
I would like to meet you for lunch and have taken the liberty
of booking a table for two at The Craven Arms, at 1pm on the 16th
(Marianne checked with Sarah that you would not be working).
I hope that you will be able to join me.
Best wishes
Gillian

"That is nice," said Tobiasz. "I have not heard of The Craven Arms. Is it far?"

"No," said Hilary. "It's not far." She began to describe where it was.

"But that's not the point. What on earth is it all about? We didn't exactly part on good terms and there's been hardly a word since."

"Perhaps she wants to apologise."

"Huh," came Hilary's doubtful response.

She was too intrigued to turn down the invitation. In addition, she had often wondered, when driving past, what the imposing Craven Arms was like. She noted that Gillian had written 'meet' and not 'take', so assumed that she would have to pay for her own lunch. But it would be worth it. She replied by email before leaving for work.

On the day of the lunch, Hilary had just parked in the hotel car park when Marianne pulled up behind her. She greeted Hilary enthusiastically, as Gillian got out of the passenger seat and straightened her coat.

"I'm taking some presents to Sarah, while you two have lunch," she said as she hugged Hilary.

Turning to her mother, she added, "I'll be back at 3.30, but don't worry if you're not ready. I can wait in the car." With that, she got back in the car and drove off.

The two older women stood in the car park staring at the departing car, until Hilary said, "Come on, let's get in out of the cold."

A waiter led them to a table by the fire in the high-ceilinged room, where he took their coats and left them to get settled.

"This is lovely," said Hilary, matching her tone to the hushed stillness of the room. "Have you been before?"

"No," Gillian replied. "Marianne found it on the internet."

"Oh," said Hilary.

In the silence that followed, Hilary racked her brains for something to say. Gillian hadn't been short of conversation on the other occasions when they met. More diners arrived. A raucous group of eight—an office Christmas party, Hilary thought—were seated at an adjacent table. At least that gave them something to focus on. The waiter brought their menus, which they studied intently, exchanging a few words about their choices. Although Hilary would have loved a glass of wine to ease the tension, they both chose to drink water.

They discussed the weather and Gillian asked Hilary about her plans for Christmas. The arrival of their starters coincided with more people joining the nearby table, and the party became even noisier. Hilary, who was unaccountably relieved when Gillian seemed pleased with her prawn cocktail, tucked hungrily into her pâté.

"I suppose you're wondering why I invited you," Gillian said at last. She leaned forwards to ensure that Hilary could hear her over the noise in the room.

"Mmmmm," Hilary mumbled through a mouthful of toast and pâté.

"Marianne convinced me that we should try again," she said. "I frightened you, didn't I?"

"Not exactly frightened but…" Hilary was unable to find a tactful way to describe how Gillian made her feel.

Gillian almost smiled.

"You won't believe me," she said. "But I was terrified when we met that first time. That's why I just kept talking. I must have sounded like an edition of *The Daily Mail*. And, then, in your beautiful home with your man who is so protective of you… It was a blessing Marianne was there. And Sarah, she seems to think an awful lot of you. You have so much. I suppose if I am honest, I was a bit jealous."

Hilary was having trouble reconciling the woman in front of her with the Gillian she had met earlier in the year.

"What made you change your mind?"

"Oh, I haven't changed my mind. I'm still jealous of you." Gillian actually laughed. "No, not really, but I do envy you your gentleness, your kindness. Marianne says I should trust people more. She is a great comfort to me."

Loud laughter rose from the next table, as Secret Santa presents were opened. Hilary smiled at the girl who turned and mouthed "sorry" to them.

"She said that we ought to talk about our parents again," said Gillian, as if she hadn't been interrupted. "I've been thinking…" The waiter came to clear their starter plates and Gillian waited until he had gone before she continued.

"I've been thinking, perhaps Dad really did love your mum but was terrified by the pregnancy. Perhaps he didn't want to leave his two little girls."

"We don't really know what happened all those years ago, do we?" Hilary gently suggested. "And we certainly don't know how they felt. Your dad might even have felt tricked by Mum. The pregnancy would have put him in a difficult position. But we can only guess. We'll never know."

"I *do* know that Mum was difficult, though," said Gillian. "She drank a lot."

She looked down as the waiter brought their main courses and fussed around offering mustard and sauces.

"I don't know," she continued, when they were alone again, "if she drank because of his philandering or if he strayed because of her drinking. I hope that, in his way, he loved her too, wanted to look after her, save her from herself, protect Georgie and me."

Gillian took a forkful of steak and chewed it thoughtfully.

"Marianne has often suggested that I should have a drink to relax," she continued. "She knows how het up I get, but I daren't. I saw Mum. I had to look after her, even had to help her to bed sometimes. I had to look after Georgie. I suppose Mum was an alcoholic but she could always just about keep up appearances. She always managed to convince people that she was coping. Georgie and I went under the radar, I suppose you could say."

"Oh, how awful. Poor you," Hilary said. She felt uncomfortable as Gillian's carefully made-up face creased and tears came into her eyes. She tentatively put her hand across the table and found it gripped.

"I really enjoyed helping Marianne look for your mum, and you. But, then, when I first met you, you seemed so self-assured, confident, happy." She let the sentence hang.

"Me?" said Hilary.

"Marianne was cross with me when we came to your beautiful home. She let me moan about you on the journey and then when we got home, she told me how upset and embarrassed she was. She said that I'd been rude to everyone. It was as if she was my mother. I'm surprised she didn't send me to my room." Gillian laughed at her own joke. "So, when you wanted to meet up again, I couldn't."

The waiter came to check that they were happy with their food. He looked askance at their joined hands, Hilary squeezing Gillian's, stopping her from taking it away. When he left, they smiled at each other and took up their knives and forks to resume eating.

After they'd finished the main course and refused dessert, the waiter asked if they would like coffee.

"Tea, please," Gillian replied.

Hilary laughed when Gillian admitted that she preferred tea but didn't dare admit it all those months ago.

"Tea is always terrible in motorway service stations and you had gone to so much trouble." She laughed.

"Perhaps we ought to start again," said Hilary.

They moved into a comfortable lounge for their drinks.

"I haven't told anyone this yet," said Hilary, leaning back into a wing-back chair at the side of another roaring fire. "I want to write a book, a novel but about my mum, the theatre, what it was like to live in those times." She hesitated. "How would you feel about your dad being included in the story? I would change the names, of course."

"That's funny. I said to Marianne, after we heard about your mother's manuscript, that you would be the sort of person to write a book. I don't think I was very nice about it then." Gillian ignored Hilary's question for a moment. She paused and took a sip of her tea. "I think I'd like Dad's part in her story to be in the book. I knew him—better than anyone, probably. I'd like to help, if you'd let me. I have no desire to write but I would like to be part of the process."

"I'd love you to be involved and I'm going to ask Marianne if I can use her dissertation as a reference. Don't tell her yet, though. I want to ask her properly."

"Have you really not told anyone else? Not even Tobiasz?" Gillian stumbled over his name.

"No. He knows I've reserved a place on a creative writing course starting next year, but I think he just thinks it is to occupy my time."

"Well, then, I am honoured to be the first you've told," said Gillian.

Hilary smiled.

Noticing the time, they asked for the bill.

"I've really enjoyed this lunch," said Hilary. "I'm so glad you suggested it. I don't think we should leave it too long before we do it again, especially if you are going to help me with research for my book."

"I'd like that," said Gillian. "Let's sort out a date."

Marianne arrived promptly at 3.30 and was surprised but very happy to find her mother and Hilary chatting like old friends.

"Did you tell her?" she asked as they drove home.

"I did. I made a bit of a fool of myself, but Hilary was very kind."

"Told you," said Marianne, relieved that her plan hadn't backfired.

Later, Tobiasz was very sympathetic when Hilary told him about Gillian's mother.

"Alcohol can be so destructive," he said.

"Yes, but I could really have done with a glass of wine when we first got there." She laughed. Tobiasz took a bottle from the fridge and poured them both a glass.

THIRTY-FOUR

Christmas

Christmas passed in a blur for Hilary and Tobiasz, as they squeezed appointments, form filling and decisions around drinks with friends, buying Christmas presents and making the bungalow look festive. Hector watched the activity from his basket and happily took any walks that were offered.

On Christmas Eve, Hilary and Tobiasz went to Midnight Mass. The church was crowded. The congregation, a mixture of regular churchgoers, once-a-year churchgoers and those on the way home from the pub, sang the carols lustily.

On Christmas morning they put the turkey in the oven, prepared the vegetables and went across the road for drinks. David was still full of their recent trip to South Africa. Hilary sat on the settee next to Betty's chair and tried not to laugh when Betty yawned exaggeratedly when her son's back was turned.

"I saw that, Mum," he said. "You might have heard it all before, but Tobiasz hasn't."

Tobiasz was treated to a monologue, complemented by the numerous photos on David's phone, until Suzanne came into the living room, having basted the turkey, and insisted that David refill the glasses and propose a toast. He put his phone in his pocket, grimaced at Tobiasz and took the bottle from the ice bucket. They all raised their topped-up glasses, and joined David in the toast.

"Happy Christmas, everyone."

"Let's hope the turkey isn't dry," he added, grinning playfully at Suzanne. There followed a series of stories of disastrous and memorable Christmas lunches.

"We should have had Christmas dinner together," Suzanne said a little later as Hilary and Tobiasz prepared to leave. "It's silly, having two ovens on for so few of us."

"I agree, but I like cooking Christmas dinner and, besides, all being well, this will be my last Christmas in the bungalow," Hilary said. "I have to admit, though, that I'm looking forward to an afternoon in front of the television with my tracksuit on. And also, if you don't cook Christmas dinner, you don't have the leftovers."

"Best bit," said David, coming up behind Suzanne to see them out.

"See you at New Year, if not before," said Hilary.

Tobiasz wished them both a happy Christmas, kissed Suzanne on the cheek and shook David's hand.

Carol and Jonathan, for only the second time in the thirty-four years that they had been together, spent Christmas alone.

"It was lovely," she told Janet on the phone a few days later. "But it meant that there was twice as much to do on Boxing Day, when everyone came around. It was completely chaotic. I haven't cleared up yet."

Janet laughed.

"But the absolute best thing about it was that the whole thing was Jonathan's idea. He did it for me."

"Perfect," said Janet. "About time."

"What about you? Did it all go to plan?"

"Pretty much," replied Janet. "We had our moments, it was all a bit difficult, but I think Dad enjoyed his day out. He even made a joke about being let out for good behaviour. Richard took him to the pub before lunch, as usual, and I think they had a good chat. Jasmine brightened everything for us. She was lovely. Didn't understand what was going on, but loved all the shiny paper. And I shouldn't say this, but I was pleased that Julia couldn't get back. It just made everything so much easier. She'll come sometime in the new year."

"I can't wait to hear how Liz got on. She was having the neighbours round for pre-dinner drinks," said Carol. "At least Lisa and her lot will have countered any difficulties with R-squared. Anyway, we'll find out at New Year. Got to go. Need to nip and get Jonathan's suit before the dry cleaner's closes."

THIRTY-FIVE

New Year's Eve

Hilary was at home, getting ready for Suzanne and David's New Year's Eve party.

"The last one we'll be able to walk to," she said, as Tobiasz zipped up her new black dress and dropped a kiss on her neck.

"Everything will be different next year."

"Yes," she replied. "And there's something I haven't told you. I thought you might think I was a bit silly and it might not come to anything."

"What?" asked Tobiasz, puzzled.

"I'm going to have a go at writing a book about Mum's life and the theatre and Lance. A novel."

"But that's amazing! Why on earth would I think that that was silly?" Tobiasz hugged her. "That's brilliant. Will you tell everyone tonight?"

"I think so."

"Well, if we don't hurry, we will be late. Come on."

Hilary slipped her feet into the black kitten-heeled shoes that had hardly been worn since her mother had sent her to change into something more comfortable four New Year's Eves ago, and tied Tobiasz's bow tie for him.

"You look gorgeous," he said. "Ready?"

"You're not so bad yourself." She smiled.

They checked on Hector and went across the road hand-in-hand.

"Everyone, Hilary is here, and Tobiasz," David boomed as he gave Hilary a hug and smacked a kiss on each cheek. Tobiasz looked slightly shocked as he, too, was enveloped in a bear hug. David placed glasses of Prosecco in their hands and propelled them into the centre of the living room.

Hilary was immediately surrounded by her friends, leaving Tobiasz feeling momentarily lost.

"Back to normal this year," said David, thumping him on the shoulder. "Would you prefer beer? Lager? Name your poison."

Unaccountably overwhelmed, Tobiasz replied, "Lager please," as he put the Prosecco glass down on a nearby table, taking care to use a coaster. Suzanne appeared with a tray of dates wrapped in warm bacon in one hand and a bowl of stuffed olives in the other.

"Lovely to see you, Tobiasz," she said, offering him the food. "I bet you're glad it's not Hilary's turn again."

"I enjoyed it, but this is perfect," he said hastily.

"I wonder if you could give me a hand, please," Suzanne asked.

"Of course. What will I do?"

"Take these around. Do you mind?"

"Of course not."

"I'll go and get the other things."

Suzanne smiled when she came back and saw Tobiasz engrossed in conversation with Jonathan, the empty tray and bowl of olives on a nearby table.

They had returned to the original format for this New Year's Eve party. Suzanne enjoyed cooking and found it much easier than dealing with other peoples' contributed dishes. There were ten for dinner this year. Although Betty was enjoying drinks with them, she wouldn't stay for the meal.

"I don't like eating late," she'd said when Suzanne had asked her. "And I'll make it an odd number. I can watch the fireworks if I feel like it, but I probably won't. I'll just come for the aperitifs and your delicious canapés."

Chahna and Jag had taken their girls to India for Christmas, combining a visit to family with a bit of research for the business.

Suzanne had made a beef Wellington, David's favourite, and hoped it lived up to expectation. She had time to sit with the others and have a drink before the last-minute preparations needed to be made.

She settled in between Liz and Janet and interrupted their conversation about infant formulas and the use of dummies.

"Come on, you two," she said. "Have a night off."

"That's why we moved over here," said Carol. She and Hilary were on the other settee, talking to Betty, who, as usual, was in the wing chair by the hearth. "At least Betty doesn't talk about babies all the time."

"No," said Hilary. "We're having a very illuminating conversation about bed socks."

At the sound of their laughter, David topped up the drinks and Tobiasz, seeing that Suzanne had sat down, picked up the bowl of olives and moved it to the table by the settees.

"It's alright, Tobiasz," said Suzanne. "We're all sorted." He followed David back to the other side of the room.

"You've got a good one there, Hilary," said Carol. Hilary acknowledged the comment with a smile.

"You need to keep hold of him," said Suzanne. "You know we went to Esmée's wedding in Amsterdam. It was all very informal, nothing like a wedding here, and the reception was in a converted factory—all exposed pipes and arc lights. Esmée was so happy and she looked lovely. Then we went to a wedding in Scotland, in a castle, completely over the top. Like something you'd see in an American film. I do love weddings."

"I do too," said Carol. "Liz's wedding was perfect."

"Absolutely," said Janet. "Shame Richard and I had to leave early. Jasmine could have waited."

"It was such a wonderful day," said Liz, looking fondly across at John.

Hilary kept quiet.

The meal was in full swing. David and Suzanne were at either end of the table and, so far, had refused any help. When Hilary started to get up to help clear the starter plates, David insisted that she remain seated.

"I have been given very clear instructions," he said, looking towards Suzanne, who was heading for the kitchen.

Hilary turned to talk to Richard, who was seated on her right.

"I seem to have spent an awful lot of time with you in the last few weeks," she said, laughing. "Thank you so much for your help."

"My pleasure," Richard replied.

"I'd be careful you don't let Janet hear you, Hilary." Liz laughed from the other side of the table.

"Oh, Liz," said Hilary, feeling herself blush. She was saved by David's ceremonious arrival into the room, carrying the beef Wellington. It was Suzanne's turn to look embarrassed as her friends broke into spontaneous applause. When they had all been served and David had made sure that everyone had the wine that they wanted, he sat back down, on the other side of Hilary.

"So, when are you moving?" he asked as he swallowed his first mouthful.

"It could be as early as the end of January," she replied. "I can't believe how quickly it has all happened and the couple that are buying the bungalow are very nice. I'm sure you'll get on. They've got a boy about twelve and a teenage girl. They're talking about building something in the garden so that the girl has her own space. I've told them you're a builder, given them your number."

"Great," said David. "I've had a look online at the flat you're buying. They've made a nice job of them. I know the developer."

"This may not be the right time to ask and, of course, I am getting a survey, but would you be willing to go round the flat with me in the next week or so? Just see if anything strikes you."

"Of course I can," David replied. "I'd like to see what they've done."

"Can we all come?" asked Janet from across the table. There was a chorus of "Can we?"

"No," said Hilary. "Definitely not. Wait till we're in." She smiled at Tobiasz, whose conversation with Suzanne had been interrupted.

"We were talking about the same thing at this end of the table," Suzanne said, putting her hand on Tobiasz's. "I have managed to get out of Tobiasz that you are talking about a flat-warming party. I hope it wasn't a secret."

"It wasn't a secret," said Tobiasz. "But even though Hilary is a very good cook, the food could not possibly be as good as this."

Suddenly, everyone wanted to say at the same time how much they were enjoying the food as they served second helpings from the dishes on the table and topped their glasses up.

Suzanne surveyed the table and smiled. She loved it when she could make people happy, simply by providing food and drink. She could hear Tobiasz, who had now turned to Janet, talking about his trip to Poland and quietly saying that he planned to take Hilary there next year as a surprise for her birthday. To her left, John was telling Carol about the American company that had taken over the pharmaceutical firm he worked for. Carol was making a very good impression of not having heard the story before, even though Liz had told them all about it at Janet's birthday do. She had made them all laugh about him having to grab ideas and run with them and how his days were becoming filled with meetings about how they could achieve more, which took them away from the work and prevented them from achieving more. At the moment, John was laughing about it all, poking fun at his new boss, but they all knew that Liz was genuinely concerned about how long he would be able to stand it.

Suzanne couldn't hear what Richard, Hilary and David were talking about but she was pleased to see that Hilary was certainly having her say. She wished she could hear Liz and Jonathan's conversation because they were both smiling. It was a long time since she had seen Jonathan looking so cheerful.

She stood up and started to collect the plates. Tobiasz helped and soon the table was clear, ready for the pavlova Suzanne had made for dessert.

"Can you bring the cheese as well?" she asked Tobiasz. "So that we won't have to get up again for a while."

As they sat down, David tapped his glass with a spoon. "Quiet please, quiet." Conversations stopped. "Hilary has an announcement. Come on. Stand up, Hilary."

Hilary was flustered. "I didn't mean to do it like this," she said to David. "I just said that I wanted to let everyone know tonight." Having just heard her news, Richard smiled at her encouragingly.

Tobiasz looked at his place mat.

Everyone else looked at her expectantly. Suzanne put down the knife she had been holding over the pavlova.

"I'm going to write a book," Hilary said, in a rush.

"You?" said Liz.

Hilary ignored the implied snub and continued. She had everyone's attention. "Marianne has been really helpful. And, believe it or not, Gillian has said she will help with the research too. And I have Mum's manuscript." Carol spluttered into her glass. "And, of course, my own imagination. I'm going to write a novel based on what I now know of Mum's life. A love story."

"What a brilliant idea," Carol said, recovering her composure.

"That's lovely," said Janet. "How far have you got?"

"Not very," said Hilary. "But I have a plan. I've made a start…"

"Brilliant. You are a dark horse. Moving house and a new career!" said Suzanne.

"Not exactly a career. But honestly, I can't believe how much I am enjoying it. I've signed up for a creative writing course in April. It's all quite exciting." She sat down with a bump. Tobiasz gave a thumbs up across the table as questions started to fly at her.

"Anyone want pudding?" shouted Suzanne above the din, waving her knife aloft.

It was just after eleven when they left the table and went into the living room. David put music on but no one was ready to dance.

Liz prevented Hilary from following Tobiasz into the kitchen to help clear up.

"There are plenty of people in there to clear up. Come and sit down with us." Carol, Janet and Liz surrounded her. They manoeuvred her to the settee.

"We are worried," said Liz. They all looked concerned.

Hilary had no idea what was going on and thought it all felt like a scene from *Little Women*.

"What about?" she asked.

"You," said Liz.

"Me?"

"Buying these properties."

"Oh," said Hilary.

"Are you doing the right thing?" asked Carol.

"Have you thought it through?" asked Liz.

"We just worry about you," said Janet.

"It was your husband who advised me."

Janet looked a little sheepish.

"Is it the drink talking?" asked Hilary.

"We were worried before we had a drink," said Liz.

"Perhaps it is coming out a bit wrong since we have had a drink," Carol admitted.

"So, what is the arrangement?" asked Liz. "You said you have an arrangement with Tobiasz."

Hilary didn't remember saying that, but then she had had a drink too.

"We want to live together," said Hilary.

"Of course you do," said Liz, lolling on the settee. "We wouldn't want it any other way."

"Shh," said Janet. "Let her speak."

"The properties will be in joint names," continued Hilary. "But I need my own space. In the bungalow, we kept our own bedrooms, even though we shared one or other of them most of the time." Hilary took a gulp of her wine. "Now we will have two properties to share, or not, as the mood takes us."

"Perfect," said Carol.

"But," interrupted Liz. "What about the arrangement?"

"I'm getting to that," said Hilary. "Tobiasz has inherited some money from his uncle, not enough to be equal partners but enough to contribute. We have arranged it so that I have twenty percent share of the cottage and Tobiasz has twenty percent of the flat."

She paused as she watched her friends work this out.

"Richard drew up the agreements," she continued. "To protect both of us. Who knows what the future holds? We have made wills. Tobiasz is too proud to be a kept man. We will have the best of both worlds."

Carol, Janet and Liz readily concluded that Hilary could look after herself and, released from worry, they re-joined the rest of the party.

"Well done," Janet whispered to Hilary as they stood up. Hilary wasn't sure if she was being congratulated on her good sense or simply for being able to stand up to them all. She smiled her thanks and went to look for Tobiasz. She found him in the kitchen talking to Suzanne. He was leaning against the sink, while Suzanne wiped the surfaces clean.

"He's all yours," said Suzanne, seeing Hilary come in. "I'll be there in a sec."

"Come on," said Hilary as she grabbed Tobiasz's hand. "The dancing's started."

They briefly stopped dancing at midnight, to toast each other, the new year and new beginnings, and carried on dancing into the early hours.

Hilary, safe in the arms of Tobiasz, surrounded by her friends, could have danced until dawn.

Acknowledgements

Thank you to everyone, particularly my family, who allowed me to escape to the south of France, giving me the space and time to write this novel.

Special thanks go to Jean-Claude, Nicole and Nicolas Viale who gave me a such warm welcome and looked after me during my stay in Menton. And to Joanna Langhorne and members of St John's English Library, Menton who welcomed me into their midst and allowed me to give a talk about my writing.

I wish to thank Gill Parrott and Margaret Beavis for being my readers, and all those who offered me encouragement to keep me writing.

Finally I want to thank Helen Hart of SilverWood Books for all her help and support the production of this lovely volume, and I wish to thank anybody who takes the trouble to read it.

If you enjoyed this book…

- Please rate or review *Journey's End* on your favourite site.
- Tell your friends.
- Add it to a genre list on Goodreads.
- Share a direct 'buy' link on your social media.
- Connect with the author on social media.
- Visit www.jacquelinejames.co.uk to sign up for news and events.

Authors work hard to be noticed in the crowded world of books, and often it's word-of-mouth that makes all the difference.

Thank you for your support and help.